ACC

The plot, the slang, the charac̲᷄_____ ̲t̲h̲e̲y swirled together with all the cinematic verve of a Billy Wilder film! Twists and turns in the story definitely had me guessing (and getting it wrong, lol). Jasmine Cross (aka Jazz), the ballsy belle the Jazz Age Mysteries revolve around, continues to be fleshed-out in BBBB and I fell in love with her character a little more. I loved being inside Jazz's head while she schemed all over town and connected overlooked dots.

Jazz is ready to move up from Society reporting and into the big time: Crime reporting. She proves to her fellow male colleagues at the *Galveston Gazette* that she's got the moxie it takes to investigate big cases.... I really enjoyed the dynamic between Jazz and her love interest and can't wait to see where it goes in the next novel.

The author does a really great job at capturing the cultural climate of Prohibition era Galveston. Everything from the customs, mannerisms, dialogue and gender roles/expectations bring this historical mystery to vivid life. Collier has a knack for describing all the decadence of the era from saloons, to brothels, to dresses, to perfume lamps. It's like walking into a magical transporting antique store when reading the author's descriptions of the 20s. In short, these books have basically made me want to ditch my modern life and become a full-time flapper journalist. Ha! —*Regina Reads (2016)*

I loved **Flappers**, and I loved **Bathing Beauties** even more. Collier did a great job of developing interesting and real characters that I've become hooked on. Mystery, intrigue, suspense, romance, and a great setting...this book has it all and is a fantastic read. Jazz is an unflappable flapper (pardon the pun) and a strong heroine. She keeps getting into hot water, but she can handle herself--she's no shrinking violet. Escape to Galveston! You'll have a blast. —*Amy Metz, A Blue Million Books Blog (2014) Author of the Goose Pimple Junction mystery series*

This is the ultimate fun read for the beach or backyard. Jazz is delightful, and her adventures take one back to an earlier age in the lovely city of Galveston. Highly recommended.
  —*Noreen Marcus, freelance reporter and editor (2013)*

ACCOLADES

I was completely charmed by Jazz Cross in Collier's first book, **Flappers,** but I was totally taken with **Bathing Beauties**, the second in the Jazz Age series following the spunky, intrepid flapper-reporter, Jazz Cross. Collier combines historical trivia with a cozy mystery beautifully, and I'm falling in love with her 1920s Galveston. Jazz is wonderfully empathetic in a way that felt authentic, not modern, which I always appreciate, and she's a lovely heroine to follow. (She passes my I-want-her-to-be-my-friend test!). *Bathing Beauties* captures the dangerous allure of glamour, fame and easy fortune. —*Audra Friend, Unabridged Chick Blog (2013)*

Jazz is a character the reader cannot help but love. She is smart, sassy and humorous. I encourage historical mystery lovers to discover the brilliance of this series...they are so entertaining and rich in historical detail. If you love sassy and quirky characters and a well-researched historical novel, then please do not pass this series up. It was a delight for me to read these mysteries. A fantastic read all around.
—*Kimberlee, "Girl Lost in a Book" Blog (2013)*

Bathing Beauties is probably my favourite in Collier's series. The exciting and glamorous setting is hugely beneficial for this colourful and enjoyable novel.... With all its fun, chemistry, authenticity, plotting and ease in style and slang, this is very recommendable.
—*ChristophFischerBooks.com (U.K., 2014), Top 500 Amazon Reviewer, Author of Time to Let Go, the Three Nations Trilogy, etc.*

So I absolutely loved this! It had everything I could ask for from a mystery. Great plot, wonderful characters to root for and all sorts of villains. Also, the author has a real flair for incorporating Jazz Age references and lingo. You feel transported to a different time and place...Fast pace, action, page-turning events, heartwarming romance and unpredictable mystery made this a completely enjoyable read.
—*Leti Del Mar, Author of The Inadvertent Thief (2013)*

BATHING BEAUTIES, BOOZE AND BULLETS

A JAZZ AGE MYSTERY (#2)

To Bootsie!

ELLEN MANSOOR COLLIER

A real bathing beauty!

EMColli

Text Copyright © 2014 by Ellen Mansoor Collier

Cover Design Copyright © 2013 by Jeff J. Mansoor
and Ellen Mansoor Collier

Interior Page Design: Ellen Mansoor Collier and Gary E. Collier

Cover Artwork: Vintage Photo (c. 1920s) Photographer Unknown

DECODAME PRESS

ISBN: 978-0-9894170-3-7

Third Edition

The text of this book is Garamond 12-point

CONTENTS

FLAPPERS, FLASKS And FOUL PLAY
A Jazz Age Mystery #1 (2012)

GOLD DIGGERS, GAMBLERS And GUNS
A Jazz Age Mystery #3 (2014)

VAMPS, VILLAINS And VAUDEVILLE
A Jazz Age Mystery #4 (2015)

Galveston Bathing Girl Revue   c. 1927

PREFACE

BY: ELLEN MANSOOR COLLIER

Before Las Vegas, Galveston, Texas reigned as the "Sin City of the Southwest"—a magnet for gold-diggers, gamblers and gangsters. Inspired by real people and places, **BATHING BEAUTIES, BOOZE AND BULLETS** is set in 1927 Galveston, where businessmen rubbed elbows with bootleggers and real-life rival gangs ruled the Island with greed and graft.

The International Pageant of Pulchritude and Bathing Girl Revue originated in Galveston in 1920 and evolved into the Miss Universe contest by 1926, attracting contestants from all over the world: including Turkey, Austria, Russia, Cuba and Egypt. In 1927, the contest became two separate events: the international contest and the Miss United States pageant, held over two days. Splash Day, held at the end of May, kicked off the tourist season. At least 250,000 people attended the 1927 pageant that weekend, increasing the city's population of 50,000 by five times.

In **BEAUTIES**, the events occur over one weekend in early June, starting with a fictitious dance performance held at the Hollywood Dinner Club. Since photos of the club's interior were not allowed or made public then, the décor is totally fabricated.

The parades and pageant, which in reality took place over two days, are combined into one day (Saturday) and one night (Sunday).

During Prohibition, the Beach and Downtown gangs fought constant turf wars for control over booze, gambling, slot machines, clubs and prostitution.

To keep the peace, the gangs tried to compromise by dividing the Island into two halves: Bootleggers Ollie Quinn and Dutch Voight headed the Beach Gang, south of Broadway and on the Seawall. The infamous but long-gone Hollywood Dinner Club on 61st Street and the Turf Club on 23rd Street (renamed the Surf Club in the novel) were located in the Beach Gang's territory.

Colorful crime boss Johnny Jack Nounes ran the Downtown Gang, the area north of Broadway, and once partnered with Frank Nitti, Al Capone's legendary enforcer. The Deluxe Club, the Grotto and Kit Kat Club were actual 1920s clubs run by Galveston mobsters.

Originally from Sicily, the Maceo brothers, Rosario and Sam (Papa Rose and Big Sam), immigrated to Louisiana with their family in 1901. After moving to Galveston, they eventually took control of the Island, known as the "Free State of Galveston" for its vice and laissez-faire attitude, for roughly 25 years, from late 1927 on, until their deaths. The Maceo empire faded when Sam Maceo died in 1951 of cancer, and Rose Maceo passed on due to heart disease in 1954.

BATHING BEAUTIES, BOOZE AND BULLETS is loosely based on actual and fabricated events leading to the Maceos' gradual take-over in the late 1920s and early 1930s.

The *Galveston Gazette* is a fictitious newspaper but the headlines in the novel are based on actual stories that appeared in *The Galveston Daily News,* the first and oldest newspaper in Texas, founded in 1842 and still in publication. Since many of the gangland crimes and activities went largely unreported and/or under-reported, the main characters and circumstances in the novel are fictitious and not intended to malign or distort actual persons or cases, but are purely the author's imagined version of possible events.

CHAPTER ONE

Sunday

Rehearsals for the Miss Universe contest—Galveston's annual "International Pageant of Pulchritude and Bathing Girl Revue"—were in full swing when Nathan and I arrived at the Grand Opera House. "You're late!" A plump woman in a snug suit pointed backstage. "Get out of your street clothes and get in line. And you can show your beau the gate!"

Swell—that's all I needed, to be mistaken for a bobble-headed bathing beauty. "But I'm not...He's not..."

"No excuses, young lady," she huffed, hands on her hips, staring me up and down. "Do you know what an honor and a privilege it is to be selected for this pageant? Young women all over the world would love to take your place."

"I'm a reporter, not a contestant!" I finally got a word in. "My name is Jasmine Cross. We're doing a story on the pageant for the *Galveston Gazette*. Nathan's the staff photographer."

A couple of doe-eyed beauties gave me the once-over and whispered behind cupped hands.

Nathan tipped his hat toward the stage. "Afternoon, ladies. Pleasure to be here."

A group of girls giggled and waved. "Hi, Nathan!" they sang out.

"I see." The matron frowned at him. "Take your seats then. Please try to restrain yourselves while we attempt to make it through one dance number without any mistakes. If possible."

"I just need to interview some contestants for the society section," I explained. "It'll only take a few minutes." Or so I hoped.

"You can wait until after rehearsals." She turned to face the stage. "Ready, ladies?"

"We're missing two girls, Mrs. Wembley," a petite blonde said. "They're not back from the beach yet."

"That's their loss. You all must adhere to a strict schedule or you'll be kicked out of the show," she snapped, resuming her drill sergeant stance.

"Yes, ma'am!" a cute brunette saluted, clicking her heels.

Nathan elbowed me with a grin. "Wait till I tell Mack and the guys that you almost got roped into this contest. Consider it a compliment."

"Says you! Be a pal and don't mention it, OK?" Sure, I was flattered, but if the *Galveston Gazette* newshounds ever found out, I'd never live it down.

As we took our seats near the center, I noticed a couple of balding men in suits parked in the front row, admiring the view. Sugar daddies or peeping Toms?

Onstage, three dozen or so young gals pranced about in various types of attire—frocks, pinafores, tap pants, shorts and smocks. Tall or short with marcelled tresses or long curls, the sea of blondes, brunettes and redheads of varying shapes and sizes made a zigzag of a chorus line.

Mrs. Wembley attempted to give the girls directions, stomping her feet for attention, her arms flailing in the air like a tipsy conductor. I remembered her as the music and dance teacher from Ball High School, acting as the choreographer—or in this case, a babysitter. A make-shift orchestra consisting of a grand piano, viola and flute played some old-fashioned tunes I didn't recognize.

"I think I'm in heaven!" Nathan smiled. "All these gorgeous girls must be angels from above. I could sit here all day and see these visions of loveliness floating about on stage."

"Angels? Floating?" I suppressed a laugh. "They're clomping around like Clydesdales!"

"It's only their first day of rehearsals. They just need more practice."

"I'll say!" I nodded. "Practice and a miracle. They'd better work around the clock to prepare for the show this weekend."

Nathan raised an eyebrow. "Jealous, Jasmine?"

"Jealous? Bunk!"

OK, maybe I *was* a bit envious. Not only did I need lots of rouge and lipstick to brighten my pale complexion, I wasn't as curvy or statuesque as the contestants. To be honest, I didn't want to let on that I felt intimidated, not only by their looks, but by their confidence and poise.

"Wanna know the truth?" I added. "I feel sorry for these girls. They're being exploited by men like the Maceos."

The beauties were performing Friday night at the Hollywood Dinner Club, a swanky hot spot owned by the Maceo brothers and Ollie Quinn, head of the Beach Gang. Rumor was, notorious Galveston gangsters Sam and Rose Maceo were the main pageant sponsors, no doubt trying to lure tourists to the gang's nightclubs for entertainment, booze, gambling and gals.

"Hogwash!" Nathan said. "These are liberated ladies, thumbing their noses at the Old Guard." Of course he was defending the beauties! He was a hound dog like all the rest.

"Oh yeah? How is flashing your skivvies in public helping women's emancipation?"

"What's wrong with girls capitalizing on their natural assets?" he argued. "The winners get plenty of publicity and opportunities. Plus two-thousand bucks is nothing to sneeze at."

Opportunities for what, I wondered? "How do you know so much about the contest?" I teased him. "Have you been hanging around the pageants, ogling the gorgeous girls?"

"My cousin Velma was Miss Galveston in 1922," he bragged. "She didn't win but she did get a few odd jobs out of it. She cut the ribbons at store openings, posed for a few pictures, even modeled for local stores. Nothing fancy, but it was fun for her while it lasted."

"You don't say." I turned to him with interest. "What happened to her?"

"She met an oilman, got married and had kids. The usual." He shrugged. "But for a small-town girl, it meant the world to her. You should've seen their crazy costumes then. Did you ever try to enter?"

"No, thanks," I snorted. "I didn't go to college to parade around in my underwear."

"Sorry I asked." Nathan frowned before he rushed off to take photos. I didn't mean to sound so snooty, but I hated to admit that I'd never finished college. I had to drop out when my dad died to get a paying job—unfortunately, I wasn't qualified to do very much.

I had my heart set on becoming a real journalist, but ended up as a society reporter, only writing fluffy puff pieces about charity balls, dances and debutantes' weddings. Not exactly front-page news.

Frankly, I blamed the editor-in-chief, Mr. Thomas—this silly story was all his big idea. When he called me into his office—"Jazz, have I got the perfect assignment for you!"—the last thing I wanted to do was interview a bunch of ditzy dames, trade make-up tips and size up their breasts and thighs.

Recently I'd risked my neck to help solve the murder of a prominent banker—and this was my reward? "Why don't you send Mack to cover it?" I'd protested, imagining our star reporter literally drooling over the idea.

"These girls don't need an old masher hanging around. A pretty young gal like you will fit right in." Mr. Thomas waved his cigar in circles. "Atlantic City may have their Miss America pageant, but by God we have Miss Universe! The contest is open to girls all over the world. Even better, this is the first year we'll crown our own Miss United States. Can you believe it? Two bathing beauty pageants for the price of one!"

He was so excited, why didn't *he* volunteer for the assignment? "Why two pageants? Isn't one contest enough?"

"Why not? The two lucky winners get to compete for the Miss Universe title. Our city officials think hosting these beauty contests will help promote Galveston as a travel resort." He gave me a devilish grin. "Bathing beauties are good for business."

No surprise. Guess who ran the city? A bunch of dirty old men.

Mr. Thomas smacked last week's paper, right on the main headline: YOUNG PROSTITUTE FOUND STRANGLED.

"As you know, the mayor wants only good news during Splash Day events, at least on the front page. Tourists don't like to read stories about dead whores and gang wars while they're on vacation."

Since when did the editor-in-chief forfeit real journalism to go along with the mayor's demands? Clearly, he had a boss like the rest of us worker bees.

"Only happy headlines?" I let out a sigh of defeat. "So what's the angle?"

"Stress the international aspect. Contestants come from as far away as Italy, France, Egypt and Spain to enter our Bathing Girl Revue!" He hit his desk for emphasis. "Find out more about these foreign beauties. What inspired them to travel all the way to Galveston to enter? Give it the personal touch. You know, the feature stories you girls are so good at writing."

Girls? Mrs. Harper, my stuck-up boss and society editor, was hardly a girl. Chances were, gossiping with a bevy of beauty queen hopefuls wouldn't exactly land me a Pulitzer.

"Don't look so glum, Jasmine. You'll even get a byline for every story printed."

I perked up. My own byline? Usually only the senior staff reporters got bylines.

"What about photos? I know Nathan will be glad to help."

I owed it to Nathan, my best friend and ally at work, who'd helped me through many a crisis, professional and personal.

"Of course." Mr. Thomas nodded so hard his spectacles almost slipped off. "What good is a story on bathing beauties without pictures? Lots of pictures! But keep him away from the dressing rooms. This is a family newspaper, not a yellow scandal sheet!"

Sure, Nathan acted like a wolf, but he was definitely more howl than growl. When I told him, he'd grinned like a sappy villain in a melodrama. "I don't even know what 'pulchritude' means, but it's got to be good if it involves beautiful women!"

"That's exactly what it means," I explained. "Physical beauty." Sad to say, looks were the contest's only criteria, as if women had no other attributes. What about brains, creativity, talent?

By now I was getting bored and restless, and glanced around the majestic theatre. The Grand Opera House certainly lived up to its name. Built in 1894, it retained the dignified air of a Victorian masterpiece with its opulent Rococo carvings, painted ceilings and plush velvet seats.

Nathan returned to sit down, leaving his camera set up in the side aisle.

"I'm going nuts. When will this debacle ever end?" I grumbled.

"Speak for yourself. I'm getting paid to admire lovely ladies. What a dream job!"

"Quiet in the back!" Mrs. Wembley glared at us. "You should be taking notes, not gabbing about the girls."

How in the world had she heard us over that deafening noise? We sank in our seats, giggling like naughty six-year-olds in class. She stood there, arms folded across her bosomy chest, shooting us the evil eye.

"Let's take it from the top, ladies!" she commanded. "Think pretty thoughts!"

Pretty thoughts? The orchestra started a new melody and the girls began fluttering about the stage like madcap fairies, reminding me of *A Midsummer Night's Dream*. Or should I say a nightmare?

Perhaps Mrs. Wembley strived for a poetic, nostalgic look at the past, but to me the girls resembled drunken butterflies, crashing into each other and falling down on stage. I had to admit, watching the girls make fools of themselves was more fun than covering crime scenes or corpses. Some gals started laughing, and I couldn't help but snicker, too.

"It's not funny," Nathan whispered. "Give them time."

"They'll be old maids by then," I cracked.

Mrs. Wembley clapped her hands like a bossy kindergarten teacher. "That's enough frivolity for one day, girls. Let's get back to the routine."

"Aw, Mrs. Wembley, we're not a bunch of boring bluenoses." The fair-skinned brunette who'd spoken up earlier stepped forward, reminding me of Clara Bow with her short dark hair and bangs. "Can't we do a more snappy routine, like a tap-dance or the Charleston?"

With that, she broke into a fast patter, her shoes echoing on the wooden stage. A few other girls joined her, strutting around stage doing a crazy mix of dances: the fox-trot, black bottom, jive, rumba and cha-cha. Even the orchestra chimed in, playing a few upbeat jazzy and ragtime tunes, livening up the somber mood. Surprisingly, the impromptu steps weren't half-bad.

"Girls! Girls! Control yourselves!" Mrs. Wembley shouted, stomping her feet.

Suddenly a couple of contestants froze in place, gaping at the theatre entrance. One by one, the girls stopped dancing, and a few pointed, wide-eyed. The orchestra quit playing and a hush fell over the auditorium.

What was wrong? We turned to see a dapper olive-skinned man walking down the left aisle, wearing a double-breasted navy pin-striped suit, a boater hat shading his face, flanked by two hulking young bodyguards, a nicer word than goons.

"Isn't that Sam Maceo?" I nudged Nathan. "What's *he* doing here? Why didn't he send one of his flunkies instead?"

Nathan cut me a smile. "Apparently he wants to check out the talent, along with their legs."

It was no secret that "Big Sam" liked dishy dames. Craning my neck to stare, I observed the two thugs, one fair, one dark, both good-looking in a gangster sort of way.

Then a gleam caught my eye, and I noticed the Italian hood was holding a shiny pistol. Why was Sam Maceo's bodyguard flashing his gun at a bathing beauty dance rehearsal?

CHAPTER TWO

"Looking good, ladies," Sam Maceo called out. "Don't mind me. Please continue your routine. I want to see your best performance this weekend."

So far, it seemed these amateurs would hurt more than help the ritzy nightclub's reputation for world-class acts.

"This is our first day of rehearsals," Mrs. Wembley replied, knotting her hands. "We're not quite ready yet, Mr. Maceo. Perhaps you can come back later?"

Maceo stood firm. "I'd like to see a short preview *now*." Then he flashed a killer smile. "I'm sure you understand. We want everyone to be prepared for Splash Day."

"We'll try our best." Mrs. Wembley nodded. "OK, ladies. Let's take our places." She waved a wand around as if conducting an actual orchestra—or hoping to cast a magic spell on this ragtag bunch of belles and turn them into a real dance troupe. Fat chance.

Slowly the contestants began their floating and spinning routine while the band cranked out some classical numbers. A few girls held back, eyes wide, clearly confused.

The two men quietly got up to leave, stopping to exchange a few words with Sam Maceo, shaking hands and slapping each other's backs. They looked like accountants or lawyers, not mobsters, with their shaved hair and spectacles, a couple of middle-aged milquetoasts. "Good to see you, congressmen," Maceo said to the duo, loud enough for everyone to hear.

I raised my brows at Nathan. "Congressmen?"

"Politicians all look the same to me. I've probably taken their photos at different events, hobnobbing with the mayor and muckety-mucks." That explained the back-slapping and bonhomie—it was business, and politics, as usual.

After they left, Maceo watched for a few minutes, tapping his foot, then loudly cleared his throat. "Excuse me, but what is this number called?"

"Originally it was based on Mendelssohn's *Dance of the Fairies*, but we've modified it somewhat," Mrs. Wembley said nervously, mopping her brow.

"I see." Maceo crossed his arms. "I'm sure you're the expert, madam, but I know what my patrons want. Do you really feel such an old-fashioned dance routine represents today's young, modern women? The flappers and suffragettes who've earned their rightful place in society?"

I was shocked. Was Big Sam Maceo a secret supporter of women's rights?

For once, Mrs. Wembley seemed to be at a loss for words. I sat up in my seat, waiting for the fireworks.

Her face flushed, she finally replied: "I wanted to allow these young ladies to express themselves in a manner befitting their natural beauty and grace."

What grace? To me, they seemed like dime-a-dance girl rejects. If they tried harder, maybe they'd earn a penny or a nickel. I turned to watch Sam Maceo's reaction, and noticed his handsome young bodyguards grinning with obvious interest.

"These young women will be pretty, no matter what they do," Sam Maceo said, walking toward the stage. "But let's try something more entertaining, more modern, for the Hollywood Dinner Club, shall we?" He spoke ever so politely and with almost perfect diction, just a slight trace of an Italian accent.

What would she do? Nathan and I traded curious looks. No one disobeyed the Maceos.

Originally from Sicily, the Maceo brothers—Big Sam and Papa Rose—found a way to make Prohibition pay big, by hook and by crook, starting off by bootlegging for Ollie Quinn and the Beach Gang. Big Sam served as the front man of the Maceo clan, a natural diplomat who knew how to meet and greet Galveston's elite, while Rose provided behind-the-scenes muscle. No wonder Rosario Maceo used his fists, growing up with a girly nickname like Rose.

"Of course, Mr. Maceo," Mrs. Wembley said, almost curtsying. "Come back later this week, and we'll have a new dance routine, just for you and the Hollywood Dinner Club." She was so humble, so ingratiating, that I suspected she was on his payroll.

"That's all I ask," he said, bowing his head.

As he turned to leave, I heard a sudden burst of tap-dancing. The Clara Bow-lookalike broke into an energetic number, her arms waving wildly while the band picked up the beat. Mrs. Wembley tried to interrupt, but the cheeky flapper only danced louder and faster, drowning out the matron's protests.

"How about this?" She flashed a defiant grin. A sharp contrast to the novice performance of these half-dressed hoofers. The gal had some gall—and how!

A few girls began clapping, but stopped when Mrs. Wembley snapped, "Quiet, Holly!" Marching toward her, Mrs. Wembley placed her hands on her ample hips. "Young lady, that type of behavior is not allowed! I'm sure Mr. Maceo wants a more dignified routine for his club. Since he's our main benefactor, we must do as he wishes."

In reality, she seemed to be the one dishing out commands, not Sam Maceo.

"That's exactly what I had in mind." Smiling, Maceo approached the stage. "Something lively, fresh, to showcase these young ladies and the Hollywood Club. What was your name again, miss?"

"Holly. I'm Miss Houston." She leaned over, holding out a dainty hand with a proud smile, not shy at all. "Pleased to meet you, Mr. Maceo."

"The pleasure is all mine." He smiled, kissing her hand.

The girls chirped while the bodyguards elbowed each other with a smirk. Maceo tipped his hat to the dancers. "Keep up the good work, ladies. Mrs. Wembley, I trust you'll have a snazzy new routine ready Friday night?"

She nodded in reply, lips pressed tight, speechless. Then I saw the dark-haired goon draw back his jacket and slowly tap his fingers on his gun, his face grim. I doubted Gentleman Sam saw the gesture, nor would he approve of such a blatant threat, but it did the trick.

Mrs. Wembley's face turned the color of tomato sauce. "Yes, sir," she rasped out. With that, Sam Maceo and his men left as quietly as they came, through the front door.

The atmosphere had clearly changed, darkening like a thunderstorm. The girls stood on stage, fidgeting and shuffling their feet, waiting for instructions. Finally someone called out: "What do we do now, Mrs. Wembley?"

She wiped her perspiring face with a hanky and took a few deep breaths. "I'll prepare a new dance routine for tomorrow. But for now, let's take a break." As she retreated backstage, she refused to look at Holly, now surrounded by girls, whispering and laughing out of earshot.

I grabbed my purse and notepad, telling Nathan, "Maybe I can sneak in a couple of interviews before Mrs. Wembley returns."

I began to feel some pity as well as sympathy for these ingénues, so far from home, even poor Mrs. Wembley. I doubted the middle-aged matron was used to getting death threats from gangsters, even if they were just for show.

Holly had piqued my curiosity, and I hoped to snare a quick interview with the bold beauty who dared to defy Mrs. Wembley.

As we made our way to the front, Holly began to sway back and forth. Suddenly she buckled at the knees, falling to the wooden stage floor with a loud thud. One girl let out a scream, while the others huddled around her.

"What is it, girls?" Mrs. Wembley rushed out from behind the curtains. "What's wrong?"

"It's Holly!" A blonde cried out. "I think she fainted!"

CHAPTER THREE

The 1894 Grand Opera house quieted for a moment, then it came alive with the sound of bathing beauties' voices, buzzing like a beehive. No wonder Holly—Miss Houston—had fainted. Poor thing probably got heat exhaustion from dancing in this humid old building. Still, I couldn't help but wonder if Sam Maceo's sudden appearance had anything to do with her timing.

We stood by the stage, waiting while Mrs. Wembley and the girls crowded around Holly, chattering in high-pitched voices. "Is there anything we can do?" Nathan asked, motioning toward the street. "I'll be glad to take her to the hospital. My car is out front."

Mrs. Wembley blinked as if she'd never seen him before. "And who are you, young man?"

"I'm a *Gazette* photographer." He held out a hand which she ignored.

"I'll be glad to go along." I offered, glancing at Nathan's eager expression. "As a chaperone."

Mrs. Wembley's eyes narrowed, studying both of us. "Maybe we should call an ambulance, just to be safe."

Then a voice piped up loudly. "What's all the fuss? I don't need to go to any hospital. I'll be fine!" Holly tried to stand up while worried voices chimed in, "Are you sure? Lie down, Holly!" They were all talking at once so it was hard to distinguish who was whom in the huddle.

Up close, I could see the smooth skin and attractive features of the bathing beauties, who appeared to be young adults, in their late teens and early twenties. Some looked like schoolgirls, only fifteen or so. I'd read that the first "Miss America" in Atlantic City was just sixteen-years-old.

"Now, Holly," Mrs. Wembley admonished. "You're in no state to argue. You need to get some rest, young lady."

"I won't get any rest in a noisy hospital," Holly pouted. She scrambled to her feet, aided by two girls who pulled on her thin, pale arms. "Then take me back to the Hotel Galvez. I just need my beauty sleep." She grinned at Nathan. "I'll be glad to hitch a ride with you. How about it?"

Nathan's face turned pink and he held his hat to his chest like a proper suitor. "My pleasure, ma'am."

"Ma'am?" She wrinkled her pug nose. "I'm only eighteen! Ma'am makes me sound like a prissy old schoolmarm, a real fire hydrant."

"Hold your horses, Holly! We don't even know who this gentleman really is," Mrs. Wembley scolded. "For all we know, he could be a lothario!"

I hid a smile. Yes, Nathan liked to flirt, but he was a clean-cut Joe College type, definitely not a drugstore cowboy.

"I assure you, she'll be in safe hands," I told her. "Feel free to come along if you wish."

Nathan shot me a warning look that clearly meant: "Keep your trap shut."

"Heavens, no. We still have too much work to do here." She put her hand to her lips and I noticed quite a few age spots. Had she been a bathing beauty in her youth, a hundred years ago? "I suppose if she had a proper chaperone, it will be all right. The Galvez isn't far from here."

Proper? Didn't Mrs. Wembley trust me to tag along? What was I, chopped liver?

"I'll help Holly!" A pretty blonde raised her hand like a goody-two shoes.

"Is that OK, Mrs. Wembley? Can she go?" Holly seemed to be pleading.

Mrs. Wembley stared at the perky blonde. "And you are...?"

"I'm Jo Beth," she drawled. "Miss Dallas. Holly's best friend."

Again Mrs. Wembley looked doubtful. She took the two friends aside and seemed to lecture them at length. Finally she turned to Nathan. "All right, young man. If you promise to go straight to the hotel, then you may give Holly and Jo Beth a ride back." She pointed toward the Hotel Galvez as if we were tourists. "But no funny business or your boss will hear from me personally!"

Was that an idle threat, or did she know the top brass at the *Gazette*? With a dramatic turn, she faced the girls on stage, herding them like sheep.

"Yes, ma'am!" Nathan said, making a face behind her back.

"Let me get my things," Holly said, disappearing backstage with Jo Beth. While they were gone, I had time to study the contestants: They all seemed so eager and hopeful, but I noticed a few girls held back from the group, appearing shy, even afraid.

From their looks and mannerisms—and the fact that they weren't interacting with the other girls—I guessed they were foreigners. Surely they spoke enough English to get by—or did they?

I wanted to ask them a few questions, but how would we communicate? My college French was passable, but my Spanish and Italian skills consisted of food and cuss words.

Moments later, Holly and Jo Beth walked down the side steps, wearing loose flowing cotton dresses and summery hats, looking like proper Sunday school teachers.   Nathan tipped his straw hat. "Pleased to be of service, ladies." He held out both elbows and the girls giggled, each one taking an arm. What a sheik. Who was he supposed to be—Douglas Fairbanks?   I trailed behind, feeling like a rumble seat on a Roadster.

Outside, Nathan made a big show of helping Holly and Jo Beth get into the back of his modest Model T. His beat-up jalopy was no Cadillac, but it managed to get us from Point A to Point B. "What a gentleman!" Holly squealed.

Sitting in front, I listened while the two beauties chattered away about the rehearsals and the other girls in the revue. Despite their heavy make-up and rouged cheeks, they were like any two young friends, gossiping and laughing.

"Let's take the scenic route, shall we?" Nathan said as he headed toward Beach Boulevard by the Seawall.

"That'd be swell," Holly said. "We've been cooped up in that stuffy old theatre for ages."

"You said it, sister," Jo Beth agreed. "Mrs. Wembley won't let us out of her sight."

"We may as well be nuns stuck in a convent!" Holly added.

Both girls broke into fits of laughter and I couldn't help but smile. Turning around, I asked, "What made you want to enter the Bathing Beauty Revue?"

"I'd like to be an actress," Jo Beth sighed. "I hear Hollywood talent scouts keep their eyes out for fresh new faces. I can't afford to head out to L.A. alone. A girl's gotta start someplace!"

I smiled at her reply, thinking about Amanda, my best friend and suitemate at my Aunt Eva's boarding house, who had a flair for melodrama and stars in her eyes. My ex-beau had left for L.A. months ago and, besides a postcard, I hadn't heard from him since. Seemed everyone I knew wanted to make it big in Hollywood. "Do you sing or dance too?"

"We'll find out soon enough," she said. "I can always take classes—or fake it. Isn't that what acting is all about—faking it? Pretending to be someone else?"

"True." I took note of her heavy make-up and bleached-blonde hair, but bit my tongue. "How about you, Holly?"

"I wanted to make enough money to go to college, maybe become a nurse," Holly said. "Even if I lost, I could make contacts, find a way to pay for school, maybe do some modeling." She paused and looked at Jo Beth. "But now...I'm not sure what I want to do."

I noticed her hesitation. "Did you change your mind about becoming a nurse?"

She looked out the window, pointing to the Crystal Palace. "I'd love to go there! I've heard it's got a huge swimming pool, and it's five stories high!"

"Sure, maybe we can go one day after rehearsals."

Why was she ignoring my question?

"I'll be glad to take you." Nathan smiled and parked in front of the Galvez Hotel like a big shot. "It's an emergency," he told the valet, taking Holly's arm. "Let me help you to your room. Just lean on me if you feel dizzy or weak."

And I thought Sam Maceo was the smooth one.

"Well, gee, all this attention on little ole me," Holly blushed and batted her long lashes, turning into Clara Bow before my eyes. "Coming, Jo Beth?" "Let's talk later, ladies," I told them as I got out of the car, but they were too busy flirting with Nathan.

I waited on a plush rattan sofa in the hotel's spacious lobby, where arched windows offered a perfect view of Galveston Beach.

Tourists milled along the Seawall, most covered head to toe in wide-brimmed hats and stuffy suits, while the sheiks and shebas wore scanty bathing costumes and pastel summer outfits. I enjoyed watching the prim and proper Galvez guests check in, smiling as a bellboy struggled to carry a wealthy matron's Louis Vuitton trunks.

A sea breeze cooled the lobby, rippling the sheer white curtains. I watched the waves crashing onto the shore, wishing I could run barefoot on the beach, feel the warm white sand under my feet. Too bad I had to return to the office soon. That's the trouble with work: it never goes away.

Inside the lobby, Jo Beth and a red-faced Nathan rushed over. Jo Beth sat by me, but Nathan started pacing around the gleaming wood floors. "How's Holly?" I asked. "Is she OK?"

"Let's just say she's not as friendly as I thought," he pouted.

My eyes widened. "You didn't try anything, did you?"

"No, he was a perfect gentleman," Jo Beth said. "It's just..." She leaned forward. "I think he has a little crush on our Miss Houston."

"Why not?" He shrugged. "Guess I'm not her type."

"What happened?" I pressed.

"I only asked if she wanted to go out while she's in town. See the sights, grab some supper, have a little fun." His face fell. "But she turned me down flat."

Jo Beth smiled at Nathan and patted his arm. "Trust me, it's not you, Nathan."

He scowled. "Don't tell me—she has a boyfriend?"

She nodded. "I suppose you can't call him a boy—he's almost twice her age."

"How am I supposed to know she's spoken for?" Nathan threw his hands up. "I didn't want to propose to her, I was just being hospitable."

"I doubt Holly's steady would like that," Jo Beth said. "I hear he can be very possessive."

"Plenty of fish in the sea." He gestured toward the beach to make his point.

"I'll be glad to introduce you to more girls in the pageant." Jo Beth struck a Theda Bara pose. "You never know. I might take a shine to you myself."

Nathan blushed a bright pink and looked away. I smiled at Jo Beth, grateful for her kindness.

"I'd better take you to the theatre before Mrs. Wembley gets worried." He stood up, holding out his hand.

"That old battle ax? She won't miss me or Holly. She's been on our backs from the start, says we're disrupting her routine." Jo Beth let out a snort. "What routine? We're supposed to be fairies, but we look like a bunch of silly mules, plodding along, bumping into each other and falling flat on our faces."

My thoughts exactly. I couldn't help but laugh out loud. This Miss Dallas was not at all what I expected. Her sweet Southern Belle act was just that—an act. Maybe she *was* destined for Hollywood. "Say, I'd like to interview you for my article when you have time."

"Absolutely!" she nodded. "Ask whatever you want, and I may even answer."

What did she have to hide? "I'd like to talk to Holly, too, when she feels better."

Jo Beth looked solemn as she walked out onto the veranda. Nathan and I joined her on the balcony, the ocean sounds like muted music. "That may not be a good idea. I don't know how long Holly will be here."

"What's wrong with her? Is she really sick?" Did she have some mysterious malady or disease, I wondered?

Jo Beth shook her head.   "It's not for me to say, really...especially to reporters. Those scandal sheets are so sensational!"

"Scandal sheet? The *Gazette* is a reputable family newspaper and I'm not a yellow journalist," I bristled. "If you tell me something in confidence, then I promise it stays that way."

Her eyes flickered toward Nathan. "OK, then you might as well know the real reason Holly won't—or can't—go out with you."

Jo Beth watched us warily as we edged closer. "Promise to keep this quiet, both of you?"

"Swear," Nathan said, crossing his chest.

"That goes for me, too," I nodded.

Jo Beth leveled her gaze at us, twirling her curls while she seemed to be making up her mind.

Finally she admitted, "Holly's not sick." She exhaled loudly, as if she'd been holding her breath a while. "She's pregnant."

CHAPTER FOUR

"Holly's pregnant?" I raised my brows. "Are you positive?" That was a scandal, all right. These young girls looked so sweet and innocent, I forgot they had real lives with real problems.

Jo Beth nodded, glancing around the hotel. "Holly's afraid to go to a doctor, but it's true..." She patted her flat stomach. "All the signs are there."

"She can't be too far along," I said. "She looks like a maypole."

Nathan seemed dumbfounded. "How can she compete in the pageant if she's...?"

"Why not?" Jo Beth seemed defensive. "She wasn't pregnant when she won Miss Houston last year. Her heart is set on entering this contest. Besides, she'll need the extra money if she decides to keep the baby."

"What about her boyfriend?" I asked. "Won't they get married?"

"That's a long story." She bit her lip, clearly nervous. "I've said too much already. I'd better check on Holly."

"Thanks for telling us." Nathan blinked. "I feel better now."

"Poor Holly," I said. "I hope she'll be all right."

"I hope so, too." Jo Beth's syrupy-sweet tone turned icy. "If you repeat one word of this, we'll deny everything. After all, there's no real proof."

Not yet. "Don't worry, it's off the record," I told her. "Your— Holly's—secret is safe."

"What secret?" With that, she flounced off into the lobby, tossing her long hair.

Nathan and I exchanged puzzled looks. "Think she's telling the truth?" he asked, still in shock.

"Good question. Why reveal something so personal about a close friend, especially to a reporter? Doesn't she realize it could disqualify Holly from the pageant?"

"Could be exactly why she told us," he said. We walked toward his car, the humid sea air as moist as a sauna. "What if she's afraid of the competition? Holly sure is a looker."

"So is Jo Beth. They're all beautiful girls," I pointed out. "I can't believe she'd lie about something so private."

"Women can be very competitive. Velma told me those girls will do anything to win."

"But to make up a pregnancy?" I shook my head. "Would Jo Beth stoop so low?"

Nathan shrugged. "If it's true, Holly sure is in a jam."

"I'll say! She can't hide a baby forever. I wonder if her parents will shuttle her off to a home for unwed mothers, and convince her to give the baby up for adoption?"

Sadly, in polite society, some scarlet women were forced into shotgun weddings, and after the baby was born, the not-so-proud parents would fudge the birth date or real father's name. Often the grandparents or distant relatives ended up raising the child, passing it off as their own—the further away, the better.

Driving back to the *Gazette*, Nathan seemed pensive. "Holly doesn't deserve to be put out to pasture, just 'cause she's pregnant. What a spitfire!"

"A baby will be a burden, especially if the father isn't willing to marry her." I shook my head. "He sounds like a palooka anyway. Holly's better off without him."

He nodded. "What kind of bum would knock up a sweet, gorgeous girl like Holly and then abandon her? He doesn't deserve her or the baby."

"You said it," I agreed. "The way she danced today, you'd never know she was pregnant. She could be auditioning for the Ziegfeld Follies! I wouldn't be surprised if Jo Beth made it all up."

Nathan raised his brows. "Let's wait and hear Holly's side of the story, if she's willing to tell the truth."

"If anyone can charm her into talking, you can," I teased, watching his ears turn pink.

As we entered the office, I noticed a group of reporters huddled together over by Mack's desk, jabbering away. Chuck and Pete, two cub reporters, wheeled their chairs around when we walked in. Then I heard Pete say, "Pipe down."

Curious, Nathan and I made a beeline for the men, who were passing around some photos or cards, like children playing hot potato. Probably nudie French postcards.

"What's going on, fellas?" Nathan asked. "What's that you got?"

"Nothing," Chuck mumbled, holding the photos behind his back. The newshawks watched me warily, obviously hiding something.

"Mack? What's the rumpus?" Nathan asked.

Once a Great War correspondent, Mack was considered the hotshot journalist at the paper. Of course I looked up to him but, as the lone female reporter, he didn't give me any breaks.

"We wouldn't want to upset the little lady here. Some things aren't meant for the faint of heart." Mack nodded my way, acting concerned, but it came across as condescending.

"Why would I get upset? Why not let me decide for myself?"

"Sure?" Mack turned to Nathan, shaking his head, and handed him some photos.

"Where'd you get these?" Nathan studied them, his back to me.

"The police shutterbug took them early this morning," Mack said. "We didn't call you since you were too busy with your girlfriends." He outlined an hour-glass figure, winking at the newsboys, who elbowed each other and snickered.

"What is it, Nathan? Let me see." I tried peering over his shoulder, but he kept circling around, blocking me like a linebacker. Finally I'd had enough of being polite. In a flash, I yanked on his arm, and snatched the photos away.

I tried to stay calm as I examined the graphic pictures, but my eyes misted and I let out a gasp: The body of a young woman lay sprawled on the huge granite boulders below the Seawall, arms twisted at crazy angles. Her simple frock looked ripped and bloodied, pierced by the jagged rocks.

What really got to me were her eyes, wide open in shock.

CHAPTER FIVE

I turned away from the reporters, and handed the photos back to Nathan, trying to regain my composure. The girl appeared so fragile, like a rag doll cast away. Was it an accident, a crime of passion or murder? If so, who'd done this—and why?

"What is it, Jazz?" Nathan looked alarmed. "Recognize her?"

I shook my head, taking a few deep breaths to calm down, but still couldn't speak.

"I told you not to show her the photos," Mack snapped. "Now look at her."

"I'm OK," I said, swallowing. "It was just a surprise, seeing a young woman killed that way. Do the police know what happened? Looks like she was pushed off the Seawall!"

"She might have tripped and fallen by accident," Nathan suggested.

"Possible, but from that angle, it looks like she was hurled out onto the rocks." I asked Mack, "Any idea who she is?"

"She's a Jane Doe. Probably a runaway or a prostitute. The cops will ask around, circulate the photos, try to locate any family. But it's hard to recognize her in that state."

"I'll bet some john broke her neck during rough sex, then panicked and threw her out," Hank, a cranky sportswriter, piped up. "She's a whore, a piece of trash. What do you expect?"

"How would you know?" I made a face at him that clearly meant: "Drop dead."

"The cops are calling it a suicide," Mack said. "No investigation. Case closed."

"Suicide? She's lying face up!" I said in disbelief. "You think she jumped off the Seawall *backwards*? Why don't they open an investigation? Sounds more like a homicide."

"I bet it's happened before." Mack shrugged. "We can't begin to guess the reasons why."

"If it *was* an accident or a suicide, wouldn't they find a purse, any ID?" I protested.

"Who brings a purse to a suicide?" Mack turned his chair around, dismissing me, and shooed away the reporters. "Get back to work, fellas. Why don't you go find some real scoops?"

Under my breath, I told Nathan, "I can't believe that's the whole story. Can you try to find out if Mack knows anything? It's not like him to cave in without chasing any leads."

Nathan nodded. "I'll do what I can, but Mack isn't exactly the gabby type."

Still upset, I trudged back to my desk, relieved that Mrs. Harper hadn't yet made an appearance. With her haughty attitude and fancy tailored clothes, my boss aspired to climb the social ladder to the top.

I tried to concentrate on the stack of papers on my desk, but my mind kept going over the grisly photos of the poor girl on the rocks, no older than the bathing beauties. Why would a young woman kill herself that way? Was it really a suicide or a cover-up?

You'd think I'd become immune to seeing a dead body, especially in photographs, after my recent experiences. But what made this so tragic was the victim: a girl whose life was snuffed out too soon.

I couldn't erase the image of her petite frame sprawled across the granite boulders like a disjointed marionette with its strings cut, her body torn to pieces by the ragged edges of rock. She looked stunned, caught off guard, as if shoved over the edge without warning. Why were the police so quick to write it off as a suicide?

To clear my mind, I decided to go downstairs to the newspaper morgue to research the pageant's history. Thumbing through old photos, I was amused by the change in attire, even attitude, over the years since the first Pageant of Pulchritude was held in 1920. Early beauties favored long, wavy locks while modern flappers sported close-cropped bobs and bangs, sleek like Louise Brooks or curly like Helen Kane. As their hair became shorter, so did their clothing.

Some contestants looked overly theatrical, not to mention uncomfortable, in their pageant costumes: from flowing Greek goddess gowns to an elaborate Viking outfit, including spears and a horned helmet hat. I especially admired the exotic beauty in a Cleopatra costume, complete with a Queen of Sheba headdress, snake bracelet and laced-up sandals. The cat's PJs!

What a contrast from the observers on the Seawall, all buttoned up and sweltering under the sun in their three-piece suits and fancy frocks, like the Galvez guests. During Splash Day events, Galveston Island attracted 150,000 tourists, three times the local population—and was expected to draw even bigger crowds this year.

Honestly, I wasn't sure what I thought about the pageant: Were the contestants being ogled and scrutinized by the public, or were they rebelling against the puritanical values of the past?

What would suffragists like Minnie Fisher think, after all the heartaches they endured to help women finally gain the right to vote in 1920? I recalled my mother and aunt Eva marching gallantly in parades on the Strand years ago, watching in fear as the crowd booed and threw shoes and random objects. I was too young to understand the significance of their actions, but I knew they were proud to join in the demonstrations.

After an hour or so, I returned to my desk and studied my notes. I wanted to know what motivated these young women to come to Galveston, flaunting their figures to strangers? How did they hear about the pageant in Europe, Denmark or the Middle East? Did they have rich relatives or friends to pave their way? Why did they risk traveling to a foreign land: to seek fame and fortune, follow the American dream, or try to escape an oppressive regime, like Russia?

I was lost in thought when Mrs. Page, the receptionist, called out: "Jasmine! Phone call for you. A gentleman. He said it was personal."

How personal? I looked around nervously, since we weren't supposed to get private calls at work. Luckily my boss wasn't around and Mr. Thomas seemed to be taking his usual afternoon nap with his office blinds closed. I picked up the candlestick phone and said formally, "Hello. This is Jasmine Cross."

"Sorry to call you at work, Jazz, but it's urgent." I was surprised to hear from my half-brother Sammy, my father's illegitimate son. Since our dad died suddenly two years ago, he watched over me like an overprotective hawk.

Trouble was, my mother and aunt considered him a black sheep, ashamed of his livelihood as a bar owner—a secret they tried to keep under their hats. Naturally, it wouldn't do for a so-called society reporter to be seen swilling cocktails at a juice joint, but it was fine for fat cats to make the rounds at the mob's swankiest night spots, like the Kit Kat, Grotto or the Hollywood Dinner Club.

"What is it, Sammy?" I frowned at the phone. "Is something wrong?"

I adored my big brother, and enjoyed sneaking out to Sammy's speakeasy, against my family's wishes. With its secret passwords, keen nautical theme and hidden basement location, I felt safe there. Still, the Oasis was located in the middle of the Downtown Gang's turf— just dangerous enough to be exciting.

"Not yet. Let's just say I need to call in a favor from your Fed friend, Agent Burton."

CHAPTER SIX

"Agent Burton? What kind of favor?" I held my breath, waiting for Sammy's response.

Prohibition Agent James Burton was the new hotshot Fed in town who'd already gained a name for standing up to bootleggers as well as local gang leaders. We'd gone on a few dates, but I had mixed feelings about being squired about town by the "tall, dashing and eligible" Fed agent, as my boss described him. Mrs. Harper might approve, but I didn't want to be the source of any Galveston gossip, with photos of me and Burton splashed all over the papers.

After all, Sammy happened to own a popular speakeasy on Market Street, the Oasis. I guess you could call it a conflict of interest. Luckily, Burton had no idea we were related. One wrong word and he could shut down the Oasis, and lock Sammy away.

"I'll tell you later. Not over the phone." His tone was brusque, anxious. "Can you come by the Oasis tonight?"

"Sure, Sammy. Why don't I bring Amanda?" My best friend Amanda had quite a crush on my handsome half-brother, so I knew she'd jump at the chance.

"Fine. But we'll need to talk privately. In my office."

Now I knew he meant business. "See you tonight," I told him, and hung up. What on earth did Sammy want with Agent Burton? The two men had met when Burton tried to raid the Oasis, so it wasn't exactly friendship at first sight. They'd interacted a few times, always careful not to be seen together in public. If the gangs found out, they could both wind up as shark food.

"What was that all about?" Nathan perched on the edge of my desk. "Something wrong?"

I looked away. "I don't know yet."

"Say, when are we going to see those bathing beauties again?" Nathan asked, a bit too eagerly. "I want to make sure Holly is all right, even if she is...you know...knocked up."

"Nathan, hush!" I frowned. "How about rehearsals tomorrow?"

"Swell. I'll be there with bells on." He smiled. "Ready to go? I'll give you a lift home."

I nodded. "Thanks, Nate." I was tempted to ask him to tag along with me and Amanda tonight, but Sammy had sounded so serious on the phone, I knew this wasn't a social call.

That evening after supper, Amanda and I took the trolley over to the Oasis and waited in line at the side door. A busy night for a Sunday. People were pouring into Galveston from all over the world, in anticipation of the Bathing Girl Revue and Splash Day festivities.

"Gee whiz, do we have to stand in line like everybody else?" Amanda complained, twirling her waist-length blonde curls, no doubt trying to imitate her idol, silent film star Lillian Gish. She'd dressed to the nines in hopes of attracting Sammy's attention, her pale blue ruffled dress setting off her crystal blue eyes. "Can't we go in ahead?"

I eyed the crowd. "I don't want to make a fuss, in case someone recognizes us."

"Says you. These folks all look like out-of-towners to me."

Thankfully we didn't have to wait long. Dino, a big, burly Italian who served as Sammy's doorman and bouncer, slid open the tiny glass door. "What's the word?" he said, gruff as usual.

Didn't Dino recognize me or was he playing games again? The tourists seemed to come and go as they pleased. I rolled my eyes at Amanda. "What's the hold up?" she nudged me. We were both anxious to see Sammy, but for different reasons.

"OK, you win. 'Jeepers, creepers, where'd you get those peepers?'" I recited. "Now can you let us in?" Sammy liked to use complete sentences as his 'password,' sort of an inside joke.

"Is that you, Jazz?" Dino acted surprised to see me when he opened the heavy door.

Once inside, I told him, "Sammy called and said it was urgent."

"Try his office." He waved his hand like he was swatting flies, then shifted his bulk on his barstool. I was afraid it might split in half any minute. "What's the word?" I heard him say to the next people in line.

"So what do you suppose Sammy wants?" Amanda asked as we crept downstairs. "Did you tell him I'm coming tonight?"

"Of course!" I smiled at her eager expression. "I'll tell you as soon as I find out myself."

Amanda and Sammy had gone out a few times, but I think Sammy was playing a tad too hard to get. With his jet-black hair, hazel eyes and olive skin, he was better-looking than the late Rudolph Valentino, a fact he used to his advantage. I tried to warn Amanda that Sammy had a roving eye, and hands, but the gaggle of gals who flocked to his bar didn't seem to mind.

As we made our way into the dimly lit room, I coughed, my throat irritated by the blasts of cigarette smoke, my eyes trying to adjust to the dark shadows. Did I smell marijuana too?

I looked for the regulars, but they'd been replaced by fresh new faces, no doubt newcomers to the underground world of speakeasies. You could tell the tourists by the way they watched the crowd, wandering around in a daze, staring at everything like it was a museum. In a way, it was.

The Oasis sported an accidental nautical theme, decorated with Doria, our life-sized masthead mascot hanging from the ceiling, ship's wheels and photos on the walls, and bottled ships by the beveled bar mirror.

A once-beautiful figurehead, Doria floated over the bar like a wooden guardian angel, watching over us, keeping us safe. I wished it was that simple. Sammy rescued her from a ship after it crashed into a jetty, and the two had been inseparable ever since.

"She's my kind of lady," Sammy often said. "She keeps her mouth shut and knows her place." So why did he always fall for floozies and flirty flappers who broke his heart?

The tourists held their glasses at a distance, clearly afraid to take a sip of any of that "vile hooch." Frankly, I didn't blame them. Of course Sammy always took careful precautions, but you never knew which batch of booze or bottle or flask contained too many of the wrong spirits. Sadly, people had to learn that lesson the hard way.

Tonight the bar was hopping with the sound of laughter and loud voices, drowning out the gramophone. Bernie, the chef, a gray-haired dandy, liked to play piano on weekend nights, when crowds preferred cocktails over cuisine. I glanced at Frank, who stood behind the bar, pouring and mixing drinks, too busy to notice us. He looked like an egghead in his trademark bowtie and spectacles and, like me, had to drop out of college due to finances.

Buzz, an orphan boy of twelve or thirteen, rushed around the joint delivering drinks, sloshing liquor as he tried to balance his tray, moving between tables. When I waved hello, he gave me a shy, frantic smile. I had a soft spot for the gangly, freckle-faced kid, who'd been a big help while I was trying to investigate banker Horace Andrews' death.

"Let's get a drink," Amanda said, carrying a dainty silk fan. Was she a geisha girl now? We pushed our way over to the bar, the men winking at her as they let us pass. "Hey, toots. What's the hurry?" A sailor tried to block our way, but Amanda elbowed him in the ribs.

Finally I got Frank's attention and we ordered our cocktails—Amanda's sidecar and my Manhattan. "Where's Sammy?" I asked Frank, leaning over the gleaming oak bar, littered with glasses and beer mugs.

"He's in the back, talking to some attractive ladies," Frank said with a sly smile.

"What a surprise." Amanda crossed her arms.

"Anyone we know?" I asked Frank, hoping to prevent a catfight.

"I doubt it since they're from out of town," he said.

I squared my shoulders and pushed a path into the crowd. Sure enough, Sammy stood in the back by a faux marble Greek statue, surrounded by a group of vamps in sheer clingy frocks, like a happy sheik with his harem.

Amanda stopped in her tracks. "I don't want to see him, much less talk to him, now. Look at him with that silly smile, enjoying every minute. What a lounge lizard."

"He's just being a good host," I said to placate her.

Amanda knew Sammy had a penchant for pretty gals, another trait probably passed on from our father, besides his dashing looks.

"Good host, my foot!" she snapped. "He's acting like a masher!"

I tried to catch Sammy's eye as he basked in the attention of all the attractive young women. As we edged closer, I let out a gasp. "There's Jo Beth!" I grabbed Amanda's arm, pointing to the blonde circling Sammy. "She's one of the bathing beauties I met today."

"Jo Beth, is it? Looks like a dumb Dora to me. Since when did you two get so chummy?"

"We're not exactly friends. Nathan gave her a ride to the hotel." I didn't mention Holly or her unfortunate condition. "Amanda, you know I have to be nice to these girls so they'll open up to me, tell me their stories. It's my job. Besides, you're just as pretty as these contestants. Prettier even!" She blushed, clearly flattered, and held her head a little higher.

I navigated my way toward Sammy, who stood by the table, a beauty on each arm. He gave me a quick smile and shot Amanda a guilty look, as if he'd been caught with his hand in the cookie jar. Two cookie jars, to be exact.

Amanda held back, shooting daggers at the bathing beauties. Sammy pulled away from the girls and went to greet us, making a big show of kissing Amanda on both cheeks. Did he have feelings for her, or was he keeping her around for sport?

"Hello, ladies. Remember me?" I said to the group over the noise. "I was there today during rehearsals."

Jo Beth's blue eyes flashed. "Nice to see you again."

"Jazz, how do you know these lovely ladies?" Sammy sounded impressed.

"Didn't I tell you? I'm writing an article on the Bathing Girl Revue. I'm supposed to interview the beauty contestants."

"You don't say!" Sammy grinned. "Let me know if you need any help with *research*," he whispered in my ear.

I poked him in the ribs, adding, "Try to contain yourself, at least in front of Amanda." He seemed to have forgotten all about our "urgent" business. Naturally, dishy dames took precedence over Agent Burton.

"Where's Nathan?" a brunette with bangs and bobbed hair piped up. "He sure was cute!"

"What's your name? I'll be sure to tell him I saw you."

"Delysia," she said. "I'm Miss San Antonio. We Texas gals like to stick together."

I glanced around the table, recognizing a few girls. "Where's Holly? Is she OK?"

Jo Beth locked eyes with me, signaling me to keep silent. "She's probably out with her fella. She wasn't in her room when we left."

"She must be feeling better." I painted on a cheery smile. "So what are you all doing here?"

"I could ask you the same question." Jo Beth's smile was equally fake. "A Galvez clerk told us this was a great spot to go to see and be seen and not get caught, if you know what I mean. Say, that rhymes! Almost." She giggled. "How about you?"

"I'm friends with the owner," I told her. "Sammy Cook. I see you two have met?" Sure, if you call clawing and pawing a stranger actually meeting.

"You don't say!" Jo Beth's voice turned to sugar. "Do you know if he's taken?"

Amanda had been hovering like a bird of prey, waiting to make her move. Now she seized the blonde, or rather, the opportunity.

"Yes, he's taken. Sammy is my beau." She batted her lashes at Jo Beth with a vengeance. Glad Sammy was out of earshot or he might have crushed her romantic fantasy.

"You lucky gal!" Jo Beth purred. "Well, I'm not surprised he fell for a sheba like you. You could be a bathing beauty!"

"Why, aren't you the sweetest thing? Look at you! Your frock is the berries!" Amanda linked arms with Jo Beth, her new best friend.

What? Did I hear correctly? Shaking my head, I left the two new gal pals to discuss their mutual admiration.

I pulled out a chair by the table of bathing beauties who clammed up as I sat down. "Mind if I join you? I'm Jasmine Cross, and I'd like to interview a few of you for the *Gazette*."

As the girls made their introductions, I noticed two exotic beauties sitting quietly at the end of the table. I reached across to shake hands, asking the chic blonde, "What's your name?"

"Excusez-moi," she said in a French accent. "My English is not so good. I'm Michelle, from Paris."

"France, not Texas!" Delysia piped up.

"Bonjour, Michelle." I nodded. "Ça va?" My high school French often came in handy with the tourists. Then I turned to the raven-haired beauty with long, thick black hair and ivory skin. "Please call me Jazz. What's your name?"

"Antonia," she said shyly in a heavy Italian accent.

"Antonia doesn't speak much English," Jo Beth told me. "But Michelle speaks some Italian and English so we get by. Besides, we talk enough for the both of them!"

"Ain't that the truth!" Delysia agreed. The girls laughed in unison as they downed their cocktails. Glasses covered their table, and I doubted drinking that much booze was smart in a bar full of woozy wolves and sailors on the make.

I pulled out my tango compact and applied 'Rose Petal' lipstick, catching a glimpse of the girls in my tiny mirror. Antonia looked uncomfortable in the corner, fingering her gold cross necklace, clearly baffled by the lively conversation.

"I'd like you to meet someone," I told her, asking Michelle to translate.

I made my way over to Sammy and Amanda, who was throwing her arms around in a jealous fit.

"I was just being nice," I overheard Sammy say.

"Do you have to be *that* nice?" Amanda tossed her long tresses toward the bathing beauties, no doubt feeling threatened.

I tapped Sammy on the shoulder. "Can Dino take a short break? I want to introduce him to Miss Italy."

He seemed grateful for the interruption. "Try not to distract the big lug too much. His ticker might give out."

I motioned for Antonia to follow me upstairs, where Dino sat on his stool, clearly bored. His big chocolate-brown eyes lit up, looking Antonia up and down with a wide grin. The petite beauty resembled a porcelain doll next to his huge frame. I wasn't playing matchmaker, for I doubted she'd find portly, bald Dino attractive, but I hoped they could be friends.

"This is Antonia, Miss Italy. She doesn't speak much English, so I thought you'd like to…"

"Would I!" Dino gestured wildly, his broad face animated, wasting no time trying to get to know the shy raven-haired girl.

In turn, she seemed delighted to be speaking in her native tongue, instantly coming to life like a wind-up toy.

"I'm interviewing the girls for the *Gazette* so any information about Antonia would be helpful." I almost had to shout to get Dino's attention.

"Sure, sure." Dino brushed me off, never taking his eyes off Antonia's angelic face. I might as well have been invisible for all they noticed, so I retreated downstairs.

By now, a few sailors and assorted gentlemen sat at the table with their arms draped around the beauties, who didn't seem to mind. In the corner, I thought I recognized the politicians from the rehearsals, sitting with a few friends. They were making toasts and nuzzling a couple of gals, their heads thrown back, clearly zozzled. Too bad Nathan wasn't around to catch these lotharios in the act.

Amanda leaned on Sammy, acting like his bodyguard, while another blonde beauty—Miss California or Miss Florida? I couldn't tell them apart from a distance—flanked his other side, trying to give him a sloppy kiss. He looked at me helplessly, as if he needed to be rescued from man-eating sharks. What a ham.

I grinned at him, enjoying the spectacle of blotto blondes surrounding Sammy. Since when did he want to run from a bevy of beautiful women? Perhaps he felt guilty, if not downright awkward, with Amanda hanging on his arm. His olive eyes wide, he cocked his head toward his office, signaling me to meet him there.

I hated to miss the live show, but I was dying of curiosity. Waiting inside his office, I admired the photo of Sammy and the Maceo brothers, taken on opening night of the Hollywood Dinner Club last year. In the background elegant couples in top hats and shimmering beaded gowns posed by Studebakers and Bentleys, the club illuminated by huge spotlights.

I'd never been to the Hollywood and had no idea what the interior looked like, since they never allowed photos of the club and casino for fear of getting shut down by authorities. I wished I'd been invited to that fancy shindig, but I wasn't exactly on the Beach Gang's guest list or in their inner circle.

Papers, pens, coins and keys littered the massive oak roll-top desk with notes and knickknacks crammed in cubbyholes and drawers. Stacks of boxes and newspapers covered the floor. Where did he hide the extra booze? Despite his pack-rat habits, Sammy was a fanatic about keeping the Oasis clean. With Bernie in charge, the kitchen always stayed spotless.

"Cleanliness is next to godliness," our grandmother used to say. Did she help raise Sammy? If so, she probably spoiled him rotten, since boys were a rare commodity on the Cross family tree.

Moments later, Sammy appeared, looking disheveled and rumpled, his shirt half-buttoned and dark hair curlier than usual.

"What happened to you?" I asked, stifling a laugh.

"All those dames!" He gasped for breath. "Get a few drinks in 'em and they turn into vultures. They were all over me!"

"I noticed. So what are you complaining about?" I teased him. "I thought you liked having a fan club around."

"I do, but..." He looked down, smoothing out his shirt, then buttoned it back up. "I just feel so bad. I don't know what to do..." His mood turned somber.

"About what? Amanda?"

"About everything..." He paced the tiny office, rubbing his unshaven face, as if trying to think. "I'm in a jam and I don't know how to get out."

"What kind of jam?" I could tell Sammy was stalling for time, so I went over to him and took his arm, to stop his pacing. "Sammy, tell me what's wrong."

"It's about the gangs. Their turf wars."

"What else is new?" Galveston gangs had a long-standing rivalry, and it didn't take much to set things off. Broadway served as the boundary separating the two gangs, and it was no-holds-barred if and when that line was crossed—the Beach Gang's turf was located north of Broadway, and the Downtown Gang was south.

Sammy wanted to stay on good terms with both gangs, who controlled the flow of booze on the Island. Agent Burton had tried, but failed, to shut down their operations, but he did manage to cut off a few sources, including a dangerous bootlegger, for a while—with our help.

"What's the latest fight about?" I'd heard Ollie Quinn had set his sights on the Downtown Gang's turf and, with his reckless wheeling and dealing, Johnny Jack seemed ripe for a coup.

"Let's just say the Maceos don't always see eye-to-eye with Ollie Quinn or Dutch Voight. They want to get out of the prostitution racket, but Ollie wants to line up houses all over the island, even set up shop in the clubs." Sammy took out a Camel cigarette and lit it, avoiding my gaze.

Only in Galveston did the Irish and Italian gangsters team up to run the Beach Gang, though I'd heard recent rumblings about an internal feud. In fact, Mack confirmed several rumors in a hard-hitting series for the *Gazette* describing the turf wars, a string of eye-opening articles the gangs didn't appreciate. In his latest piece, Mack quoted anonymous sources who claimed the Maceos were trying to oust Quinn and Voight, vying for the top spots in the Beach Gang.

"Really? How does that affect you?" I downplayed my concern.

"Word is, the Maceos want to break away from the Beach Gang, branch out onto new turf, start their own operation." Sammy puffed away, hiding behind a cloud of smoke. "Johnny Jack knows we're friends, and he didn't care as long as they kept out of his way and left Market Street alone. But after the ice man hit, all hell broke loose. Now Johnny Jack wants to stop the Maceos cold before they muscle in on his territory."

"How does he plan to do that?" After a string of recent killings, I saw first-hand how vicious the Galveston gangs could be if you double-crossed them.

"He's got one hare-brained idea." Finally Sammy quit pacing and plopped down in his worn banker's chair. "Jazz, you've got to help me. I need a favor, a big favor. "

"What kind of favor?" I eyed him, skeptical. Sammy always made it clear that I was supposed to stay out of his business, for my own safety, but now he wanted my help?

"Remember the night I spent in jail? Somehow Johnny Jack got the idea that your Prohibition friend bailed me out. So now he thinks Burton and I are best buddies."

"That's not true." I bit my lip, feeling guilty, since I'd asked Agent Burton to get involved, to help get Sammy out of jail. Fortunately he'd managed just fine on his own.

"I just tolerate the guy 'cause of you. But now I need his help." Sammy leaned forward, elbows on his knees. "Johnny Jack's putting the squeeze on me. He threatened to tell everyone in the Downtown Gang that I'm Agent Burton's squealer if I don't do what he wants."

I froze. "His informant? Bunk! What does he expect you to do?"

His shoulders slumped. "He wants me to convince Burton to raid the Hollywood Dinner Club and shut it down—during the bathing beauty routine this Friday night."

CHAPTER SEVEN

"A raid? Why in the world would Agent Burton agree to raid the Hollywood Dinner Club on Friday night?" I stared at him in disbelief. "Besides, aren't you pals with the Maceos?"

"Believe me, it's Johnny Jack's idea, not mine. He wants to embarrass Ollie Quinn and the Maceos, get the Hollywood shut down during Splash Day weekend." Sammy blew out a blast of smoke. "If I don't get Burton on board, he threatened to close the Oasis—for good."

"What about the girls? They may get hurt or thrown in jail. It'll ruin the bathing beauty contest—the whole weekend!" I jumped up, feeling a wave of anger and frustration. The gang wars had extended into my personal turf, and I couldn't do anything to stop them.

Sammy nodded. "That's the idea. But Johnny Jack doesn't care. He's so hell-bent on bringing down the Maceos that he doesn't give a damn if it hurts his business too."

"How can *I* help?" I fidgeted with my long bead necklace.

"Talk to Burton. Explain the circumstances." He looked hopeful. "I can't ask him directly, but he'd hang the moon for you."

Was he serious? Sammy rarely asked me for favors, but this was an impossible task. How could I ever broach the subject with Burton? 'Say, James, if you're not busy Friday night, would you mind raiding the Hollywood Dinner Club, just this once? Pretty please?'

"You're putting me in a very awkward position, Sammy." I let out a heavy sigh. "I can't give orders to Burton."

"Hell if I know what to do. I'm just caught in the middle." Sammy shoved back his chair and stood up. "Forget it. Forget I said anything. I have no right to ask you this favor. Maybe I'll just shut the Oasis myself and leave town. Then everyone will be happy."

Sammy tended to be a tad melodramatic when things didn't go his way. "Please, don't do anything drastic. There's got to be a solution." My mind was reeling. "What about a peace offering? Some cases of liquor or cash?"

"Johnny Jack has all the booze and clams he needs." Sammy paced the tiny office, waving his hands. "This is about power. Control. He wants to prove that he's still in charge, calling the shots."

"He must be daffy, expecting you and Burton to jump through his hoops. It's not fair."

"Who said gangsters play fair? He's daring me to disobey, testing my loyalty." Sammy blew out a blast of smoke. "Johnny Jack doesn't trust his own dog."

Outside, strains of "Ain't We Got Fun?" almost drowned out our conversation. Too bad everyone else was having so much fun.

"Say Burton agreed to do it, just this once. Then what? Johnny Jack will treat him like his personal puppet." I frowned. "He won't be satisfied with only one raid."

"That's his plan. I think *he* wants to take over the Beach Gang."

"If you turn him down, what happens to you? And Burton? You're damned either way."

"Killed is more like it. Johnny Jack wouldn't think twice about putting a bullet in our brains." Sammy rubbed his temples, as if he had a bad headache.

My heart sank. If anything happened to Sammy, I'd be devastated. Yet it wasn't fair to involve Burton, to jeopardize his job. Frankly, I had no sway with Burton. He was just a friend, not my fella. Even if he agreed, if the Maceos ever found out Burton and Sammy had sabotaged the show, they could end up in Galveston Bay.

"Don't worry. We'll think of something." I heaved a sigh.

"Think fast." He ground out his cigarette on a rusty Coca-Cola tip tray. "We've only got five days till Friday."

Swell. Now I knew how Houdini felt, trapped in a tank underwater, wearing a straightjacket. Somehow he always managed to get free, but I had no escape hatch.

Turning away, I flung open the door, wanting to rush outside, where music and gaiety filled the air, not talk of danger and death. In the club, I watched the crowd drink as if there was no tomorrow, as if a cocktail or a bottle of booze was the solution to all their troubles.

Bernie played "Five Foot Two, Eyes of Blue" on the grand piano, surrounded by a few bathing beauties, mixing up the Charleston, jive and fox trot. A row of girls had their arms around each other's waists, doing an impromptu can-can.

Without breaking a step, Amanda motioned for me to come over and I squeezed in, glad for a diversion. "If you can't beat 'em, join 'em," Amanda cracked, while we tried to keep up with the long-stemmed beauties.

Antonia appeared then, her mood now jovial, and gave me a grateful smile as we linked arms. The rest of the girls joined us and the crowd fanned out to give us room, cheering as we tried to kick our legs up to the sky. "Hollywood, here we come!" Amanda cried out while the crowd whistled and applauded.

Sammy came out of his office, his dour mood changing to bewilderment, then relief as he clapped along with the boisterous crowd. Finally Bernie finished his medley of jazz tunes with a flourish, and we all doubled-over with sweat and laughter and exhaustion. I had to admit, the bathing beauties were a lot more fun than I expected.

Despite my initial impression, I really liked the girls, especially as individuals, not one monolithic chorus line. "I'll be at rehearsals tomorrow with my pencil and pad!" I had to admit, these contestants weren't all subservient schoolgirls or bird-brained belles as I'd expected—rather, they seemed to be free spirits seeking adventure, perhaps fame and fortune, trying to improve their lot in life.

"You gals are great." Jo Beth grinned at us. "Have you ever thought of entering the pageant?"

Amanda nodded. "I've competed twice for Miss Galveston, but I was always a bridesmaid, never a bride."

I turned to her in surprise. "I didn't know that, Amanda. When did you enter?"

"I was too embarrassed to admit that I kept losing. My Grandma Bertha pushed me to enter—first, when I was sixteen, then eighteen. She was like your typical stage mother, and wanted me to make some money, but after two tries it became humiliating."

"It must be who you know, not what you look like," I assured her. "Politicians playing politics."

"Well, that's a shame. You sure can move those gams," Jo Beth told her. "Hope you can come see us Friday night at the Hollywood." With a practiced parade wave of her hand, she flounced off with the other beauties. "See you gals later!"

I was surprised Sammy didn't offer to pile them all in his Roadster for a ride back to the hotel—but tonight, he had more on his mind than his love life. We said our good-byes, with Amanda lingering a while. Sammy offered to drive us back to the boarding house, but I begged off, much to Amanda's disappointment.

Frankly I was rather upset at him, and needed to think, to make sense of his "request." As we walked toward the trolley stop, Amanda chattered non-stop. "So what did Sammy want? Did it have to do with Agent Burton?"

How did she know?

She gave me the once-over. "What's the matter? You look like you've seen a ghost!"

I sat there tight-lipped, as the trolley bounced and jerked down the street. Avoiding her gaze, I watched the people nodding off on the trolley, either from drink or fatigue or both.

That night, Amanda and I sat on my bed with my Japanese dancer perfume lamp on, orange blossom scenting the room, whispering in the dark. "You've got to level with me," she said, eyes wide. "Is Sammy in trouble? What's wrong?"

I always had trouble keeping secrets from Amanda.

"Johnny Jack wants a favor from Sammy," I admitted. "He's trying to force Agent Burton to raid the Hollywood Dinner Club on Friday night, and shut it down!"

"During the bathing beauties' performance? Why?" Amanda sat up in surprise.

"Sammy told me Johnny Jack is trying to destroy the Maceos."

"You don't say." After I filled her in, she said, "If anyone can talk Burton into it, you can. I like the girls, but Sammy comes first."

"What if Burton says no? Then they'll both be on the Downtown Gang's hit list." I shook my head. "But if they go through with it, the Beach Gang will get their revenge. Either way, it's a lose-lose situation."

CHAPTER EIGHT

Monday

That night, I tossed and turned in my small bed. When I finally fell asleep, I dreamt Amanda and I were dancing at the Hollywood Dinner Club with the bathing beauties in sexy sailor outfits: satin tap pants, striped tops and Navy caps. Burton and Sammy burst in the front doors, brandishing guns and badges, and closed down the production. Everyone panicked, running out the back doors. Sammy let everyone else go, while Burton dragged me and Amanda away, kicking and screaming, to jail.

I woke with a start, disoriented. Then I remembered Johnny Jack's threat, Sammy's plea for Burton's help. Unfortunately, we didn't have many options. We could call his bluff, see if he made good on his threat—but did we really want to take that chance?

Preoccupied, I got ready for work and arrived at the *Gazette* a bit late. A stack of stories to be proofread sat on my desk and I diligently dove into the pile, glad for the distraction. Still, I had trouble concentrating on high school graduations, fancy fundraisers and engagements. All I could think about was helping Sammy. He usually remained calm during a crisis, but this time his desperation broke through his brave façade. I knew he didn't want to involve me or Burton, but he clearly felt he had no other choice.

Nathan came by my desk, and must have noticed the dark circles under my eyes. "Burning the midnight oil?"

"I had trouble sleeping last night," I admitted, wanting to tell him about Sammy's predicament. But if Nathan told the reporters, we'd really be in hot water.

"So when are we going to see the bathing beauties again?" he asked with a grin. "Don't you have more girls to interview?"

"Sure, how about now? We had so much fun last..." I bit my lip. Uh oh.

"Last night?" His eyes flashed. "Did you go out with the girls?"

"I ran into them at the Oasis." I felt guilty for not inviting Nathan, but I had no idea the girls would show up at Sammy's speakeasy, of all places.

"What a coincidence," he said dryly. "Where'd you go?"

I gathered my clutch and notebook. "Let's talk in the car. I'll leave a note for Mrs. Harper." Thank goodness she wasn't there to spy on me.

On the way to the theatre, Nathan peppered me with questions, sounding like a nosy reporter. "Why wasn't I invited to this shindig? Ain't we got fun?"

"It was last-minute," I fibbed. "Amanda is sweet on Sammy, so she wanted to see him last night. We ran into the girls by accident."

"Oh, yeah?" He looked skeptical. "Was Holly there?"

"No, but I met a few new girls you may like. Maybe we can all go out this week?"

"Why not? If you don't mind me tagging along." He shrugged, still sore at me. "So how's Sammy? Bet he enjoyed seeing all those bathing beauties. Even with their clothes on."

"You slay me!" Changing the subject, I said, "Hey, Nate, I've got a question. Let's say you wanted to help a friend in a jam, but it was a big risk. What would you do?"

"What kind of jam?" His eyes widened. "You mean Holly? Or Jo Beth?"

I tried to keep a poker face. "I'd rather keep my friend nameless." Let him think it involved the beauties.

"Is it dangerous? Illegal? I wouldn't stick my neck out unless you had a damn good reason." Nathan glanced at me sideways, alarmed. "Could anyone get hurt?"

"Possibly," I sighed. "In more ways than one."

"Hard for me to give advice when I don't know the full story. But I'd try to help in any way possible, before it's too late."

Easier said than done.

As we drove along the Seawall, I watched the waves crashing and churning on the beach, and thought of the poor girl on the rocks. "Say, did you find out anything about that dead girl? Strange that no one bothered to investigate her so-called suicide."

He shook his head. "I tried to ask Mack, but he clammed up. Seemed kinda fishy to me.

"What are they hiding? Maybe they're looking into it privately, keeping it quiet?"

"I hope so," Nathan said. "What a way to go."

At the theatre, the girls I'd seen at the Oasis last night waved with knowing smiles as we took our seats. "Hi Nathan! Hi, Jazz!" they called out. Mrs. Wembley frowned her disapproval, as if our mere presence threatened to be a bad influence on her wards. If she only knew what her angels were really up to. Still, I doubted the Hollywood Dinner Club crowd cared about their high-jinks as much as their high-kicks.

The contestants didn't seem as disjointed and disorganized as before, but you'd hardly mistake them for the Rockettes. During the break, I did a short interview with Delysia, who came from a military family in San Antonio and had lived all over the world. Some girls chatted about rehearsals and the "swell time" they'd had at the Oasis.

Nathan set up his camera onstage and the contestants happily posed for pictures, hamming it up like silent film stars.

Jo Beth sashayed over and sat on the edge of the stage, her face puffy. "Looks like you tied one on last night." I winked.

"I feel like I was hit by a train," she nodded, rubbing her red-rimmed eyes.

"You said it." I glanced around the theatre. "Where's Holly? Is she still sick?"

Jo Beth's baby blues popped open and she whispered, "She never came home last night."

"I hope she's OK." I frowned, worried. "Any idea where she is? Can you contact her boyfriend?"

She shrugged, looking as helpless as a lost child. "I don't trust that no-good bastard."

Hands on her hips, Mrs. Wembley marched over in her laced-up leather boots. "Jo Beth, where on earth is Holly? If she's late to rehearsals again, she won't appear in the show."

"She's not feeling well," Jo Beth stammered.

"Sorry to hear she's still ill. Perhaps she's too sick to participate in the show *and* the beauty pageant." Mrs. Wembley stomped her foot like she was chasing away a stray cat.

Jo Beth's face flushed. "I'll show her the routine. I know she'll feel better by tomorrow."

"Tomorrow?" Her brows rose to her hairline. "I expect her to show up for rehearsals *today*." She motioned toward us. "Ask your new friends to help you fetch Holly." Then she clapped her hands, barking, "Girls, let's break for lunch. Meet back here in an hour."

Nathan helped Jo Beth to her feet. "Nathan's taxi, at your service. Where to?"

"Let's try the hotel first. After that, I'm stumped."

We rushed outside and jumped into his car. Jo Beth sat in back, biting her pink nails.

"What about Holly's boyfriend?" I suggested. "He might know where she is."

Jo Beth stared out the window, her face blank. "I'd rather not get him involved."

"Why not?" I wondered. Wasn't he already involved, as the father of Holly's baby to be?

"Long story," she sighed, her face like a sphinx. "Holly keeps quiet about her private life. There's not much I can do."

During the drive, I watched the tourists wandering around the Seawall, some on bikes, some in bathing suits. At the Galvez, Jo Beth asked us to wait in the lobby while she went to their room. "So what do you think Holly is up to?" Nathan asked after she left.

"Maybe she and her beau eloped? Considering the situation, it may not be a bad idea."

"Always the romantic, aren't you, Jazz?" Nathan smiled. "You must be covering too many weddings."

"I'll say!" He knew how society news bored me to tears.

Then Jo Beth rushed out of her room, breathing hard. "Holly's not here and there's no sign of her. Come take a look."

We followed her inside the small, tastefully-furnished room with walnut furniture and maroon brocade curtains to match the bedspread. "See, all her clothes are here and she didn't take her vanity case or her suitcase." She knelt by the bed and tried to pull out something from underneath. "Nathan, give me a hand with this thing, will you? It weighs a ton!"

He tugged on the suitcase and almost fell over with the effort. "Damn, what's she got inside? A load of bricks?"

"Gold bars?" I joked. "Wishful thinking."

"It's probably filled with books. Holly wants to be a nurse so she's studying for the exams to get into nursing school." Jo Beth frowned as she tried to open the suitcase. "It's locked. But I can fix that. Should we open it?" She hesitated, waiting for our approval.

"Go ahead," I told her. Yes, it was an invasion of privacy, but my nosy reporter's side couldn't wait to see the contents.

She pulled a bobby pin from her hair and fiddled with the lock like an experienced burglar. Where'd she learn that handy trick?

The lock snapped open and Jo Beth looked at us with a gleam in her eye. "I sure hope Holly doesn't mind."

Jo Beth popped open the lid and we all gasped at once: A row of amber liquor bottles snuggled side by side, flipped head to toe, like new toy soldiers in a box.

CHAPTER NINE

"Oh my Lord. What's all that booze doing in here?" Jo Beth covered her mouth. She plopped down on the bed, her blue eyes as round as the buttons on her ruffled cotton frock. She wasn't the only one in shock: A suitcase full of hooch was the last thing I expected from a budding beauty queen.

Was Holly using her hotel room, and even her title as Miss Houston, to sell booze on the side? At least she had good taste: Johnnie Walker Black brought a premium price.

"Would you get a load of that!" Nathan whistled under his breath. "I had no idea Holly was a rum-runner."

"She's not involved!" Jo Beth said, standing up. "This is all Rico's fault. He's using her, setting her up, in case he gets caught."

"Rico? Is that her boyfriend?" Nathan asked. "Sounds like a gangster to me."

Jo Beth nodded, lips trembling, trying to hold back tears. "That son of a bitch. He's up to something. And he's got Holly all messed up in his business."

"Bootlegging?" Clearly, this was a dilemma I'd never anticipated.

"Among other things." Jo Beth lowered her voice, her breath coming out in short bursts. "He does whatever his boss wants him to do. Rico is his right-hand man."

"Who's his boss?" I blurted out.

Jo Beth hesitated, wiping her hands on a hanky, as if trying to remove germs from the suitcase. Then she whispered, "Sam Maceo."

"You don't say." Interesting. "Did he show up with him yesterday at the theatre?"

"Couldn't miss him. He was the big guy with the gun," she said, eyes downcast.

No wonder Holly had fainted. Was he threatening her, too, when he flashed his gun?

Jo Beth paced the room, wringing her hands. "Damn it! I don't feel safe as long as that bootleg booze is under the bed. What should I do? Y'all won't tell anyone, will you? Being newspaper reporters and all?"

"You can trust us. Want me to take this loot off your hands?" Nathan grabbed the case.

"Nathan!" I swatted away his arm. "What if Rico comes looking for the liquor? Then you'd be putting both Jo Beth and Holly in even more danger."

"I'm sure Rico is hiding it for Sam Maceo. I doubt Holly even knows it's there," she said.

"What if he swiped it from the Maceos, so he can make some extra cash?" I suggested. If Sam Maceo ever found out his right-hand man was lifting his top-shelf booze, who knew what Rose Maceo would do? Frankly, I didn't care about Rico, but I was worried for Holly's sake.

"Sounds like Rico," Jo Beth fumed. "Using Holly as a cover."

"Remember Sammy from last night? I could ask him what to do, get his take."

Her eyes lit up. "Yes, please do. He's a sheik." Figured she'd get googly-eyed in a crisis.

"Want Sammy to get in hot water with the Maceos?" Nathan gave me a warning look.

"Good point. Let's leave the suitcase under the bed. Pretend nothing has changed."

"Why don't we take a couple of bottles with us, just in case?" Nathan suggested.

Jo Beth looked aghast. "Whatever for?"

"Evidence. It's a lead. I could show the bottles to Mack, see if they're the real McCoy. He may know where they get the stuff. Then if we find Rico, we can locate Holly."

"Sure that's a smart idea?" I had second thoughts. "What if Rico comes back, looking for the booze? He could accuse Holly of stealing them, selling the bottles herself."

"We'll return them this evening. Maybe Holly will turn up by then," Nathan consoled her.

"I hope so. You won't mention me or Holly, will you?" Jo Beth bit her lip, blinking.

Nathan squeezed her arm. "It's our little secret."

Was Nathan that easily swayed by her blonde curls and a few tears? I believed Jo Beth's story, but I didn't completely trust her "damsel in distress" act.

"Serves that jerk right if he's short a couple bottles of his precious liquor. I doubt he even knows how to count." Jo Beth held out two bottles to Nathan. "I'll get my vanity case and you can hide them in there."

Vanity case? The garish bag could double as a valise, it was so huge, covered in pink roses and lacy designs. While Nathan watched, amused, Jo Beth expertly powdered her nose and face with a fluffy pink swan's down puff, outlined her eyes in kohl, and applied a quick dab of rouge and lipstick. Where did she think she was headed—to the Cattlemen's Ball?

Then she removed a full tray of make-up and hid the liquor in the bottom. Carefully she rearranged the bottles, then pushed the case under the bed. "That should fool Rico," she said with a smile.

Smart gal. After locking the door, Jo Beth linked arms with Nathan and pasted a big smile on her freshly made-up face. Then we strode out into the lobby and right out the exit, looking as innocent as three friends out for a stroll.

Trailing behind, I felt like Jo Beth's humble handmaiden clutching her lethal vanity case.

How did I get stuck holding this neon-pink bag? The sun radiated off the busy and bright floral design, making it even more of an eyesore. What would the prim-and-proper Galvez guests think if they knew this garish case actually contained two bottles of brand-name booze?

CHAPTER TEN

Outside the Hotel Galvez, we piled into Nathan's jalopy, sadly out of place among the Bentleys and Cadillacs parked in front.

"Can you drop me off at the Opera House first?" Jo Beth asked.

"What should we do with these bottles?" I wondered, struggling with the blinding bright vanity case. There was hardly any room in back for the both of us.

"I can't take a case of booze inside the theatre!" Jo Beth declared, a hand on her throat, a poor imitation of Greta Garbo. "If anyone found it, I'd be disqualified from the pageant for sure, not to mention locked up like a common criminal."

Nathan grinned like it was all a big joke. "Don't look at me, girls. Can you imagine the ribbing I'd get if I carried that neon-pink vanity case into the newsroom? It's not safe here in the car. The booze may be stolen or explode in this heat. For all I know, it's full of gasoline."

True, I'd heard horror stories of the toxins suppliers added to bootleg booze—rotgut or not, liquor was flammable.

Nathan eyed the vanity case, then gave me a pointed look. "Seems you're the natural choice, Jazz. No one would suspect you of harboring hooch at work."

"Gee, thanks." I began to panic. "What if the newsboys see me with this thing? They'll think I'm running away to join the circus!"

"Go chase yourself," Jo Beth snapped, glaring at me. "I think you're just jealous."

"Jealous? Of what?" Her clown make-up? Her fake bleached-blonde hair? I wanted to mouth off, but Nathan stared at me like a lion guarding his prey. True, I may not be a beauty queen, but I'm no bug-eyed Betty.

"Girls are always jealous of us bathing beauties." Jo Beth flipped her long hair, hitting me right in the face. "I can't miss any more rehearsals or they'll throw me out on my can."

"We wouldn't want anything to happen to your *can*." Nathan stared at her with a suggestive smile. "Don't act so guilty, Jazz. You'll be fine. Relax."

Relax? Was he joking? How would I explain this frilly, silly pink case to all the jaded male reporters? They considered me a ditzy dame anyway, a distraction from their overly important jobs.

Nathan parked in front of the Opera House and jumped out to open the door for Jo Beth, who giggled like a helpless Southern belle. "Be sure to call us if you hear from Holly."

She batted her long lashes. "Why don't you call me later at the Galvez for an update?"

"I can go one better." Nathan beamed. "How about if I pick you up after rehearsals?"

"What a gentleman! See you at six!" Jo Beth waved and flounced off into the theatre.

I swear, watching them flirt made me as uncomfortable as carrying the garish case with two bottles of illegal hooch in public. "What about *my* ride home after work? I feel like a felon."

"Sure, after we pick up Jo Beth." He glanced at the case like it was a picnic basket, nothing more. "Why not stick it under your desk for now?"

"My desk? You're screwy. How can I hide it in a newsroom full of reporters?" I glared at him, getting nervous. "I don't want to get anyone in trouble, especially me. Can't we stop by Sammy's and leave it there?" What were we thinking, stealing two bottles of booze from Rico, a Beach Gang thug? Why did I go along with this dumb idea?

"If we're late to work again, people will really start asking questions. Want Mr. Thomas and Mrs. Harper to keep you under lock and key?"

I had to admit, he was right. "OK, I'll carry the vanity inside if you hide it in the darkroom so it stays cool. If not, you'll have a lot of explaining to do."

"Fine, you win." He let out a defeated sigh.

As we drove to work, I mulled over the possibilities. If we showed Mack the bottles, would he turn it into an exposé and end up endangering Holly and Jo Beth?

"I'm having second thoughts about telling Mack," I admitted. "If he finds out where we got the liquor, the girls could get kicked out of the pageant. Worse, the Beach Gang might take matters into their own hands."

Nathan nodded. "You may be right. I know how Mack likes to dig up a good story, poke his nose around town."

I almost mentioned Agent Burton, but I knew Nathan wouldn't approve. His contacts on the police force were the best chance we had to find Holly, yet I was hesitant to get in touch. I knew flappers called fellas all the time, but my upbringing was more on the old-fashioned side.

In front of the *Gazette* building, I gave a nickel to Finn, the newsie, and attempted to cover the vanity case with the newspaper, trying my best to look like a hard-working reporter instead of a debutante on her way to the Midsummer Night's Dance.

Naturally, my decoy was a flop. A couple of jokers whistled across the newsroom, and Hank, the smart-mouth sports reporter, pointed to the case. "Say, Cinderella. You're late for the ball!"

"Go jump in the lake!" I rolled my eyes, my face flushing as pink as the frilly floral case in my hot hand. I followed Nathan to the darkroom, avoiding Mrs. Harper, who looked puzzled.

"Going somewhere, Jasmine?" my eagle-eyed boss asked suspiciously.

"My cousin is in town for the beauty pageant," I fibbed. "I'm just holding onto her valise until she finds a hotel room." I shoved the vanity case at Nathan, flashing a fabricated smile. "Don't forget this! Thanks, you're a pal!"

He panicked, eyes darting around, hoping the newshounds weren't paying attention. But I heard quite a few snickers going around the office. "Hey, Nate, don't forget your face paint. Don't you wanna look beautiful this weekend?" Chuck called out.

Nathan grimaced and shot him an ungentlemanly gesture, then disappeared into the darkroom. If the rude reporters only knew that eyesore was full of liquor, they'd be fighting over it like stray dogs with a T-bone.

As I sat down, Mrs. Harper looked up with interest. "How are the contestants?" she asked, glasses dangling off her nose. "Anything exciting yet?"

"They're busy with rehearsals. Not much time for interviews, but I'm working on it," I reassured her, wheeling my oak chair around so she wouldn't keep drilling me.

A stack of stories sat on my desk, ready to be copy-edited and typed, including one from Mack, a big deal coming from him. True, I wasn't the fastest stenographer in the Southwest, but with his big meaty hands, Mack was a giant tortoise. I'd edited a couple of his articles, full of misspellings and typos. Pity the would-be scribe who tried to tamper with Mack's solid-gold words. Sure, he could write, but he definitely couldn't spell.

After I finished typing and quietly correcting his many typos and mistakes, I walked over and tapped his shoulder to break his trance. He was so engrossed in his work, his craggy face was only inches from his typewriter.

Startled, he looked up, then beamed. "Jasmine, you're just the person I want to see."

"Really?" I blinked in surprise. Mack tended to reserve his smiles for special occasions. "Why?"

"I need some information for this story, and you're the only one who can help."

"Sure, Mack, anything." I felt flattered. "What can I do?"

He pushed back from his desk and placed his glasses on his head. "You can get me a meeting with your friend, Agent Burton."

Not again. Why did everyone assume Agent Burton was my personal genie, granting wishes and favors at my command?

"Did you try to call him?"

"He must be too busy to answer." Mack thrust the candlestick telephone at me, handing me the receiver. "Why don't you try to reach him? Here, you can use my phone."

"Now?" Oh, brother. "Can't you call him yourself?" I stalled, fingering my beads. Not the best way to impress our star reporter, but he'd put me on the spot.

"As I recall, aren't you two good friends?" He gave me a wink, referring to the infamous Surf Club fiasco. "Look, I've tried to get an audience with him, to no avail. I think this needs a woman's touch. *Your* touch."

Blushing, I racked my brain for a way out. Sure, I needed an excuse to call Burton, but I didn't want a captive audience full of nosy newsmen. Luckily Mrs. Page's voice yelled out across the room, "Mack, it's the police. They say it's urgent."

Saved by the Bell telephone.

Mack tried to shoo me away but I sat down in the oak banker's chair by his desk, trying to eavesdrop. He mumbled into the phone, scribbled a few notes and said, "I'm on my way."

"What is it, Mack? Bad news?" That was obvious from his sour expression.

"None of your beeswax, kid. This ain't your department." He spun around in his creaky chair, scanning the newsroom. "Where's Nathan? I need him to take photos right away."

No doubt hiding in the darkroom until the pink vanity case humiliation died down.

"I'll go get him," I offered. "Need any help? I can take notes, ask questions, whatever you want."

I hated to be a pest, but I'd learn more from Mack in a day than a year behind my desk. My last story with Mack made me crave the excitement, the thrill of chasing a big story.

He brushed me aside and jumped up. "Just tell Nathan to meet me at the post office. Make it snappy!" he barked, grabbing his satchel, notepad and hat.

"The post office?" I followed him to the door. "Why? Was there a stick-up?"

"You really wanna know?" He leaned over, his voice low. "OK, kid, you asked for it, but keep this quiet. They found a young girl behind the P.O., about your age."

"Is she dead?" I held my breath, hoping it wasn't Holly. "Any idea who she is?"

"Probably a hooker, like the rest." Mack shrugged. "She was dumped off in the alley like a sack of mail." He snapped his fingers. "Aha! I think I just found my lead!"

CHAPTER ELEVEN

My heart dropped. Could it be Holly? Post Office Street was known as the red-light district so I suspected the victim was a prostitute. Was it related to the other young woman's death? Was the same killer targeting "working girls?"

Sad to say, Galveston had gained a reputation for sporting the highest number of "houses of ill repute" per capita—even more than Paris. France, not Texas. Nothing to brag about, just a depressing fact. Whorehouses lined Post Office from 25th Street to 29th Street, and everyone from sailors to students to tourists knew where to go after dark for that kind of indoor sport.

I rushed to the darkroom to get Nathan, pounding on the door. "Quick, it's an emergency. Mack needs you to take photos, and pronto!"

Nathan stuck his head out, blinking, like a sleepy turtle. "What's the ruckus?"

I looked over my shoulder, but luckily most of the reporters had left. Only Mrs. Harper remained, alert as a squirrel. "He wants you to meet him at the post office. Now!"

"What, he's got a special delivery?" he cracked.

"This is no joke. I'll tell you on the way there."

"On the way? Sure you want to tag along?" He frowned.

I tugged on his arm. "Grab your gear and let's skedaddle."

Then I remembered my boss, who probably had heard every word. I doubted she'd let me out of sight without "permission."

When I explained the situation to Mrs. Harper, she seemed skeptical. "Mack wanted you to go, too? I wish he'd asked me first."

Who was she, my mother?

"It involves a girl my age, so I think he wants a woman's touch," I fibbed, quoting him out of context.

My boss shook her head and sighed. "Honestly, Jasmine, I don't see why on earth you want to involve yourself in these sordid crimes. A nice young lady like you…"

She had a point: Why *was* I so interested in crime and murder?

I certainly didn't have the stomach for it: I got upset watching *Frankenstein*. I didn't relish the thought of seeing dead bodies or crime scenes, especially a female victim, but I needed to know if it was Holly.

"Fine, go ahead." She waved me away like a pesky fly. "Don't forget a stack of work is waiting for you!"

"Yes, ma'am," I said politely, grateful she agreed.

Nathan stopped by my desk, overloaded with camera equipment. "Got your permission slip?"

Nodding, I stuffed a notepad in my leather handbag and grabbed my straw hat. As we walked out to his car, I told him what little I knew. "Mack didn't mention if the poor girl was dead or alive." I touched his arm. "Are you thinking what I'm thinking?"

He nodded, eyes cloudy. "I just hope to God it's not her."

I felt for him. I knew he was attracted to Holly the minute they met. Who wouldn't like such a vivacious, fun-loving girl, so different from her stuck-up "friend," Jo Beth.

The post office was a large imposing building with huge columns and steep front steps, as majestic as any Federal landmark in D.C. Half a dozen police cars formed an arc around the entrance off Post Office Street and 25th Street, blocking the corner; the cops had barricaded the back lot. A few gawkers milled around, looking for excitement, but from the front lot, we couldn't see much of anything.

"Wait here." Nathan parked across the street and we got out, dodging traffic as we rushed to the lot. "I'll see what's happening."

"Good luck." I watched him disappear into the crowd, dreading the verdict, yet dying of curiosity.

The heat felt stifling as I paced the parking lot, trying to work up the nerve to sneak in past the barricade. Maybe I could tell the cops that I was a journalist, though I'd never gotten an official press pass to prove it. The editors' excuse was that it "made the society crowd uncomfortable." So what?

As I waited, I anxiously mulled over possible scenarios: If it was Holly, I prayed she was still alive, still conscious. Or was the victim a working girl who'd angered some client? A gangster's moll?

I shuddered to think of the possibilities. But why deposit her behind the post office? Was the location significant? Could it be a message, a warning, the start of another gang war?

Looking for clues, I scanned the parking lot, wondering if the girl had been assaulted here or dumped off later. No signs of blood or torn clothing so far.

Out of the corner of my eye, I saw a tiny, shiny gold-colored object and rushed over to pick it up. I barely glanced at it, but it appeared to be a religious charm, engraved with a saint and a few Latin words underneath. Quickly I pocketed the charm, hoping no one noticed. Did it belong to the victim or was it lost by accident?

Losing patience, I waited until the cops had turned their backs to make my way across the lot. So many rubberneckers had gathered around the building that I couldn't clearly see the crime scene.

Quickly I snuck under the rope blocking the side alley, acting as if I belonged there. Who was I kidding? In my pastel summer outfit and hat, I looked more like a tourist than a reporter.

I spotted Nathan and motioned him over. Reluctantly, he approached me, breathing hard, his face flushed. Oh no…was it Holly? I tried reading his expression, but he wouldn't meet my gaze. "Is it…?" I asked, my voice a whisper.

"No, thank God. The cops think she's a prostitute, maybe around 18 or 20? She's a pretty young thing, but it's hard to tell her exact age due to her injuries."

I let out a relieved sigh. "Poor girl. What happened?"

He shook his head. "The M.E. said it appears she was strangled. I hate to think of what she went through right before she died."

"What do you mean?" Despite the balmy weather, I shivered. "Is she all in one piece?"

I pictured the diabolical Jack the Ripper, who I'd heard dissected young prostitutes in London's East End. Did Galveston have a copycat killer?

"Yes, but trust me, you don't want to know the details. The victim is probably around your age and size." I made a move toward the victim, but he held tight to my arm. "Sure you wouldn't rather go watch the bathing beauties rehearse?"

"Nathan, you can't keep trying to protect me." I struggled against his grip. "Mack's there, isn't he? I need to learn how to handle crime scenes if I want to cover real news."

"Don't say I didn't warn you." He let go of my arm and held up his hands in defeat.

My heart hammered as I tiptoed through the crowd, saying, "Excuse me" as they made room.

A burly cop faced me, blocking my way. "Say, girlie, what are you doing here? You know this girl? Is she a relation or something?"

"No." I blanched, taken aback. "Why would you say that?" Now I was really curious.

He looked down. "Excuse me, miss. Just asking."

"I'm here as a reporter." I tried to put on a brave front.

I carefully crept into the inner circle, then covered my mouth, recoiling at the sight. On the pavement, a petite young woman with long dark hair lay at an awkward angle, her right eye bruised and swollen, a few cuts on her face and bloodied lip. She wore a silky print frock ripped down the middle, her small frame partially hidden under a man's jacket. Thank goodness someone had the decency to cover her bottom half.

Red and purple bruises wreathed her neck, evidence of strangulation. But what really bothered me were her eyes, a blue-green like mine, open in surprise, accusatory, as if she knew her attacker. I blinked back tears, trying to remain composed in front of this hard-boiled bunch of cops and reporters.

Across the huddle, Mack frowned at me, stone-faced. Clearly he thought the poor girl's death was none of my business.

Still, I felt nothing but pity for this young woman, wondering about her final moments, her past. Was she a runaway? An orphan? What had made her turn to prostitution?

Granted, I hadn't grown up in the Moody mansion, but my family had never lacked anything, thanks to my father's store.

In a daze, I turned away, my face hot, stumbling over to the M.E. who was examining her neck and shoulders. "What happened to her?" I blurted out.

"And you are?" He cocked his eyebrow. "Do you know the victim? Are you a relative?"

Why did everyone assume we were related? How could they tell if we looked alike with her swollen and bruised face?

"No, I'm with the *Gazette*," I informed him. "I'm a reporter."

A shiny gleam caught my eye and with a start, I noticed the dead girl wore a gold charm bracelet on her right wrist. Good luck charms, gold-plated I assumed, not worth stealing. How ironic. Seems the gold charm I found may have belonged to the victim. Too bad all those charms didn't help her luck one bit.

"It's OK, Charlie. She's with me," Mack called out across the group of onlookers.

I thanked him with a nod, then thought, Mack didn't do favors for nothing. I bet he still wanted me to set up a meeting with Burton.

"So what's the verdict?" I asked the M.E.

"Why don't you ask Mack?" he shrugged. "I've got work to do."

"I can't quote Mack, but I can report you," I snapped, standing tall, glaring back at him.

"Fine." His brown eyes were dull as dirt, no doubt weary of seeing so many dead bodies. "Obviously she was strangled, choked to death by the perpetrator's hands, as indicated by these bruise marks in her flesh." He pointed to her neck, signs of dark red half-moons still obvious. "But this little wildcat put up a good fight. Luckily I found traces of tissue under her fingernails, and strands of hair stuck to her gown."

I bit my lip, trying not to picture this fragile creature fighting for her life. "Anything else?" Did I really want to know?

"What's unusual is the hairs are different colors, fair and dark. Short hairs, not hers."

"Not that unusual for a hooker," one joker snickered. "The more, the merrier."

The M.E. watched my reaction. "Seems the victim was raped, more than once, perhaps by different men. Mack can tell you the rest." He turned away and sighed, the first sign of compassion. "Poor girl didn't stand a chance."

I grimaced and gripped my stomach, as if I'd been struck in the gut. Was that the response he wanted? "Do you have any idea who she is? Any ID?" Hadn't I asked these same questions before? Except for location, the similarities between the two prostitute deaths were uncanny.

He shook his head. "No clue. All she had on was her gown. What's left of it."

Did he have to be so matter-of-fact, so indifferent? I suppose if examining corpses was your chosen profession, you'd need to develop a hard shell, preparing for the worst. Not unlike cops or reporters. Maybe I wasn't cut out for this business.

"What about the gold charm bracelet? There, on her right wrist?" I pointed toward the body, but averted my eyes from her battered face. "It may have an inscription, her initials?"

"We'll look into it," he scowled. "But unless someone claims the body, it's of no use."

"No use? It's evidence!" I replied. "Must you examine her in public? Can't you take her someplace private?"

"She's ready to go to the morgue. Just call off your newshounds and shutterbugs."

My newshounds? I looked up to see Mack and Nathan comparing notes behind his camera. Figured. I turned to go, feeling sick. I didn't want to ask any more questions anyway.

The M.E. stood up and waved away the crowd, now doubled in size. The burly cop took his cue, dismissing the onlookers.

"Let's go, people. Show's over. Nothing to see."

Most people wandered away in silence, heads bowed. At least they showed some respect for the victim. Of course the reporters stood their ground, tapping their feet and pencils on pads.

Nathan reappeared and took my arm, leading me away. "I'm sorry. I tried to stop you."

"The M.E. was right." I squeezed my eyes shut. "That poor girl didn't stand a chance."

CHAPTER TWELVE

"I told you not to come, kid." Mack ambled over. "Not a pretty sight."

"Seems so unfair, to rape and kill a young woman, then toss her out like old news," I said, trying to calm down. "What did she ever do wrong? Even prostitutes deserve better."

"I doubt it was pre-mediated murder," Mack said. "Appears to be a crime of passion. Strangulation is the killer's method of choice. Quick and easy."

"We need to find out who did this to her." I balled my hands into fists.

"How do you propose we do that?" Mack shrugged. "No one cares about these whores, not even their madams. They'll deny everything, even their existence 'cause they don't want any trouble. To them, these girls are a dime a dozen."

My face started to flame. "This girl was someone's daughter, sister, friend. I'm sure *they* cared about her!"

Mack scratched his chin, a mix of gray and brown stubble. "Well, maybe you're just the person to help me investigate her murder. I'd bet these prostitutes wouldn't mind talking to you, but be careful snooping around. They might get their feathers ruffled."

Was he serious or pulling my leg? I hadn't thought of helping Mack solve a real case. "What do you suggest? Where would I start?"

He pointed down the street. "I'd go to Madam Templeton's house first since it has the best reputation. She's got the cleanest shop around, and keeps a close watch on the neighborhood."

Clearly Mack had been around this particular block quite a few times. Grinning, he elbowed Nathan in the ribs. "But don't be surprised if she tries to recruit you on the spot. If you really want the scoop, you may have to go undercover, do the legwork, so to speak."

"That's not funny." I scowled at him, and crossed my arms.

Nathan frowned. "Don't listen to him, Jazz. He's just joking."

Mack shook his head. "No, I'm not. You have to gain their trust, make them think you're one of them, or at least that you don't judge them. Sympathize with the girls. That's how you get closer, find out what they know."

I considered that a moment. What a contrast from the beauty queens I'd interviewed just yesterday. Could I actually pull it off? Then I remembered what the cops had said. "Say, I have an idea. What if I pretend that I'm looking for my sister or cousin?" I made a face at Mack. "Then I don't have to pose as a prostitute."

"Now you're talking." Mack nodded.

"Jazz, that's too dangerous." Nathan seemed worried. "How would it look for a society reporter to get caught in a whorehouse?"

He was right. "Then I won't get caught."

"Caught doing what?" A long shadow fell, and I looked up to see Agent Burton, towering over us. He stared at me, his mouth tight. "I'm surprised to see you here. Sorry about the girl."

"So am I." I studied him head to toe. For a Fed agent, he sure was a natty dresser, his double-breasted suit snug on his muscular frame. A far cry from the local yokels who barely filled out their uniforms, or stretched them out of shape. "What brings you here?"

He raised his brows. "Same question to you. Since when do *society* reporters show up at crime scenes?"

Flustered, I said, "Why not? I'm just trying to help."

Nathan wasn't Burton's biggest fan, but now he turned to him like an old pal. "Say, maybe you can talk some sense into her. Jazz wants to investigate this girl's death on her own."

Why was it any of their business? "Nathan, keep Agent Burton out of this. If I need any help, I'll be sure to ask. Or I can bring Amanda along."

"Right. You and Amanda are gonna take on a ruthless killer." Nathan let out a snort. "Now instead of two murders, there'll be three or four."

"Says you." I glared at him, miffed. "Gee, thanks for the vote of confidence."

Mack cleared his throat. "Aren't you going to introduce me to your..." He paused, as if searching for the right word. Please don't say fella, I thought. "Friend?" He reached over to shake Burton's hand. "I'm Mack Harris, city reporter at the *Gazette*. We haven't officially met yet, but I've been trying to reach you by phone."

"Really? Why?" Burton's voice was flat, his blue eyes wary.

I decided to help Mack out, since I owed him a favor. "Say, don't you remember me telling you about Mack? He's the one who bailed me out with my boss."

A small smile played across his face. "How can I forget?" Burton winked at me. "The infamous Surf Club photos. OK, sir, why don't I come by the paper later today?"

"See you then." Mack nodded his thanks. "Come on, Nathan, we need more photos."

Nathan looked apologetic. "Sorry, Jazz. Maybe you can catch a ride back to work?"

Great, they were leaving me stranded with Agent Burton.

"Don't feel obligated. I can take the trolley back to the *Gazette*." He was so tall, I had to squint in the sun.

"You're welcome to tag along with me." He tipped his hat. "Beats the trolley."

"Thanks." I recognized his Roadster, parked across the street. "So what brings you by here? I didn't think you got involved in death investigations, especially on Post Office Street."

"Only in special circumstances." He gave me a sly smile, referring to a recent case. "I'll tell you, but only off the record. We got a tip that some bootleg was stored in the Pretty Kitty, another brothel on Post Office Street."

"Pretty Kitty? Sounds like a pet shop. What did you find?" Besides naked women.

"Nothing. It was a bust. The whole place had been cleared out. Even the girls were gone." He let out a frustrated blast of air. "So we heard about this crime scene and rushed over." Burton stopped walking, and motioned toward the area. "I suspect this killing was related, the body left here as a distraction, to keep the police busy. What do you think?"

Was Agent Burton really asking for my opinion? "It's possible, depending on the timing. What if she was killed there first, so they decided to clear out the house?"

Burton nodded. "Her death could be happenstance, and they used it to their advantage. Both scenarios are plausible."

The heat beat down on us as we walked to his car. "If you're serious about investigating this girl's death, I'd like to help. How about if we work together?"

"In this area? They'd see us coming a mile away." I tugged on my peach floppy hat with its striped sash. "We don't exactly look like the criminal element."

He held open the car door. "What about searching for your long-lost sister or cousin?"

So he *had* been eavesdropping. "What else did you hear?"

"Enough to know that you shouldn't go to Post Office Street alone. A cute young gal like you? They might mistake you for...well, you know. One of those girls."

Was that an insult or a compliment? "I hardly think I'd pass for a lady of the night," I bristled, smoothing out my skirt.

"You'd be surprised. Lots of nice girls show up on Post Office Street when they have no place else to go. They may be runaways, trying to escape an abusive father or husband and need to hide out, to make money fast." He started the engine, looking at me sideways. "Sad, but true."

How did he know so much about prostitutes? I wondered. Then I recalled his dad had been a cop in New York. "I can't imagine how horrible their lives must be, to run away from one abusive situation to another. What a life, having to gratify men just to pay the bills."

"Bad luck." He nodded and stared ahead. "Tell you what. Why don't we hit a few houses, ask some questions, see what happens. I'll be your bodyguard, so to speak."

"Both of us? Now?" Caught off guard, I turned to see if he was serious. In an instant, my bravado floated away like mist. "I'm not exactly prepared."

Stalling, I pulled out a red enameled compact and powdered my nose. What on earth do you wear to a bordello?

CHAPTER THIRTEEN

Burton seemed nonchalant, like visiting whorehouses was the most natural thing in the world. "We're in the neighborhood, so why not? Best to show up now before word gets out about the dead girl."

Now what? "I'm not used to making social calls at cathouses. What do I do? How do I act?"

I admit, the idea of parading around the red-light district of Post Office Street, even in broad daylight, terrified me.

"I'm afraid you might be overdressed. Anything more than a nightgown is considered formal wear," he teased me, then shrugged. "Never mind. I thought you wanted to help."

"I do, but..." I hesitated. "What if someone sees me? My job, my reputation is at stake."

"Then you can ask them what they're doing on the wrong side of town." He grinned. "Say, how about if I go with you? Tell them you're searching for your cousin, like you said. I could be her broken-hearted beau."

I had a feeling he wanted me to be his decoy, an excuse to poke around the place. As I mulled it over, I watched a sad black lab lumber along the street, looking for food, its ribs sticking out. He wagged his tail and looked at me with hopeful brown eyes, breaking my heart. How I wished I had some scraps of food so I could feed the poor stray. Was that how it felt to be a runaway, lost and alone, begging for hand-outs?

"I need to get back to work soon," I told him, plucking at a loose thread on my cotton frock. OK, I admit, I was a scaredy-cat.

"Where's your moxie? Are you all talk, no action?" Burton thrust out his chin, challenging me. "Come on, it'll only take ten minutes at most. Just blame me for being late."

He was right. How could I refuse? "Mack mentioned Madam Templeton's house?"

"I happen to know where that is." Oh really? Was he a regular?

Burton drove a few houses down and parked in front of a bright pink Victorian mansion with flower pots lining the wide wrap-around front porch. A black wrought-iron fence surrounded the property with an unlatched gate, welcoming gentlemen callers. On the porch, a wooden swing faced the street, covered with puffy pillows, inviting us to stay a while.

From the outside, it looked like a colorful three-story house that belonged to a well-to-do matron, not a madam. Only the big pillows, lace curtains and Pepto-Bismol pink paint gave it away.

How fitting: A painted lady housing the painted ladies.

I rearranged my hat, trying to shield my face. "Sure you want to do this?" My legs felt shaky as we climbed the expansive steps.

He nodded and knocked on the rose-colored wooden door adorned with ornate stained glass, colors bright in the sunlight. "Just follow my lead."

A plump older woman in heavy make-up answered the door and stepped outside, blocking the entrance. She resembled a gypsy, her arms covered in bracelets, a print scarf wrapped around her long wavy hair. With her ample cleavage squeezed to its full potential in a long flowing floral burnt-velvet dress, she certainly didn't look like anyone's grandmother. Who wears velvet in summer, in the middle of the day? Her dark kohl-rimmed eyes darted back and forth, her expression guarded. "Yes?"

Agent Burton took off his hat and said in a courtly Southern accent: "Excuse me, ma'am. We're looking for a miss Annabelle Smith. She told us she's living in a boarding house on this street but didn't give us the exact address."

I turned to him in surprise. I thought Burton was born and bred in New York, so how did he manage such a convincing Texas drawl?

The woman pressed her lips together, as if trying to stifle a smile. "Sorry, but this isn't..." She cleared her throat. Behind the gauzy curtains, I could see two or three made-up female faces peeking out the windows. "No one here by that name. What does she look like?"

"She's got dark hair and pale skin, about my height and coloring. I'm her cousin," I piped up, adding a tremble to my voice.

Then I remembered the victim's bracelet. "By the way, she always wears a gold charm bracelet. Not real gold, of course. She said it brought her good luck."

Her stern expression softened. "Sorry about your cousin. We do have a few young ladies who are *boarders* here." That was a new name for the oldest profession. She cleared her throat, studying Burton. "Sometimes they change their names because they don't want to be found."

I dabbed my eyes with my hanky. "She's been gone a few months and I really do miss her. I hate to think she's lost!" I wailed. Who knew I could act on demand?

"Dry your eyes, hon." She smiled at me, perhaps looking for her next recruit. "I'll keep my ear to the ground and in case I hear of anything, I'll let you know. Where can I reach you?"

What now? "We're from out of town, wanted to see the Bathing Beauty Revue. Why don't I check back later this week?" I ad-libbed.

"That's fine. I'll ask my girls...I mean, my *boarders* if they've seen her around."

"Thanks so much!" I forced a smile, waving as we bounded down the stairs.

"See, that wasn't so hard," Burton said as we got into his Roadster. "Are you sure you're in the right profession? You could always make it as an actress."

"Thanks, but my little performance didn't help much." I looked out the window, trying to shake off the image of the dead prostitute. I pitied the poor working girls who wanted to escape their past and were desperate for income. Yes, my job and my boss gave me a headache, but at least it was honest and often interesting work—when I was let off my chain.

"The fact she even opened the door at all says a lot. Seems she hasn't heard about the dead girl yet or even realized she was missing. For all she knew, I was a cop." Burton turned to me with a smile. "And that was a good move, inventing an excuse to go back there."

"Maybe she's looking for her next breadwinner," I said glumly.

"Could be," he nodded. "Take it as a compliment."

"A compliment? Do I look like a streetwalker to you?" I huffed, hands on hips.

"Not at all, but that's the idea. The movers and shakers who patronize these places don't want used goods. They like fresh young faces and girls next door."

"I don't look like the girl next door," I pointed out.

"You look like the girl they *wished* live next door." He gave me the once-over.

"Thanks, I think." Was he teasing me again?

Flustered, I decided this was a good time to ask him about Sammy's predicament. Anything to keep my mind off the victim. Time was running out since the bathing beauties' performance was this Friday.

"James, I need to ask you for a favor. A big favor." I tried to butter him up by using his first name, then changed my mind. "But not now. Later."

"Sounds serious. How about if I pick you up after work, and we can grab a bite to eat, maybe on the beach? Say, around five?"

"That'd be swell." I nodded, grateful for the chance to talk to him alone. "I'll take off early. After today, I'm in no mood to write about bathing beauties."

The moment Burton dropped me off at the *Gazette*, I began to worry. Sure, I wanted to help Sammy, but I couldn't very well talk about the weather, then suddenly blurt out: "Why don't we go see the bathing beauties Friday night at the Hollywood Dinner Club? By the way, while we're there, would you mind raiding the place for me? Just this once?" After all, he wasn't a Prohibition agent-for-hire, charging by the raid.

What was I thinking, letting Sammy rope me into this mess?

CHAPTER FOURTEEN

At the *Gazette*, I slunk back to my desk but couldn't concentrate. Ignoring Mrs. Harper's glower, I hunched over my stack of papers to be proofed or edited or filed, yet my mind kept drifting off.

Despite Mack's assessment, I couldn't shake the feeling that something didn't add up. True, I didn't have much experience with crime scenes, especially "crimes of passion." The second victim didn't look like any ordinary prostitute, hardened by years on the street. To me, she seemed fragile, innocent even, as if she'd taken a wrong turn, literally. Her silk gown looked expensive, her charm bracelet, brand-new. Could anyone have helped her?

As my mind swirled, Nathan leaned over my desk. "Took your time coming back, I see. How'd things go with your fella?"

"What fella?" I rolled my eyes. Who was he to razz me, after his crush on Holly—or was it now Jo Beth? "We only went to one house, but that was a bust. I'd like to go back and try to interview some girls, but I doubt the madam, Mrs. Templeton, will let me near the place again."

I let out a frustrated sigh. "Mack's right. There's not much we can do unless someone reports the girl missing."

"Fat chance." Nathan studied his fingers, stained with chemicals from processing photos. "If anyone does report her disappearance, they'll be considered the prime suspect in her killing."

I hadn't considered that angle. "It just doesn't seem fair. Why should this poor girl's death get ignored while the fat cats get away with murder in this town?"

"Who said it was a fat cat? Could be a jealous boyfriend or john." He tapped his fingers on my desk. "Say, I know what'll cheer us up. Let's go see the bathing beauties rehearse."

"How would that cheer *me* up? You, definitely." I lowered my voice, and motioned for him to follow me. We found an empty office and ducked inside. "Don't forget, we have to figure out what to do with...the stash. What should I tell Agent Burton?"

"Why tell him anything?" Nathan frowned. "You wanna get the girls in trouble?"

"They're already in trouble. Burton is coming by here after work later."

"Here? Tonight? Let's hope you do more telling than showing." He winked, but it was more of a warning than a joke.

I assumed he meant the booze. "This isn't personal, it's purely professional, believe me."

"May not be safe, hiding a bunch of booze in the darkroom, especially with a Fed agent around." Nathan stared at the worn wooden floor. "Sure we should come clean?"

"Got any better ideas?"

"We could take the bottles to Sammy, find out what he knows, like you said."

"After seeing that dead girl, I don't think that's such a bright idea. Burton said they tried to raid a brothel today, but the whole place had been cleaned out. Makes me wonder if somehow the two events are related." I scratched my head, trying to make sense of it all. "What if this booze was part of that same stash? Even two bottles can be incriminating."

"Who knows?" He slid off my desk, shaking his head. "Good luck with Burton tonight. You'll need it."

And how. I didn't know which was worse: Telling Burton about Holly and the hidden booze at the Hotel Galvez, or Johnny Jack's request to raid the Hollywood Dinner Club during the bathing beauties' dance routine?

Either way, I felt as doomed as the heroine in "The Perils of Pauline."

Across the newsroom, Mack motioned me over and I obeyed, like a good foot soldier. I'd heard he was an Army sergeant in the Great War before a leg injury sidelined him. Even after he became a war correspondent, he still acted like a bossy drill sergeant, issuing commands at will. He eyed me, his bushy brows raised.

"So, did you take a detour to Madam Templeton's?"

"As a matter of fact, we did. She was quite a character, but it seems to be a dead-end."

"Sure was a dead-end for the victim," Mack cracked. "Did she offer you a job?"

"Of course, but I turned it down. Not enough pay." I gave him a deadpan look. "I wonder if the girls know anything? She could be covering for her clients."

"Maybe she's telling the truth. Those kinds of girls don't last long in the biz."

"I'll bet," I nodded, looking away. My eyes stung, thinking of the victim's mangled body in the alley behind the post office. "Do the police have any leads?"

"Not yet. Until there's a missing-person report, their hands are tied." He shrugged. "A lot of these girls are orphans or runaways and have no relatives, or the family just doesn't care."

"Wasn't there any sign of the killer? The M. E. said she put up a good fight. Did they check the forensics? What about fingerprints, tissue, hair? Any clues?" Somehow I doubted the police had put much effort into gathering evidence.

"Sure, the cops can look for prints, but unless the killer is on file, there's not much to go by." Mack shifted his bulk around in his beat-up banker's chair. "Let's be realistic. A dead whore isn't high on their to-do list. They don't want to waste time on an unclaimed, unidentified body."

Did he have to be so cold? This case rattled me, perhaps because the victim was close to my age and people thought I resembled her. "What can we do?"

"Just sit tight." His eyes darted around the newsroom. "Keep asking questions and something may turn up soon. Cops can't solve every case. The bad guys are good at disappearing."

"I'll bet." I fussed with the buttons on my frock, working up my nerve. "Say, have you gotten any more information about that dead girl on the rocks? Any clues or leads? I wonder if their deaths are related in any way?"

Mack stretched his arms. "Not yet, but I wouldn't hold my breath, kid."

I leaned forward. "But now there are *two* dead young women. What if it's a serial killer targeting young prostitutes? Isn't that worth a serious investigation?"

"I'd hope so." He nodded. "For now, the mayor wants to keep these cases quiet, and out of the papers. The cops are too busy handling the extra traffic and tourists in town for the pageant. To be blunt, city officials don't care about a couple of dead hookers."

"How can they be sure they were working girls?" I asked. "Maybe they were college students or secretaries or maids? They might be from out of town, looking for a job?"

"I'll tell you this much." He lowered his voice to a husky whisper. "The girl on the rocks was branded. She had a seashell tattoo on her wrist."

"*Branded?* Like cattle?" I made a face. "How do you know? What does the shell mean?"

"My M.E. friend told me about the tattoo." Mack looked me dead in the eye. "It means she belonged to the Beach Gang."

CHAPTER FIFTEEN

"She *belonged* to the Beach Gang?" I shook my head in disgust. "I thought slavery was abolished during the Civil War."

"To them, it's just business." Mack shrugged. "They don't want to confuse their gals with the Downtown Gang's girls. The goons like to keep tabs on their women, especially their best performers."

"Guess the girls all look alike to those thugs. Use them up, then toss them onto a heap pile, like an old jalopy." I let out a sigh. "No one deserves to die that way."

"All I know is Ollie Quinn has high standards. Maybe she didn't make the grade." Mack surveyed the newsroom. "Hey, let's keep this quiet. The only reason I told you is 'cause you got me a meeting with Agent Burton." He turned around in his chair. "Back to work. No more questions for today."

I knew when I'd been dismissed. In a daze, I reluctantly returned to my desk, Mack's words echoing in my ears. That explained why the police were letting these girls' deaths go unsolved so far. They cared more about placating the Beach Gang than investigating the lives of two young women, maybe not entirely innocent, but both victims of brutal crimes.

I thought about the seashell tattoo Mack mentioned, wondering if the Post Office Street prostitute also had a similar tattoo. Is that why she wore a charm bracelet, to hide the seashell, cover up her shame? That reminded me: I made a mental note to go to a jeweler and find out more about the charm, try to get some answers.

Despite all these distractions, I still had deadlines to meet. In two hours, I managed to write a rough draft of my conversation with Miss New Orleans, Sara, who was orphaned at an early age and raised by her aunt and uncle.

I began to sympathize with these beauty queens, to understand their perspective. So many girls depended on their good looks and wits to survive, and had to develop a competitive spirit by sheer necessity. Most Southern women I knew were taught to be demure, to defer to men, to avoid conflict. Competing for anything—good grades, a beauty pageant or a sports event—simply wasn't considered ladylike or genteel. Horse feathers!

As I was editing my profile, a long shadow crossed my desk: Agent Burton, six-foot-two with eyes of blue, as my mom would say. He stood over my desk, hat in hand, his tanned face cracking into a smile. "Hello, Jazz. Fancy seeing you here."

I almost jumped out of my chair. "Hello, yourself. What's wrong? Any news?"

"Don't let me interrupt. I'm meeting with Mack, then we can get together." Burton's tone implied we had a date, not an appointment. More like a sentencing.

I painted on a smile. "Ready whenever you are."

Mack waved from across the room. "Burton, over here." Burton tipped his hat at me as he sauntered over to his desk, then followed him to the back. What was the big secret?

Speaking of secrets, how could I bring up Holly and the stash of booze? Better to leave it in the darkroom with Nathan. But knowing him, he'd try to polish off the booze himself, maybe with Mack.

Worse, I dreaded asking Burton to get involved in Johnny Jack's crazy scheme. Truth be told, I could never say no to Sammy.

Mrs. Harper waddled over, staring at the back office so intently that I thought she was trying to read lips. "Why is Mack meeting with Agent Burton?" She smoothed away stray auburn hairs by her face, adjusted her skirt. Was she preening for Mack or Burton?

"Wish I knew." I shrugged. "Mack probably needs information for a story."

"So how is your young man?" Mrs. Harper's rosy-hued lips curved upward.

"We're just friends," I told her for the umpteenth time. "We're not seeing each other socially."

"Oh, really? You seem very sociable to me." With that, she gave me a smug smile and returned to her desk, taking one last lingering glance at the corner office.

I tried to work, but was too distracted by Burton and Mack to concentrate. So I gave up and grabbed a tango compact from my purse, applying peony pink lipstick and rouge, holding up the mirror for a better angle. What were they discussing: the gangs or the dead call girls or what?

Nathan strolled over and cocked his head toward the back. "What's Romeo doing here now? What does he want with Mack?" Nathan had taken an instant dislike to Burton since the night he'd raided the Oasis.

"Good question. Mack asked me to set up a meeting with Burton today." I wheeled my chair around, craning my neck for a better look.

Nathan perked up. "I'd love to be a fly on the wall."

"You and me both. Why don't you find out what you can from Mack? I'll try to get the scoop out of Burton."

"What scoop?" Agent Burton had an uncanny habit of sneaking up behind me without warning. Nathan disappeared into the darkroom, like a second-string actor taking his cue.

"Never mind," I said, flustered. How much had he overheard?

"Ready to go?" Burton asked me.

"Give me a minute, then I'm all yours," I told him, then winced at my choice of words.

"Fine with me." He made himself at home, pulling up an old banker's chair, watching as I sorted through a few papers. Then Nathan strode over to my desk, holding up the flashy case at arm's length like it was a ticking bomb. In a way, it was.

"Don't forget this, Jazz!" Nathan mimicked me from earlier. "Your vanity case?"

I shot Nathan the evil eye. Was he trying to get me in trouble or save his own skin?

"Planning a trip?" Burton asked, curious.

"It's not mine." I blinked, and turned to Nathan. "What about Jo—?"

"She said you can borrow it." He cut me off, shoving it across my desk.

"Gee, thanks, but I don't really need it now." I gave it a hard push. "Sure you don't want to deliver it to her yourself?"

Amused, Burton watched us slide the case back and forth across my desk like a giant hockey puck.

"It suits you better." Nathan tapped his straw boater. "Gotta run. You two have fun."

Fun? I wanted to strangle that little Judas. Now I had no choice but to explain the vanity case full of booze to a Prohibition agent—and fast. Mrs. Harper watched with interest while I fumbled with the handle, trying to act casual, avoiding her beady eyes.

Outside, I followed Burton to his car, carefully holding out the case, feeling guilty as a wanted criminal.

To distract him, I asked, "So what did Mack want?"

"Wouldn't you like to know?" His smug smile spread across his handsome face. "Maybe we can catch up over an early supper? How about Gaido's?"

"I'm not hungry now. I'd rather go someplace where we can talk in private, maybe the beach?"

"How private?" Burton raised his brows and opened the car door. As I struggled to get inside, vanity case and all, he grabbed the handle. "Let me take that for you." He lifted up the case and stared at it, then knocked on its side. "Say, what's in here? A ton of bricks?"

I froze in place, reaching for the case. "Nothing," I sputtered, trying to snatch it away, but he held it out of my reach.

"Nothing?" He lifted it to his ear and shook it, the glass clinking while the bottles rolled around. "Sounds like something to me. Perfume bottles? I can put the case in the trunk if you want."

I held my breath. "Please be careful...it's full of face lotion and jars. You know, make-up, ladies' things."

I tugged on the handle and managed to pull it out of his grip, praying the damn thing wouldn't suddenly burst open like a pink piñata. With my luck, the liquor bottles would fall out and shatter on the sidewalk. Then I'd really have a lot of explaining to do.

"Why all the fuss over some silly face paint and perfume? You don't need a load of cosmetics." Burton seemed puzzled, as if trying to comprehend the whole female population. "You don't really want to look like a streetwalker, do you? Or was it all just an act?"

Was he joking?

"You slay me. I'm just holding onto this for safekeeping."

I slipped inside the car, and placed the vanity case safely on my lap, cradling it like a newborn baby. Close call.

As we drove, his eyes narrowed. "What's so special about some girly train case?"

I chewed on my nails, worried about his reaction. "If I tell you the truth, promise you won't get mad or do anything rash?"

"Why would I get mad?" He stopped the car along a deserted stretch of road, and turned toward me. "Tell me the truth."

I let out a sharp breath. "A friend of mine may be in trouble..."

"Really? What kind of trouble?"

"For one thing, she's missing. She's been gone for a whole day."

"Is she in danger?" He frowned. "Any idea where she is?"

"She's probably with her fella." I tapped my nails on the case.

"Why don't you contact him then?"

"I don't know him and I hear he's not exactly a nice guy."

I hesitated, toying with the case. Was I doing the right thing? Doubtful, but Nathan had left me no choice.

"This may help explain her situation." I popped open the case, removed the top tray of cosmetics and unwrapped one fancy bottle of Johnnie Walker Black.

CHAPTER SIXTEEN

Agent Burton grabbed the Johnnie Walker Black, eyes wide as he studied the label. "Looks like the real deal. Where'd you get this? And what in hell are you doing with it now?"

"I can't tell you." The case felt like a lead barbell, pinning me down, trapping me.

"Can't or won't?" He looked exasperated. "Jazz, don't you trust me by now?"

"Sure, but...I don't want my friend to get in trouble."

"Sounds like she's already in trouble."

"I'll say. No one knows where she is." I let out a sigh. "We searched her room, but all her things were still there, including her suitcase."

"So she couldn't have gone very far. What's the problem?"

If only I knew. "Turns out, her suitcase is filled with bottles of Johnnie Walker Black. We think her boyfriend is hiding it there for his gang."

Burton worked his jaw. "Which gang? Where's the booze now?"

Did I have to spill all the beans? "In her room. We left it there, under her bed."

"Does your friend know it's there? If so, she could be considered an accomplice."

"I doubt it." I shook my head, trying to defend Holly in absentia. "But if she does, it's because her so-called beau forced her to hide it there. She's a nice girl who's taken up with the wrong people. What should we do?" I asked, hoping to share the burden.

"Just leave it there for now or the gangs could come after your friend. If they haven't already. And I know firsthand what they're capable of doing."

"You said it." Playing dumb, I asked, "Any idea who sells this type of liquor?"

"Both gangs have expensive taste when it comes to booze." He rolled the bottle around in his hand. "But I know Sam Maceo's liquor of choice is Johnnie Walker Black."

That confirmed Jo Beth's story. But why was Rico hiding the bottles at the hotel? Did Smooth Sam know about the extra stash or was Rico trying to peddle booze to rich Galvez guests?

Burton narrowed his slate-blue eyes. "Tell me, Jazz. If you want to protect your friend, why did you show me these bottles?"

"I thought it might lead us to Holly." Ooops. I covered my big mouth with both hands. How could I let her name slip out?

"Holly? Who's Holly?"

"I just met her. Her boyfriend's name is Rico," I added, to take the heat off her.

"Rico? Rico Giovanni?" Burton hit his fist on the steering wheel. "He's Sam Maceo's right-hand man. A brute. From an old Mafioso family in Sicily. How'd your friend get involved with a gangster? And why are you mixed up in this mess?"

"Long story." I sighed. "Can you help us find her, before Rico does? I'm really worried."

"Sure, if you answer some questions." He eyed me as he started the car. "First, tell me where she lives. Maybe she's there, trying to hide from Rico."

"She's from Houston. That's all I know." I shrugged, worried that I'd said too much.

His eyes glazed over with impatience. "Want me to help you find your friend or not?"

"Of course, but I don't want her to get in any more hot water, " I admitted.

He made a quick U-turn in the middle of the street, then parked by the beach. Burton stretched an arm across the back of my seat. From outside appearances, we could be sweethearts, having a lovers' quarrel. "Jazz, I can't help you or Holly if you only tell me little bits and pieces at a time. I need to know what you know, the works."

I watched a flock of seagulls fly overhead, wishing I could fly away with them. A few gulls landed near families picnicking on the beach, squawking as they scurried for food crumbs. Finally, I told him the whole story…well, almost.

"I met Holly after she fainted during a dance rehearsal. Nathan gave her a ride back to the hotel. That's the first and last time we saw her. Jo Beth told us she went out that night with her boyfriend, but never returned to her room or showed up for rehearsals."

I took a deep breath, steeling myself for more questions.

"She's a bathing beauty?" His head snapped to attention.

I nodded. "When they found the dead girl behind the post office, I was afraid it was Holly." Now I felt exhausted, spent, as if I'd been in confession. Frankly, I'd never make it as a Catholic.

As I talked, his expression changed from curious to concerned. "I'm glad it wasn't your friend. Say, I need to question Jo Beth." Burton started up the car. "She's staying at the Galvez?"

"Now? Yes, she's still there." Swell. I dreaded facing Jo Beth almost as much as Burton. She'd probably accuse me of being a tattle-tale, ratting on Holly, trying to get them both kicked out of the Bathing Beauty Revue.

He gunned the engine and raced down Seawall Boulevard, parking in front of the Hotel Galvez. When a bellman came out to protest, Burton flashed his badge, and the man backed away, eyes wide with fright. Was he expecting a raid or an arrest? Burton jumped out of the car, forgetting to open my door, but a valet did the honors. Nice to be treated like a princess for a change.

We were in luck. Apparently Nathan had also taken the scenic route with Jo Beth after chauffeuring her from rehearsals. The pair stood in the lobby, laughing and talking, as if Holly and her bootlegging beau were yesterday's news. When we approached, Jo Beth eyed Burton, her face lighting up like a Christmas tree.

"Jazz, I don't believe I've met your *friend*," she cooed.

Her tone implied that we could only be friends, since he was way out of my league. She held out her dainty hand, taking Burton in as if he was a chocolate ice cream cone with sprinkles on top. He shook her hand formally, then removed his hat.

"I'd like to ask about your friend, Holly. How long has she been missing?" I tried not to gloat over Jo Beth's disappointed expression, pleased he'd ignored her obvious charms.

Burton tried to take her elbow, but she yanked away from his grasp. "Say, what is this? Are you a cop or something? No police!" Her eyes flashed daggers at me. "What did you tell him?"

"Don't worry, he's not a cop." I lowered my voice. "He's a Prohibition agent."

"What? A Fed?!" Jo Beth screeched and recoiled as if Burton was on fire. "That's even worse!"

"Pipe down," I warned her as guests turned to watch her antics. "He just wants to help."

"How is *me* getting arrested going to help Holly?" She stomped her feet, throwing a temper tantrum right there in the lobby. What a show! She could give Amanda lessons. Burton and Nathan watched, amused. A dandy wearing a yellow bow tie behind the front desk scowled and shushed her loudly, putting a finger to his lips like an overzealous librarian.

"Why don't you calm down and talk to Agent Burton? Give him a chance. Got it? All you need to do is answer a few questions so we can find Holly." I'd had enough of her theatrics. Taking her by the shoulders, I positioned her right in front of Burton. No way out.

Jo Beth seemed to shrink in size. "Sure I can trust him not to squeal on me or Holly?"

"Let's go," Burton said, steering her to a quiet area off the lobby, out of sight.

Nathan dug his hands into his pockets. "Didn't expect to see you here with Burton. What were you thinking, bringing him by to interrogate Jo Beth?"

"Interrogate her?" I faked a sweet smile. "I had to return her vanity case. Just like you asked." Then I slapped my forehead. "Oh no! I almost forgot—it's still in Burton's car!"

Frantic, I rushed outside, where a few hotel employees circled the car. Worse, I'd left the lone liquor bottle on the floorboard, with the vanity case on top, in plain sight.

"Is this your car?" A short valet with a ruddy face asked me. "We're looking for the owner so we can move it to the back lot. It's blocking the entrance."

"This belongs to my friend. He'll be back soon." I got inside, flattered that they believed I drove such a snazzy hay-burner. I waited until the valet returned to the lobby before I crammed the bottle into the case, hoping no one noticed.

Juggling the case, I gave a grateful smile to the bellman who held open the door. I could get used to this lifestyle of luxury!

"Are you checking in? Need help with your bags, miss?" He eyed the bright-pink valise with suspicion.

I clutched the case tight. "No, thank you." What if he dropped it and the liquor bottles rolled out into the lobby?

Inside the hotel, I saw Jo Beth leading Burton toward her room. If I didn't know any better, I'd assume she ran a thriving *escort* business out of her hotel room. As they passed, a heavyset man in a Panama hat elbowed an older gentleman smoking a cigar.

"Would you get a load of that dame? Some guys have all the luck." Typical tourists, looking for excitement.

I nudged Nathan. "Think we should follow them?"

"Why? Don't you trust your boyfriend?" Nathan smirked.

"What about your new girlfriend?" I shot back. "Don't you want to see Burton's reaction?"

"Ready when you are!" he nodded.

We tiptoed down the hall, trailing behind Burton and Jo Beth like kids playing "Follow the Leader."

Glancing around, Jo Beth unlocked the door to her hotel room.

"Glad you could join us," Burton said with a straight face. We crept inside and crowded around Jo Beth, watching her reach under the bed for the suitcase.

"Here, let me help you," Nathan offered gallantly.

"I've got it." Jo Beth had no trouble pulling it out this time. She sat on her haunches, legs daintily positioned to one side, staring at the suitcase, stalling.

"What are you waiting for?" Nathan told her. "Hurry, before anyone catches us."

"Go ahead, unlock it," Burton demanded, arms crossed, tapping his foot in anticipation.

With a flourish, Jo Beth fiddled with the locks and flung open the case, contents clearly on display. Burton let out a low whistle as he surveyed the rows of Johnnie Walker Black stacked neatly as logs.

As we leaned over for a better look, Jo Beth gasped, "Oh no! Half the bottles are gone!"

CHAPTER SEVENTEEN

"That means Rico's been here!" Jo Beth jumped up.

"So where in hell is Holly?" Nathan frowned.

"I hope to God she's OK." Frantic, Jo Beth searched the room, flung open the walnut triple armoire, and rummaged through the clothes. "Looks like Holly took a few frocks with her, so maybe everything is jake. But if she doesn't show up soon, she'll miss the whole pageant!"

"It may be best if Holly doesn't participate, at least not in the dance routine Friday night." I glanced at Burton.

"Who cares about that stupid show?" Jo Beth wailed. "We're doing it to make that damn mob boss happy, sell a few drinks to his boozed-up customers. He thinks we're just a bunch of floozies with great gams. He doesn't know how much this means to us, how important it is if we win." Then she flopped onto the bed, pulled out a hanky and dabbed her baby blues.

Were those real tears, I wondered? If not, she was giving the performance of a lifetime.

Never one to miss an opportunity, Nathan rushed to her side and stroked her curly blonde hair. "Don't worry about the pageant. We need to focus on finding Holly now."

Burton seemed unfazed by her act. "Do you have any recent photos of Holly?"

"Sure do." Jo Beth fumbled around the dresser drawer and handed him a tinted photo of Holly in full regalia: a Miss Houston banner across her chest, and a tiara glistening atop her dark curls. With her big eyes and red bee-stung lips, she was a spitting image of actress Helen Kane.

"Thanks. I'll ask around, see if I can help find your friend."

"Please keep it quiet. I don't want the police or anyone to know Holly's missing."

"I'll be discreet," Burton nodded. "And the less you say, the better. Don't tell your friends or the pageant organizers. Just say Holly is ill. Anything to avoid suspicion."

Jo Beth nodded sullenly, blinking back tears. "I'll do my part."

As we were leaving, Burton turned to face Jo Beth. "I hate to mention that you may be in danger. Carry on as if nothing unusual has happened. If the mob comes looking for Rico, act like you don't know anything. If not, you could be their next victim."

"Victim? Me?" She looked terrified, and fresh tears appeared, as if she'd sprung a leak.

Nathan glared at Burton. "Now look what you've done!"

Burton looked apologetic before he bolted out the door. Worried, I followed him into the hall and shut the door quietly.

"Sorry, I didn't mean to upset her." He sounded sheepish. "She sure can turn on the waterworks."

"If my best friend was dating a gangster, and then went missing, I'd be ready to call the cavalry!" I told him.

An elderly couple walking down the hall paused, giving us curious looks. The old man leaned on his cane, his cloudy eyes darting back and forth, gnarled hand cupping an ear.

"It's not the best place to have this conversation," Burton said in a low voice.

"I'll say," I agreed as we dashed out to the front, heads down.

"Before we leave, I need to ask the hotel clerk a few questions. Wait for me in the restaurant if you want. Feel free to have a drink. A *soft* drink." Burton winked. "It's on me."

In the lobby, I saw a few contestants who waved, including Antonia, the Italian beauty. She walked over, beaming, saying the only two words she thought I'd understand: "Dino. Grazie."

Naturally I knew all the important words, including pizza, lasagna and spaghetti, even a few curse words, courtesy of Dino.

I smiled back, glad he'd made her feel more at home in a strange country. No doubt she regarded him only as a big brother or uncle type, though I guessed he'd fallen hard for the striking, raven-haired "Miss Italy."

In the restaurant, the hostess seated me in a plush half-moon booth overlooking the beach. I ordered lemonade, craning my neck to watch Burton in action. From my vantage point, I saw him at the front desk, checking his watch as the clerks rushed around like clucking hens, looking for the manager on duty.

After Burton flashed his badge, a balding man with a handlebar moustache magically appeared. He pulled Burton aside, obviously trying to avoid a scene. Then Burton showed him the photo of Holly, I assumed, and the man shook his head.

Nathan took a seat at my table, following my gaze. "What's that gumshoe think he's doing? Is he ratting out Jo Beth and Holly?"

"Bunk." I lowered my voice. "He wants to help us find Holly and her no-good boyfriend. Who knows where he went with all that...stuff."

"Let me know if he turns up any leads. Jo Beth is terrified Rico may show up and demand the rest."

"I'd be scared, too." I looked around the hotel. "By the way, where is she?"

"Taking a nap with the door locked good and tight." Nathan reached over, took a sip of my lemonade and gave me a sly grin. "Just checking. You don't wanna be caught drinking giggle-water with a Fed agent around."

A young couple looked startled, and got up to leave. "Pipe down," I told Nathan. "We're in public."

"Big deal. They're on vacation. Time to let loose." He stood up. "Going my way?"

"Thanks, but I think I'll tag along with Burton, see what we can dig up."

"Keep me posted. Personally, I don't trust the fella but it's your call." He patted me on my shoulder. "See you at the paper, toots."

As Burton approached my table, he and Nathan faced off like opposing quarterbacks, bumping shoulders as they passed. Would those two ever learn to get along?

When Burton sat down, a plump waitress rushed over, and asked, "How about some dinner, hon? Coffee and dessert?" Her gaze lingered on him, implying she wished she was on the menu.

I shook my head, my stomach too knotted up to eat. "Thanks, but I'm not hungry."

"Later?" He placed a dollar on the table, took my elbow and we crossed the lobby.

A couple of bathing beauties made a beeline for us, appraising Burton with a smile of approval. "Hi, Jasmine," they purred. "Who's this—your fella?"

Not again. "He's a friend," I said, my face flushed.

"Well, does your friend have a name?" said a tall, tanned blonde. Miss California?

Before I could recall my manners, Burton beat me to the punch. "I'm Agent James Burton. FBI, Prohibition Bureau." He stuck out a hand, enjoying the scenery, watching their reaction.

Both girls blinked and visibly blanched. The blonde gal mumbled, "Pleased to meet'cha," then they slunk away like alley cats.

"Happens all the time." Burton gave me a sly grin. "And I never get tired of it."

I had to admit, I enjoyed watching him douse their flames.

Outside, Burton held the car door open for me, and gave the valet a dollar, probably as compensation for blocking the hotel entrance.

"Say, I didn't mean to get Jo Beth so rattled," he said, starting the car. "But it doesn't look good. The mob thinks nothing of killing one of their own, so why not ax a girl who got in the way?"

"Ax?" I touched his arm, alarmed. "Who's talking about murder? Holly's just missing, that's all. Maybe she ran away with her fella so she can have the baby, and they can raise it together."

Burton braked suddenly and stared at me. "Baby? What baby?"

CHAPTER EIGHTEEN

I covered my mouth, again. Why couldn't I keep my trap shut? "There is no baby—yet."

"Are you sure Holly's pregnant?" Burton frowned. "If so, that puts a whole different spin on the situation."

"According to Jo Beth, it's true." I shrugged. "But I don't know if I can trust her. Wish I could talk to Holly myself and get the facts straight."

"Isn't Rico married? I doubt his wife would be happy if she knew he had a squeeze on the side, especially with a baby on the way. That gives him a valid motive."

"A motive?" I swallowed hard. "Maybe his wife doesn't have to find out. What if Holly won the contest? Then she could afford to raise the baby alone."

"Nice thought, but not very realistic."

"Poor Holly," I sighed. "So what did the hotel manager say?"

"He hasn't seen Holly around lately, but I told him to keep an eye out for her," Burton said. "I made it sound as if her parents were worried, nothing more. He doesn't know who I am. They think I'm a cop, that's all. No point in alerting him or the staff."

"A cop with a fancy Ford. What if he gets suspicious?"

"So what?" He squared his jaw. "Then Rico and Holly may come out of hiding."

"I hope so." I tried to change the subject. "Say, how about some supper? Fish and chips on the beach? We still need to talk."

"Sounds serious." Burton gave me a sideways glance.

"I'll say." Sure, I had second thoughts, but Sammy was counting on me to persuade Burton.

By now it was after seven o'clock, but the beach was still full of families and couples enjoying the fading sunlight and the cool evening breeze. The salty sea air felt warm and moist on my face.

Despite the crowd, we managed to find two striped canvas chairs near the ocean. While Burton left to get our food, I paced on the beach, the breeze whipping around my hair and frock. Several youths charged into the surf, daring the waves to chase them back. A fair-haired boy and girl were building a sandcastle, bright metal pails gleaming in the sun.

Burton soon returned with two loaded baskets of fish and chips. I sank down into the beach chair, trying to balance the basket on my lap without spilling greasy food all over my pale blue frock. The basket bounced on my knees like a seesaw. I finally gave up attempting to use a knife and fork, and decided to eat with my hands. My etiquette teacher would be so proud.

Burton smiled as he watched me, no doubt a picture of loveliness and grace. "I thought you weren't hungry?"

Flustered, I grinned at him with clenched teeth while trying to swallow. A shaggy mutt covered in wet sand bounded up, begging for food, its tail wagging hopefully, spraying sand all over us. Burton petted the rascal and I tossed her a few fries, afraid she'd jump in my lap. That's all I needed: the aroma of wet dog mixed with greasy fish to complete my aura of femininity.

A young man raced down the beach, dragging a leash, chasing the energetic pup, calling out, "Roxy!" We laughed as he chased Roxy all over the beach, funny as a Sunday cartoon.

Burton reached over to wipe some sand off my arm. "So, what did you want to discuss?"

How to begin? I watched the waves turn to foam, the ocean a soothing background for my jumbled thoughts. "Well, it has to do with Sammy, and the Oasis. He's in a jam."

Burton rubbed his chin, wiping off sand from Roxy's overactive tail. "What kind of jam? Are the gangs giving him trouble again?"

"And how." I nodded. "After his night in jail, Johnny Jack got the idea that you bailed him out. Now he thinks you and Sammy are best buddies. Johnny Jack practically accused him of being a snitch for the Prohibition squad."

"You don't say." Burton blanched under his tanned skin. "Sorry about Sammy. Guess that's my fault. Maybe word got out I paid him a visit, asked him to help me out with the gangs. Damn it, I didn't mean to cause him any problems with Johnny Jack." His words trailed, his voice lost in a strong gust of wind.

I grew silent, well aware that he was the one who'd raised Johnny Jack's suspicions. If Burton hadn't approached Sammy in the first place, then his reputation wouldn't be tainted. So didn't it make sense to ask him to undo the damage he'd already done?

"Jazz, what is it?" Burton studied me, concerned. "Is there anything I can do?" Now he seemed so remorseful that I couldn't blame him. After all, he was only on the job a few weeks when he'd met Sammy, and me.

My face felt hot, damp. "Remember those bathing beauties you saw at the Galvez? They're performing Friday night at the Hollywood Dinner Club. Invitation only."

"Hard to miss them." He gave me a sly grin. "Why? Are you asking me on a date?"

"Not exactly." I started babbling. "I saw Sam Maceo at rehearsals, making sure the dance routine went smoothly. You do know the Maceos are the main pageant sponsors?"

He nodded. "What does this have to do with Johnny Jack and the Downtown Gang? I doubt Sam invited his biggest rival to his fancy shindig."

I hemmed and hawed, trying to find the right words. "Johnny Jack thinks Sammy has pull with you, so he's asked him for a favor. A big favor."

"Oh yeah? What's he planning to do?" He raised his brows. "Spit it out, Jasmine."

There was no polite way to say it, so I blurted out: "Johnny Jack wants you to raid the Hollywood Dinner Club Friday night, during the bathing beauties act."

Burton stared at me in surprise. Then he traced the sand with his finger, making a zigzag pattern. Finally he spoke up, fury in his tone. "Johnny Jack has some nerve. I'm not one of his guns for hire."

I knew he was angry, yet I hoped he'd understand the gravity of Sammy's situation. "If you don't, he threatened to shut down the Oasis. He swore he'd tell everyone in town that Sammy is your informant. A stool pigeon."

I took a deep breath. "You know what the gangs will do to him if they suspect he's a rat."

"Who in hell does Johnny Jack think he is?" Burton picked up a shell, much like the dead girl's tattoo, and threw it hard into the surf. "Why would I risk my badge, my job, to do his dirty work? He must be loony to think I'd agree to do something so ridiculous, so risky."

"Aren't raids part of your job?" I forced the words out. "I just thought, maybe..."

"You thought what—I was a pushover? Your personal lapdog?" He turned to face me, eyes blazing. "What I want to know is, why in the world did Sammy put you up to this? Why are you playing his messenger girl? Doesn't he have the guts to ask me this goddamn favor himself?"

CHAPTER NINETEEN

I wished I could take my words back. I'd never seen Burton lose his temper and, for a moment, I couldn't breathe, couldn't speak.

"How in hell could Sammy get you involved in these gang wars?" Burton demanded. "Doesn't he realize how dangerous it is?"

"Johnny Jack gave him no choice. Can't you see? He's desperate." I tried to think fast, covering for Sammy as usual. "Besides, it was my idea. I offered to help him out."

"Oh yeah?" He crossed his arms, shaking his head in disbelief. "Do you think I'm so easy to manipulate? Maybe I should shut down the Oasis instead. For Sammy's own protection."

"You wouldn't. Would you?" I panicked. Instead of helping Sammy, seems I'd made everything worse.

"I've heard enough of this bullshit." Burton bolted out of his beach chair effortlessly, while I scrambled out, like a clumsy crab flailing its claws. Silently he pulled me up, then stormed off down the beach. I trailed behind, wishing I could tell him the truth. I'd asked him to compromise his principles, sell out to a gang leader, because of our friendship. How could I be so stupid, so naive?

I caught up with him, trying to talk over the crashing waves. "James, I wish I could explain everything."

"Try," he snapped, his face twisted, a mask of hurt and anger.

I watched the foamy tide, trying to think, my mind in a fog. Should I tell Burton the truth? If I admitted Sammy was my half-brother, would he understand why I got involved?

Maybe it made no difference at all. Even so, it was too risky. Frankly, I didn't know Burton well enough to trust him completely. If any of his cop buddies found out, they might let it slip to the dirty cops on the force. Worse, they could squeal to the gangs, perhaps use me as leverage to get to Sammy, or even blackmail us both.

Who knew what could happen? Truth be told, I didn't want to take that chance.

"I'll be honest, Jasmine. I thought we were friends, that we had something special." His eyes narrowed. "Now I realize you're only using me to help Sammy. I get it. You're sweet on him."

I made a face. "You're all wet. We're just friends. He's like family." Did I say too much? I reached for his hand, but he pulled it away. How could I explain the promise I'd made to my dad before he died, to look out for Sammy?

"Guess I expected more from you." Burton walked to his car, silent, and I could see his jaw working, trying to control his anger.

What could I say that wouldn't jeopardize Sammy, my job, my family? "I'm sorry" didn't seem to be enough.

On the ride home, I stared out the window, fingering my pearl necklace like a string of worry beads. Now I'd lost Burton's trust and respect, if I ever had them at all. Did he really think we had "something special?" Now I'd never find out.

At the boarding house, Burton opened the car door for me, as formal as the Galvez valet, and walked me to the front steps like a proper escort.

Normally I'd be nervous, worried he'd try to make advances. Tonight I had no such fears. His brusque manner spoke volumes.

I stood awkwardly on the porch, searching for the right words to make amends. The tension felt like a brick wall, keeping us apart. Why was I so determined to protect Sammy, to fight his battles? Now I'd alienated the one ally who could help. Never mind my personal feelings.

"Thanks for dinner," I mumbled, my face flaming, waiting for his reaction, anything besides the silent treatment. His cold eyes met mine, his face stony. I hoped Eva wasn't watching this icy exchange from behind the curtains, waiting for her cue to pounce on Burton.

When I couldn't stand the silence any longer, I asked, "What are you going to do?"

He stared at me a few beats. "I think I'll have a little talk with your *friend* Sammy."

My throat felt dry. "It's too risky. What if the gangs see you?"

Burton's eyes looked like glass, cold and hard. "Don't you know by now? I'm not afraid of any gangsters."

Head held high, he turned on his heel and got into his car, slamming the door so loud I'm sure the neighbors heard. The he gunned his engine and raced down the street.

Shaken, I stood there feeling alone, blinking back tears. Damn it, what had I done? He was right: I'd treated him like a mere errand boy, blinded by Sammy's dilemma, too scared to think rationally.

Thanks to me, our relationship had ended before it even had a chance to get started.

I made my way inside, rushed upstairs to my bedroom and locked the door, wanting to hide. Luckily Amanda was working late so I didn't have to face her yet. A few minutes later, I heard a soft knock. Eva called out, "Jasmine? What's wrong?"

"I'm not feeling well," I mumbled. "I'm going to bed early."

She paused, then, "How was your evening with James?"

"Fine." I added a lilt to my voice, not wanting to worry her, relieved when I heard her walk down the hall. Head pounding, I got undressed and crawled under the covers, wishing I could erase the evening, forget the fiasco with Burton ever happened.

That night, I tossed and turned, replaying the whole exchange in my mind, reinventing different, more satisfying endings.

If only life could be rewound and revised so easily.

CHAPTER TWENTY

Tuesday

The next day, I stumbled around the newsroom like a sleepwalker, bleary-eyed and exhausted. I avoided contact with the male reporters and tried my best to concentrate on work, but Burton's betrayed expression remained stuck in my mind.

When Mrs. Harper barked out her latest orders, I barely looked her way, propping up my head to stay awake.

Nathan stopped by my desk around noon. "What happened to you? You look like hell."

"Gee, thanks. You sure know how to make a gal feel pretty."

"Seriously, Jazz." Nathan looked concerned. "You seem upset. What happened?"

"I can't talk now." Mrs. Harper was glaring at us like bad kids acting up in detention.

"Well, why don't we go to the bathing beauty rehearsals this afternoon? Don't you need to do some more interviews?"

"Thanks, but I'll catch them at the Galvez." I wasn't in any mood to interview the girls. "Say, did you hear from Jo Beth after we left last night? Any word about Holly?"

"Not a peep." Nathan's face fell. "That's why I wanted to go down to the Opera House. Guess she'll call when she has news."

At lunchtime, I walked down to the street vendor and ordered a BLT on sourdough. As I rummaged around for coins in my purse pocket, I felt the gold charm that I'd swiped from the crime scene, feeling guilty. Guess I was so distracted, I'd forgotten it was there.

"What's eating you?" the Polish vendor asked. "Your fella got you down?"

"No fella." I managed a smile. "Just a cat."

Golliwog, the black stray adopted by the *Gazette* staff, followed me to the small park nearby and rubbed my ankles as I tried to choke down the sandwich. Her warm silky fur felt soft on my bare legs, and I rewarded her with several bites of food. After we'd both finished eating, I enjoyed hearing her purr while I stroked her glossy fur and scratched under her chin. The small stray always had a knack for cheering me up, especially when life seemed so bleak.

As I passed by Cucci Jewelers, I decided to ask about the lost gold charm, now weighing heavily in my bag and on my mind. Should I have turned it over to the cops? The way my luck was going, they might consider me a suspect. The jeweler had always been friendly and kind when I window-shopped on the way to work.

"Come in, come in, take a look," he said today, holding open the door. After I pulled out the charm, he examined it with a magnifier.

"Saint Jude. Latin," he told me in a heavy accent, fingering the charm. The patron saint of lost causes. How fitting for a prostitute. "Looks old, antique. Good stuff. Solid gold."

"What?" I stepped back, surprised. "This is made of real gold?"

"Twenty-two karat. Foreign." He rubbed the charm, a gleam in his dark eyes. "Where you get this?"

"From a friend," I stammered, acting guilty as a cat burglar. No wonder he seemed suspicious. "Is it worth very much?"

He nodded again. "Gold always expensive."

"Thanks for your help," I told him. "Next time, I hope I can afford to buy something."

"Let me know if you want to sell. Real gold hard to find."

"OK, I will." I headed back to the office, wondering what was a prostitute doing with an expensive gold bracelet—and a charm of Saint Jude to boot?

Clearly ladies of the night got paid a lot more than I did. Sad, but true. Was it a gift from a sugar daddy or an old beau, or perhaps a cherished family heirloom? I wrapped the charm in a silk hanky and tucked it in my bag, wondering if it might help identify the victim. Who could I show the charm to, but trust to keep it a secret?

At the *Gazette*, I stopped by to see Mack, who'd had his fair share of run-ins with the gangs, risking his life to expose their secrets. I wouldn't be surprised if he sat at the top of their hit list. With his experience, I hoped he could provide some insight into Johnny Jack: Was he bluffing or did he always carry out his threats? Mack stopped typing, stubby fingers poised over his typewriter keys. "What's on your mind, Jazz?"

"Can we talk in private?" I glanced around at the newsboys. "It's important."

"Sure, kid." He led me to an editor's empty office, probably thinking I had a hot scoop.

"About that young woman they found behind the post office...Did the cops ever ID her?"

"She's still a Jane Doe, probably a hooker like the first girl."

"Did she also have a seashell tattoo on her wrist? I noticed she wore a charm bracelet."

"I can double-check with my M.E. pal. Why do you ask?"

"Just wondering." I shuffled my feet. "She didn't seem like the type to me."

"You never know what drives a nice girl to turn tricks." He shrugged. "Hate to say it, but it's often the boyfriend or husband who becomes their pimp, makes them earn their keep. Or the family kicks them out, so they wind up on the street."

I shuddered, thinking of the girls who ended up as prostitutes because of circumstances or bad choices and worse judgement. Then there was Holly, whose married gangster boyfriend used her hotel room to stash his booze. Was it any different?

Mack studied me, arms crossed over his barrel chest. "Anything else, Jasmine?"

I looked at the framed photos on the wall, a panorama of Texas history: shots of the Spindletop oil well, the Alamo, the Seawall construction, Bishop's Palace, the University of Texas campus. Finally I told him: "A friend is in trouble with the Downtown Gang."

"What kind of trouble?" Mack perked up.

"Call it a disagreement. They threatened to get revenge if he didn't do as they wanted."

I swear his face brightened, hoping for his next big lead.

"You mean Agent Burton? Did he cross swords with Johnny Jack?" Mack puffed on his cigar. "That *is* serious. What'd he do?"

"I'd rather keep my friend anonymous." I eyed him. "Question is, do you think Johnny Jack will make good on his threats?"

"Depends. Does your friend owe him money? If so, he'd better watch his wallet *and* his back." I could tell Mack was fishing for more information, but he wouldn't get a peep out of me.

"Nothing like that." I shook my head. "It's more like a favor. A test of loyalty."

"Hard to say, without knowing all the details." Mack studied me, rubbing his stubbled chin. "Johnny Jack can be unpredictable. One day he's donating thousands to charity, the next he's fitting his best friend for lead boots. But I hear if you double-cross him, he'll find a way to make you pay. He likes to dole out the punishment slowly, torture you a while, till you wished you were dead."

"That's what I was afraid of." I shuddered, thinking of the way Golliwog and the other cats batted mice and birds around, playing with their dying bodies like it was a sport.

Was Johnny Jack baiting Burton and Sammy, setting them up? Or would he keep raising the stakes, to see how high they'd jump? Knowing them, they wouldn't put up with his demands for long.

I couldn't concentrate all afternoon, and it didn't help that Mack kept casting worried glances my way. Why had I blabbed my problems to him, of all people? I hoped he wouldn't mention it to Agent Burton. Even if by some miracle Burton agreed, Johnny Jack would no doubt use the raid as leverage to blackmail him into doing more of his dirty work. And if the Maceos ever found out Sammy put him up to it, he'd never live it down. Damned if you did, damned if you didn't.

These thoughts swirled around my head all day like a mini-tornado. Finally, after five o'clock, I gathered up my hat and purse, feeling useless and unproductive. As I turned to leave, the operator rang me at my desk. "It's a gentleman. But he wouldn't give his name."

Sammy? What new threat did Johnny Jack make? Did he also expect Sammy and Burton to tap dance and sing along with the bathing beauties at the Hollywood Dinner Club?

"Sorry to disturb you at work, but it's urgent." Burton's even voice sounded much calmer than it had earlier—too calm.

"James? I'm so glad you called." I felt almost giddy with relief, and swiveled my chair away from Mrs. Harper's prying eyes and ears. "I thought you weren't speaking to me."

"This isn't a social call." He kept his tone formal. "I'm afraid that I have some bad news."

I sucked in my breath. "What is it? Is it about Sammy?"

"Why is everything always about Sammy?" He paused, exhaling into the phone. "Hate to bother you at work, but I thought I'd tell you first, before your snoops got the police report. Sorry to say, a young woman fitting your friend's description was found on the Beach Gang's turf, behind the Deluxe nightclub."

CHAPTER TWENTY-ONE

"Holly?" I almost dropped the phone. "Is she OK?"

"She's alive, but barely," Burton said. "She's at John Sealy Hospital. I thought you and Nathan would want to know."

"Thanks for telling me." I held my breath. "Can we talk to her?"

"I don't know. She was in pretty rough shape when they brought her in early today."

I tried to contain my irritation. "Why didn't you tell me before?"

"Hey, I just found out myself. I don't work in Homicide, remember? As you know, I'm not exactly on the best of terms with these local yokels."

"I noticed." It was no secret the cops resented Burton, a Yankee and a Federal agent. "Did anyone question her?"

"That's one reason I called. I hoped you could get her to talk. Find out if Rico is the culprit. If so, she may turn on him, tell us more about the stash of booze. That's *my* department."

"I'll do my best," I promised. "But I'm not sure how much she'll confide in me."

"Need a lift to the hospital?" Burton asked. "I'd like to be there when you question Holly."

I knew there was a catch. "Thanks, but I'll get a ride from Nathan. He wants to see Holly as much as I do. Will they let us into her room, even though we're not family?"

"I'll get you in. Be sure to ask for me and give them your name. We've got a cop posted outside her door, just in case."

"OK, thanks. One more thing. Can you keep this hush-hush for now? For Holly's sake?"

Sure, I wanted to tell Jo Beth, but she'd probably start blabbing and possibly put Holly in even more danger.

"Of course. That was the plan all along. See you soon."

When I told Nathan the news, his face lit up like a Ferris wheel at night. "Holly's alive? Hallelujah! It's been so long, I got worried."

"Unfortunately, Burton said she's in bad shape. Want to go to the hospital now?"

"Sure!" He frowned. "What about Jo Beth? Should I call her?"

"Let's see how she's doing before we tell anyone." Tell the truth, I didn't completely trust Jo Beth after squealing on Holly. "It's safer if we keep Holly's location a secret, for now."

"Good idea," Nathan said, practically pushing me out the door. "Let's go."

At the hospital, I noticed two cops stationed by the front entrance and corridors. Was this all for Holly's protection? When we asked about Holly, a matronly nurse eyed us with suspicion.

I was ready to give her a piece of my mind when Burton appeared, sporting his badge. "She's with me." He led us down the hallway, not giving the nurse a backwards glance.

"Thanks," I told Burton, grateful. "She acts more like a prison guard than a nurse."

Burton shrugged, avoiding my eyes. "Don't mention it."

"So how's Holly?" I braced myself for the worst.

"Hanging in there," he said. "From what I hear, she was unconscious when they brought her in last night. Someone gave her a good going-over."

"How bad was it?" I was almost afraid to ask.

"You'll see for yourself."

Burton led us down a gloomy corridor and we followed single-file, like schoolchildren on a field trip. How I hated hospitals, the antiseptic smell, the moans and groans of patients suffering, in pain or dying. I rarely visited for happy occasions, like births. To me, hospitals represented death.

Still, I wasn't quite prepared when I entered Holly's room: Her pale, fragile frame was cushioned by several pillows, her right arm in a cast, her face bruised, her eyes black and blue, one eye almost swollen shut. No longer did she resemble a perky Clara Bow, she looked more like a worn and torn rag doll.

Nathan inhaled sharply when he saw her, his eyes flashing in anger, but he held his tongue. She appeared to be in a deep sleep, perhaps medicated. I tiptoed to the back of the room, and whispered to the young attending nurse. "How is she?"

"It's touch and go," she replied.

"What about—?" I began, patting my stomach. "Wasn't she ...expecting?"

The young nurse shook her head sadly. Did that mean Holly had lost the baby—or there was never a baby at all? I wanted to find out the truth, but now wasn't the right time to ask.

Nathan stood in the corner, balling his fists, trying to restrain himself. Slowly Holly stirred, and the nurse rushed over to help her sit up, adding extra pillows.

Burton stood by my side and gave me a slight nudge, prompting me to ask questions.

"Not now," I whispered. I felt uneasy, as if I'd come under false pretenses. Holly needed a friend, not a nosy reporter hovering over her bed.

Holly leaned forward, glancing at me and Nathan, puzzled, as if trying to place us.

"Remember me?" Nathan took her hand, his face softening when she nodded. "Who did this to you?" he demanded. "Rico?"

Holly refused to reply, and shut her eyes, falling back against the pillows as if exhausted, poor thing.

The nurse frowned. "Please don't upset her. She needs her rest."

Nathan didn't hold back. "I'll bet it was Rico..." he said in a cold, distant voice. "So help me God, if I ever see that bastard again, I swear I'll kill him."

CHAPTER TWENTY-TWO

"What did you say?" Burton snapped to attention, edging closer to Nathan.

Holly's eyes popped open, frightened, and she pulled the bed sheets up to her chin.

"He didn't mean it," I cut in to defuse the tension, and stood in front of Nathan. Frankly, I was surprised by his reaction, unaware he'd developed such intense feelings for Holly. His eyes turned frosty and without a word, he stormed off down the hall.

I followed him out the door, Burton at my heels. "Before you go off half-cocked, we need proof that Rico is responsible," he warned Nathan. "There's nothing we can do now unless Holly presses charges against him."

"Wanna bet?" Nathan glanced at Burton and kicked at the floor. "Never mind. I'm just frustrated, that's all. You know me, Jazz. I'm all talk."

Burton seemed to relax, clamping a hand on Nathan's shoulder.

"I know how you feel," Burton told Nathan. "Seeing a beautiful young woman lying in a hospital bed, all black and blue...it's not right. Makes you want to give the lowlife a taste of his own medicine. If Holly is willing to press charges, we can probably get Rico on assault and battery."

Nathan gritted his teeth. "How about attempted murder?"

I stared at Nathan in alarm, and tried to change the subject.

"I'll say my good-byes to Holly now." Burton started to follow me into her room, but I shook my head, closing the door behind me.

Holly's eyes opened wide when I approached her bed. "Don't tell Rico I'm here," she pleaded. "He tried to take me…to one of those doctors in Houston… but I refused to get rid of my own baby." She bit her lip. "Then he made sure I lost it anyway."

I agreed with Nathan: Rico needed a good, solid beating, just like the one he gave Holly. If I could, I'd pummel the bastard myself. Better yet, shoot him in the gut.

"Don't worry, we'll keep this between us," I told Holly. "Who else knows you're here?"

"My parents. They're coming to get me later this week."

"Good." I patted her hand. "What do you want me to tell Jo Beth and the girls?"

"Tell them I got sick, broke a leg or got food poisoning…anything but the truth." Her big dark eyes flashed, panic on her face. "For God's sake, keep it quiet. I don't want the girls to see me like this." She stared at the wall, blinking, her voice monotone. "I used to be a smart gal with a bright future. Now I'm a disgrace, a real dumb bunny."

"That's not true. Your bruises will heal. You can still have a good life," I squeezed her pale hand. "Promise me you won't contact Rico, that you'll stay away from him…"

She nodded, dark eyes welling with tears. "After what he did to me and my baby, I'll never forgive him. He made sure I couldn't compete in the contest. What can I do?"

"You can fight back, press charges against him for assault and battery," I suggested.

"I can? But won't he get mad and try to come after me?" She looked worried.

"Talk to Agent Burton. Meanwhile, you can recuperate at home in Houston." I gave her a reassuring smile. "If you're ever in a hospital again, I hope you'll be there as a nurse, not a patient."

"Me, too." Her swollen face brightened for a moment. "Wouldn't that be swell?"

My heart went out to this delicate beauty who'd learned and lost so much, yet still remained hopeful. "You'll make a great nurse. Take care of yourself, Holly. Keep in touch." I patted her frail arm.

"Thanks for coming by, Jazz. Tell Nathan not to worry about me." She gave me a weak smile. "Please tell the girls to be careful."

"Careful of what?" I whirled around to ask what she meant, but she appeared to be nodding off.

In the hallway, Nathan and Burton looked at me with interest. "You sure were in there a long time. What were you two jawing about?" Nathan asked.

I motioned toward the nurses congregating in the halls.

"Let's go outside where we can talk." A few heads turned and we heard whispers as we walked out the exit. Obviously word had spread about Holly's condition and her uniformed visitors.

We stood on the sidewalk away from the hospital, shaded by a palm tree. "So what happened to Holly?" I asked Burton. "How'd they find her? Did they know who she was?"

Burton rubbed his chin and I noticed in the sunlight that he hadn't shaved that day. Long night? "We got an anonymous tip, but the cops couldn't ID her, thought she was some floozy."

"How'd *you* get involved?" I asked. "You're not in Homicide."

"I didn't know anything till this afternoon," he said. "I heard a few cops talking and made the connection. I showed them the photo of Holly and they confirmed it was her."

"When did they find her?" Nathan asked.

"After the bars closed, around four a.m. They were afraid to move her. It took hours to locate a medic who could examine her on the scene. He didn't show up till eight this morning."

"So poor Holly was laid out all night, like rotting garbage?" Nathan sputtered.

"What did the doctor say?" I cut him off, trying to erase that mental image.

"Apparently her bruises were several hours old, like she'd been beaten somewhere else and dumped behind the Deluxe Club, in his own backyard, so to speak." He shook his head. "Seems Rico is trying to implicate the Beach Gang."

"What if he's feuding with Sam Maceo?" I suggested. "That might help explain the stolen liquor under the bed."

"But it doesn't add up," Nathan said. "If everyone knows Holly's his girl, then isn't he just incriminating himself?"

"True, but this tarnishes Sam Maceo's good reputation even more—and it puts a black eye on the beauty pageant and Galveston. Literally," I added, thinking of Holly's bruises. "As one of the main sponsors, Maceo has a lot to lose. A scandal like this could shut down the entire Miss Universe contest."

Nathan nodded. "What if Rico wants to join forces with Quinn, take the Maceos' place?"

Burton crossed his arms. "Well, well. You two detectives are ready to solve this case all by yourselves. We don't even need the police force to help. Should I call off the hounds?"

I didn't appreciate his sarcasm. "What do you suggest, Agent Burton?"

"Actually, I just assumed it was a lovers' quarrel, a fight over the baby." He shrugged. "Who knows? Maybe you're on the trolley."

"Sure we are." Nathan gave me a triumphant smile.

Burton lowered his voice. "Listen up. We got orders from the mayor himself to keep this hush-hush. He doesn't want anyone to know one of the bathing beauties had an *accident*."

"The mayor is involved? Is that why there's extra police protection?" I raised my brows.

Burton nodded. "The Beach Gang is afraid Holly might squeal. If anything happened to Holly, that may be the end of the beauty pageant." He faced us, eyes narrowed. "Besides the bad press, the mayor doesn't want any ill will between Houston and Galveston. Can I trust you two to keep this quiet? Out of the papers? The city's orders, direct from the mayor, not mine."

So it was politics as usual. The big brass didn't give a damn about Holly. They just wanted to use bathing beauties like her to promote tourism, bring in big bucks. Why wasn't I surprised?

Of course I'd cover for Holly, even if it meant kowtowing to the rich and mighty.

"You have our word," I told him. "Besides, we could lose our jobs if this got out."

"I wouldn't drag her name through mud," Nathan said. "A classy dame like Holly deserves better."

Burton turned to me. "So what did she tell you? Did she admit Rico was her attacker?"

I nodded. "She said he forced her to go to a doctor in Houston for an abortion. When that didn't work, apparently he tried to cause a miscarriage, beat the baby out of her."

"Heartless bastard." Nathan clenched his fists, his mouth tight. "He'll get his due."

Burton gave him a pointed look. "Anything else?" he asked me.

"Turns out she wants to press charges, but she's afraid of Rico's reaction. Fortunately her parents are coming to get her later this week, so she can hide out in Houston."

Nathan looked hopeful. "That's swell! Finally she sees the light."

"What about the stash hidden under her bed? Did she mention the booze?" Burton asked.

I shook my head. "I didn't want to bring it up. I'm sure it was all Rico's idea."

Burton frowned. "We still need to ask Holly more questions. But your visit helped break the ice. Since she knows we're friends, she may be willing to talk."

Friends? I wondered at his choice of words. Was he being sarcastic, or were we still friends? Sure, he was polite, but overly formal. I felt a distance between us that left me all balled up.

"Go easy on Holly," Nathan told Burton. "Make sure she's safe. She's a good girl. Don't treat her like a gangster's moll."

"I'll do my best," Burton said, before he walked off.

He stopped to talk to the cops by the door, without bothering to say good-bye. Could I blame him for still being sore at me?

"Coming, Jazz?" Nathan stormed out to his car, breathing heavily, no longer able to control his temper.

After we got in his Model T, he slammed the door so hard, the car seemed to vibrate. Then he sped down Seawall Boulevard, passing the turn-off for the *Gazette* building.

"Where's the fire?" I gripped the door straps tightly as we bounced down the city streets. "Where are we going?"

"The Opera House. I want to be the first to tell Jo Beth and the girls the good news." He sounded sarcastic. "Then I want to find Rico and show him just how it feels to be a personal punching bag."

"Don't you dare do anything rash," I told Nathan. "The Beach Gang will take care of Rico, especially when they figure out he's stealing Sam Maceo's prize liquor."

Nathan slowed down as he considered my words. "Let's hope so. But those wiseguys protect their own. Rico could lie and say it was all Holly's idea. And she can't defend herself while she's laid up at Big Red."

He jerked to a stop in front of the Opera House and flung open the car door. "What are we going to tell the girls?"

"Wait...we can't just blurt it out. We need a convincing story."

"You're the writer. You'll think of something." He leaned back in his seat, both hands kneading the steering wheel like bread dough. "Go on ahead. I'll wait here. I'm too riled up to see the girls."

Taking a deep breath, I entered the cool, dark theatre and headed toward the stage. Luckily Mrs. Wembley appeared to be taking a break. The girls loitered on stage, gathering their things but a few looked up, wide-eyed, as I entered.

Jo Beth rushed over, squatting down. "Is it Holly? Is she OK?"

I tried to paint on a sunny smile. "Holly's fine. She just wanted me to tell you that she's decided to drop out of the contest. The strain of rehearsals was too much for her."

"Why couldn't she tell us that herself?" Jo Beth eyed me. "I was worried sick. Why'd she disappear like that, out of the blue?"

"Man trouble?" asked Miss California.

"You know how it is, girls." I nodded, grateful for the impromptu cue. "She and Rico were having a lovers' quarrel and they finally made up. Guess they lost track of time."

Jo Beth didn't look convinced as she scrambled down the stairs and pulled me aside. "Did you really talk to Holly? This sounds like a lot of baloney to me. What's the real story?"

I looked around, indicating the bevy of beauties who'd suddenly gotten quiet. "You know the real reason," I said in a hushed voice.

"You mean...the baby?" Jo Beth cupped a hand to my ear.

I nodded and whispered back: "The dance routines, especially the high-kicks, made her nauseous. She's afraid of losing the baby. "

I also felt sick to my stomach, lying to her face. Yet there was a kernel of truth in that statement, so it wasn't a complete fabrication.

"Why didn't Holly tell me herself?" Her face fell. "I'll miss her."

"I'm so sorry, Jo Beth. I'm sure she'll be in touch soon. I'd better get back to the paper now." I turned to go, afraid I'd break down and tell her the truth.

"What if Rico comes by the hotel room, looking for the bottles?" Jo Beth held my arm. "What'll I do then?"

She walked with me to the exit, out of earshot. "Let him take the rest. If he asks about Holly, tell him she left town and you don't know where she went. It's for her own protection."

"I knew your story was a load of hooey. Knowing Rico, he probably tried to keep her out of the contest." She placed her hands on her hips. "The sooner she gets away from that jerk, the better. He never wanted that baby anyway. I hope we never see him again."

"I second that. Just in case, I'd find a new room and roommate."

"Good idea. Thanks for the lowdown on Holly." She waved good-bye as I returned to the car, still feeling guilty for lying, waiting for lightning to strike me down.

Nathan asked, "So how'd it go?"

I let out a sigh. "I told the girls that Holly decided to drop out of the pageant, then I secretly told Jo Beth she was doing it for the sake of the baby." I paused. "She's a lot smarter than I realized."

"I hope they bought it." He started the car. "All I can think about is the way Holly looked in the hospital—like a helpless little ragamuffin. Tears me apart."

"Why do these nice girls always fall for gangsters and hoods? What do they see in them?" I shook my head.

"Beats me." Nathan shrugged, his face hardening.

"Say, I know what will cheer us up. Why don't we go to the Oasis tonight with Amanda?"

"I'm not in the mood to make whoopee, but I can give you gals a ride. Say, eight o'clock? Remember it's a school night," he joked.

"Are you sure? You don't want to sit around and mope all evening. That won't help Holly recover."

"I may go check on her tonight." He stopped in front of the boarding house. "Do you mind if I don't go? It's been a rough day."

"You said it." I nodded. "Hey, you'd better watch what you say about Rico, threatening his life. I think Burton got worried."

"So what?" He frowned. "I'm just mouthing off. But if I run into Rico in a dark alley, who knows what could happen?"

The menacing way he said it gave me chills, if that was possible in this heat wave.

CHAPTER TWENTY-THREE

That evening, I had no trouble convincing Amanda to accompany me to the Oasis—any excuse to dress up and see Sammy. She looked extra-pretty in her blue print frock with ruffles at the neckline and hem. I wore a fitted pale peach number with cap sleeves that I'd picked off the sale racks at Eiband's.

When Nathan arrived promptly at eight, he gave a loud wolf-whistle. "You two gals look like the tiger's stripes! Wish I hadn't made other plans."

"Still going to see Holly?" I asked.

"Something like that." He gave me a Chesire-cat smile.

"Why don't you bring her some flowers?" Amanda suggested. "Girls love flowers."

"Good idea, but all the shops are closed." He looked sheepish. "Can I borrow some from your aunt's garden? If Eva doesn't mind."

"Be our guest. Please give Holly my best."

After he dropped us off at the Oasis, I gave the customary three taps on the unmarked wooden door. Before I could say the password, Dino opened the door wide, glancing behind us.

"Welcome, Jazz. Amanda," he beamed. "Is Antonia with you? Or will she come later?"

What—no interrogation? No third-degree at the door? I'd never seen Dino smile so wide, and the effect was startling.

I hated to disappoint the baby grand. "Sorry, Dino. I'll try to bring her next time."

His jowly face fell, and he returned to his lonely barstool. "Tell her I said hello, will ya? They don't make gals like that here."

I wasn't even offended. "Sure, big guy. Say, why don't you go see her and the bathing beauties dance at the Hollywood this Friday night?" I winced the minute the words were out.

Dino's expression indicated he knew all about Burton's possible raid. "I'll try, but gotta get the A-OK from the boss."

Amanda tugged on my arm. "Speaking of, where's Sammy?"

"Downstairs, making the rounds." Dino signaled with his stubby thumb, like a hitchhiker. "It's gonna be a full house again tonight."

We clattered down the stairs, inhaling the aroma of sweet cigar smoke and lilac perfume. A higher class of fumes than the usual sweat, grease and tobacco smoke.

The Oasis was more than half full, and as we made our way past the bar, I nodded at Frank, who wore his trademark red suspenders. In the dim lights, I spotted Sammy at a corner table, talking in earnest to a young, good-looking guy with chestnut hair.

I held back, but Amanda charged forward, plopping down on the chair closest to Sammy.

"Hello, Sammy, how are you?" She said it with a cheery smile that only I knew was forced.

"Been busy. The joint is jumping with all the tourists in town." He looked over at me for help, mild panic in his eyes. "Hey, are any of your friends with you? Got a lot of customers asking about the bathing beauties."

"Aren't you two dolls in the pageant?" The cute guy stood up and held out a chair for me, motioning for me to sit down by him. "Sammy, why don't you introduce me to these dishy dames?"

"No, but thanks for the compliment. I'm Jasmine," I told the handsome stranger. "I go by Jazz. This is my friend Amanda."

I motioned toward her, but she and Sammy were quarreling again—no doubt Amanda was feeling ignored. What else was new?

"Jazz," he repeated. "I like jazz. I'm Colin, by the way." He stuck out a hand, and shook mine with a firm grip, his fingers lingering until I pulled away.

"Nice to meet you." He looked familiar, but I couldn't quite place him.

"How about a whirl across the dance floor, Jazz?" He flashed a smile that lit up the room. Very tempting, but first I needed to talk to Sammy about Agent Burton.

"Maybe later." Yes, he was attractive, but I wasn't in the mood.

"Well then, how about a drink, Jazz?" Colin leaned forward, his arm thrown over my chair.

"Sure, why not? Make it a Manhattan." Normally, I didn't drink with strangers but he seemed to be a friend of Sammy's and besides, I didn't expect to hear from Burton anytime soon.

After Colin left, I tried to nudge Sammy's foot under the table, to get his attention.

"Ouch! That hurt!" Amanda glared at me. "Let's go talk in private, shall we, Sammy?"

Sammy shrugged, looking helpless, as she took his hand and dragged him to the back.

Colin returned with two drinks, and scooted his chair over so our knees touched under the table. The cocktail felt cool and refreshing and I began to relax. "So what do you do?" I asked him, wondering where I'd seen him before.

"I'm in sales. How about you, doll?" He gave me an easy, confident smile.

I didn't reply, since saying "I'm a reporter" usually scared people off. "What do you sell?"

"Whatever people need. Some import and export, some local." Rather a vague answer, but then again, this wasn't a formal interview. "So what's a lovely lass like you doing here all alone? I take it you're not married?"

I grinned, feeling flirtatious. "Do I look like I'm married?"

"Just checking." Maybe it was the cocktail, but I felt comfortable around him and soon we were chatting, almost like old friends.

"How do you know Sammy?" I wondered.

"We have mutual friends," he said. Another cryptic answer.

Bernie began playing "Ain't She Sweet?" on the piano, and Colin held out his hand, helping me up from the chair. "What are we waiting for? Let's dance."

I hadn't danced with anyone since my rendezvous with Agent Burton at the Surf Club. Naturally I was rusty, but I loved to dance and for once, I didn't worry about anything or anyone, least of all Burton. Colin kept up with my Charleston and even did an impromptu Irish jig when the song ended.

When the tempo slowed down, Colin pulled me close, his big arms crushing my chest. Uncomfortable, I tried to push him away, but his grip only tightened around my waist, one hand wandering down my backside. "Leave me alone! Get your hands off me!"

As I struggled to get free, he forced his mouth on mine, his lips rough, the whiskey strong on his breath. "Stop it, you're hurting me!" I cried out. "Who do you think you are?"

Finally I jerked back and slapped him hard across the face. Even in the shadows, I saw his cheeks turn bright pink.

A small semi-circle gathered around and Bernie stopped playing, his fingers hovering above the keys. Sammy stormed across the small dance floor, grabbing Colin by the shoulder and knocking him to the floor. The crowd fanned out, gaping as if it was a boxing match.

A few onlookers shouted and cheered: "Fight back, you palooka! "Get up, you sorry Mick!"

Embarrassed, I fled to a corner, wishing I could hide, disappear in the dark. The last thing I wanted was to make a scene, or cause trouble for Sammy.

Colin stood up shakily, his eyes blazing, while Sammy circled him, fists up. Then he took a swing at Sammy and almost fell over. Frank and Bernie yanked on Colin's arms, marching him up the stairs. Buzz cowered behind the bar, watching, wide-eyed with fear.

"Stay out of my joint!" Sammy yelled after him. "Or else!"

Colin managed to break free of Frank's grasp and whirled around, pointing at Sammy, his hand like a gun going off. "You're a dead man, hear me? A dead man!"

A dead man? Now what had I done?

Amanda rushed to my side. "Jazz, what happened? What a masher! Are you OK?"

I leaned against the back wall, waiting for the commotion to subside, trying to calm down. "Colin was getting fresh, that's all. But I can defend myself. I didn't expect Sammy to knock him out, in front of everyone."

I tried to brush it off, but I admit, I felt vulnerable, violated, not to mention stupid that I fell for Collin's act. Still, did I really want my big brother to bail me out every time I had a problem?

Sammy rushed over, waving his hands in the air. "Jazz, what were you doing, dancing with that asshole? What were you thinking?"

"Clearly I wasn't thinking straight." I stared at Sammy, confused. "I assumed Colin was your friend."

Sammy snorted. "Friend? Far from it."

Sure, some of his friends were on the unsavory side, but with his cropped hair, striped shirt and khaki pants, Colin looked as clean-cut as any BMOC, big man on campus, or fraternity member.

"Did you have to slug him like that?" I told him, my face on fire. "So he got a little too friendly. I didn't want to cause a big ruckus."

"Don't you know who he is?" Sammy frowned. "He's in the Beach Gang. Colin is one of Sam Maceo's thugs."

CHAPTER TWENTY-FOUR

"Colin is in the Beach Gang?" I froze. "I thought he looked familiar. He must be one of Sam Maceo's bodyguards. They stopped by to see the bathing beauty rehearsals early this week."

"Oh yeah?" Sammy snapped. "So why'd you make goo-goo eyes at a goon like him?"

"Goo goo eyes? You're screwy!" I frowned, glad Sammy couldn't see me blushing. "How could I recognize him in the dark?"

If only Nathan had come with us tonight, he'd have remembered Colin and warned us to stay away. When it came to faces, he had a photographic memory.

"That bully was a gangster? I'm so worried about you!" Amanda flung her arms around Sammy's neck. "What are you going to do?"

"Don't worry," he said, carefully peeling off her arms like faded wallpaper. "I've dealt with worse punks than Colin before."

"So what was he doing here?" I repeated. "I thought the Beach Gang is supposed to stay off the Downtown Gang's turf."

"You got that right." Sammy nodded. "But Colin doesn't like to play by the rules."

"No surprise." Thinking of Holly, I began to understand why a nice girl like her could get involved with a gangster. If Rico was anything like Colin, he had charm and good looks to spare—until you really got to know him.

Sammy pulled up his collar and gestured for Buzz, who rushed over, carefully balancing a tray. "What do you gals want to drink?"

"I'll take a Coke. I don't trust myself with any more giggle-water," I admitted, blushing again.

"Make that three bottles," Sammy told Buzz.

After he left, I tapped Sammy's arm. "We need to talk, in private. About Burton."

Amanda caught my eye. "I think I'll go powder my nose."

Buzz bounded up, handing us our frosty bottles of Coca-Cola. "Thanks, sport," I told the gangly boy, tousling his sandy hair.

Sammy raised his brows. "You talked to Agent Burton? When? What'd he say?"

"Yesterday. On the beach." I followed him to his office, a cluttered cubbyhole not much bigger than a pantry. "Don't worry, no one could hear us there."

How could I break the news? I'd gotten so distracted by Colin and his advances that now Sammy was in an even bigger dilemma.

I took a swig of my Coke, settling in a squeaky old bank chair, marveling at the amount of stuff he managed to cram into such a small space. Photos of special events and club openings and past beauty pageants—and conquests, I suspected—covered the exposed brick walls.

"Tell me what Burton said," Sammy demanded, drumming his desk with impatience.

I looked to make sure the door was closed. "First of all, he was angry that I asked him to do this favor, that you didn't approach him directly." Best not to quote Burton's exact words.

"What does he expect?" He shrugged. "Burton knows I can't be seen in public with a Fed agent. That's suicide. What else did he say?"

I hated to let him down. "Sorry to tell you, he made it clear he won't take orders from gangsters, and we had no business getting him involved. I swear, I've never seen him so angry."

"In other words, he said no." Sammy buried his face in his hands. "Now what in hell am I supposed to do? For all I know, Johnny Jack has me on his hit list."

Hit list? I racked my brain for ideas. "How about leaving town, waiting till he cools off? Open a bar in Houston or New Orleans. Change your name if possible. Get away for a while."

"Splash Day weekend pays all my bills. I can't drop everything and skip town. Then what?"

"Whatever you do, watch your back," I warned. "Agent Burton is getting suspicious, jealous even, wondering how we're connected. He may decide to raid the Oasis, just to get revenge."

Sammy leaned forward, shoulders slumped as if he carried the weight of the world. "Sorry, Jazz. I didn't know what else to do. This may be the end of the Oasis."

What about me, my career? Still, worrying about my job seemed silly compared to a mob hit.

"Didn't you say business is booming? Keep giving Johnny Jack his take, plus a bonus. Tell him a raid would drive the tourists away from all the bars, not just the Hollywood Club, for good."

Who was I to give advice on gangsters? I wasn't even qualified to give tips to the lovelorn.

Sammy seemed to mull it over, a glimmer of hope in his eyes. "Maybe I can try to reason with him. It's worth a shot." He shrugged. "What have I got to lose?"

"Frankly, I'd be more worried about Colin than Johnny Jack. Calling you a dead man?"

"Colin's a hothead. He's just blowing smoke, trying to save face, impress my customers."

I shifted in my seat. "So tell me the truth, Sammy. What was Colin doing here?"

"No big secret. Colin tried to sell me some top-shelf booze. He said the Maceos were keeping him on a tight leash, and he needed to make some dough on the side."

I held my breath, heart racing. "You don't say. What kind of top-notch booze?"

Sammy shot me a stern look. "What difference does it make?"

"Did it happen to be Johnnie Walker Black?"

He sat up. "How in hell did you know? Did Burton tell you?"

"Of course not. I'm not his confidante." Not even his friend.

"Was it your reporter pals? Did they spill the beans?" Sammy shoved back his chair and stared at the ceiling like he was looking for the Big Dipper. "If word got out that I'm buying booze from the Beach Gang, then I *am* a dead man."

I frowned, upset. "Wait, I thought you turned him down?"

"Sure I did. But Colin could spread rumors and lie to Johnny Jack or the cops." Sammy started to pace around the tiny office. "When he found out I'm pals with Big Sam and Papa Rose, he tried to turn it around, pretend like he's got the Maceos' blessing. He's afraid I'll rat him out to Ollie Quinn, and start another gang war."

In a way, I felt relieved. "So I'm not the cause of your fight tonight?"

"Well, it didn't help." He scowled. "It's obvious he didn't like being humiliated in public."

"Don't you have the upper hand? What if you do tell the Maceos or Ollie Quinn, isn't *his* life on the line?" I was trying to make sense of the gangs' laws, which usually made no sense at all. If you looked at a gangster funny or said the wrong word at the wrong time, you could get bumped off in a heartbeat.

"Exactly. The way he sees it, better my neck, than his." Sammy pulled out a Camel, and lit it, daring me to talk. "Now it's your turn. How'd you know he was hawking Johnnie Walker Black? I figured it was fishy 'cause that's Big Sam's favorite brand, and the price was good. Too good."

I paused, wondering how much to reveal. "All I know is one of the bathing beauties was hiding bottles at the Galvez for her boyfriend, Rico. Seems Colin and Rico are partners, trying to skim off Sam Maceo's booze and make some cash on the side."

"Rico Giovanni, that lowlife?" He jumped up, alarmed. "Which tomato? Not Dino's gal?"

"No, not Antonia." I couldn't help but smile. Since when had Miss Italy become Dino's girl? If she only knew what a big torch he carried for her.

Amanda peeked in the office. "I'm getting bored. And lonely."

"Sorry, toots." Sammy crushed out his cigarette on a tip tray, while I grabbed my Coke bottle and followed him out the door. "How about a ride home? I don't want you gals riding the trolley alone tonight. Colin could be outside, waiting to make his move."

Amanda and I traded worried looks. "We'd love a ride home!"

Boy, I really knew how to pick them: First a Hollywood-bound actor with stars in his eyes, then a Prohibition agent who despised me and wanted to lock up my big brother. Now Colin, a dangerous gangster, was after both me *and* Sammy.

Like the song says, "Ain't we got fun?"

CHAPTER TWENTY-FIVE

All the way home, Sammy lectured us on the dangers of two unescorted young dames going out alone at night. "Watch out for wiseguys and hoodlums. They're nothing but trouble," he warned.

Was he talking about himself? What about all the wild flappers and floozies he liked to fool around with? They weren't exactly over-the-hill spinsters and blue-nosed schoolmarms.

Amanda ran her hand through Sammy's dark curls. "So have you seen the bathing beauties lately? The way they were hanging all over you the other night...Should I be jealous?"

"Maybe." Sammy shrugged, keeping his eyes on the road. "Some girls came by the other night, but I can't tell them apart out of their costumes."

"What do you mean, *out* of their costumes? Did you get fresh? Or did they?" she yelped.

In the moonlight, I could see Sammy's devilish grin. He loved attention from women, even jealous gals like Amanda. I'd never met his mother, and he rarely mentioned her, but I imagine she doted on her handsome son. "Don't be a dumb Dora. You know what I mean. I'm too busy running the Oasis to go all bug-eyed over every dame who looks my way."

"Who's looking your way?" Amanda demanded.

"Only you, sweet pea. I only have eyes for you."

Sweet pea? Sammy never used such sappy words. Was he teasing her? Eavesdropping in the back, I began feeling sorry for him. Amanda could be a pit bull when she wanted something, especially when it came to men.

Honestly, I didn't want to be in the middle of their lovers' spat or fling, or whatever their on-again, off-again romance was called.

Thank goodness Amanda changed the subject. Or maybe not. "What are you going to do about this Colin character?"

"Keep my mouth shut and my eyes peeled. What else?"

"What about getting extra protection?" I piped up. "A big bouncer or a security guard. You need protection inside the club, not only Dino at the door."

"That's the Maceos' racket, not mine. Hell, I'm giving Johnny Jack a big enough cut of my take as it is. There's no dough left over for any muscle." He worked his jaw. "Dino's all I got."

"What about guns? Ammunition?" I couldn't believe I was suggesting that Sammy stockpile weapons since my Quaker mother abhorred guns and violence of any kind.

He gave me a sideways glance. "Let's just say I'm not lacking in that area. I did learn a few things during the Great War."

"Good to know." A sore subject. Thank God Sammy came back in one piece, unlike many of his soldier buddies. I leaned against the car seat, momentarily relieved, but began to worry: Would Colin return to the Oasis with Rico, looking for revenge? If they were reckless enough to steal from Sam Maceo, they could easily start a gang war and pin the blame on Sammy.

When he dropped us off at the boarding house, I told Sammy, "Whatever you do, please be careful. You're my only brother. I don't want anything to happen to you."

"Don't worry, Jazz." He gave me a thoughtful smile. "I feel the same way about you."

Wednesday

The next day, I arrived late to work, sleepy and red-eyed, and looked around for Nathan. I couldn't wait to ask him about Holly, and tell him that Colin tried to sell the Maceos' booze to Sammy, a rival gang member. What a hot potato!

Strange, but the newsroom was eerily quiet. No clacking typewriters, no huddled group of reporters sharing war stories. Where was everyone? Even Mrs. Harper seemed engrossed in her society column, so I walked over to the editor-in-chief's office.

I lightly knocked on his door, and Mr. Thomas motioned me inside. "Where is everyone? Seems the whole staff has disappeared."

"You didn't hear?" Mr. Thomas pushed back his bowler hat, scratching his forehead. "Oh, I guess you wouldn't, working for the society section. Mack heard some poor sap got killed last night and was dumped off at a club near downtown. No ID on the victim. Couldn't tell if he was a member of the Beach or Downtown Gang. I'll find out when Mack gets here with the details."

My body stiffened and spots appeared before my eyes. I leaned against his desk, feeling faint. Was it Sammy? Did Colin return to the Oasis last night and carry out his threat?

Mr. Thomas studied me through his thick spectacles. "Aren't you feeling well?"

"Excuse me while I go freshen up." No need to admit I planned to upchuck in the women's restroom. Not very ladylike behavior for a society reporter.

In the bathroom—more of a makeshift closet with primitive facilities—I sat on top of the toilet seat for a while, my head throbbing, my eyes watering. For one night, I let my hair down and allowed myself to have fun, dancing with a lothario who turned out to be a gangster, in a rival gang to boot. And now my stupid, foolish act may have resulted in my brother's death.

Hold your horses, I told myself: I didn't even know the whole story, or even half the story. What had I learned so far as a journalist? In a nutshell, I'd learned by observing the best: Get all the facts straight, then double and triple-check your facts before any story goes to print. Make sure all of your quotes are accurate, and don't quote anyone out of context. Don't presume anything or jump to conclusions—and don't always assume the worst.

So far I'd failed on all counts.

Taking a deep breath, I splashed water on my face and went out to face the music, or rather, the newsroom. As I passed by Mrs. Harper's desk, she scolded me: "Where were you, Jasmine? We've been looking all over for you!"

"I don't feel well." I tried my best to stay calm. "Why? What's wrong?"

She gave me a sly smile. "That handsome Agent Burton called. Said it was urgent."

"Urgent?" I scanned the newsroom, but none of the staffers had magically reappeared in my absence. "What does he want?"

"Why not call him and find out? He sounded very nice. Maybe he's calling for a date?"

Here we were, in the middle of a crisis, and Mrs. Harper still wanted to play matchmaker. Reluctantly, I entered an empty office and picked up the candlestick phone, asking for the police department. After the connection, I said in my best reporter's voice, "Agent Burton, please."

Agent Burton's deep voice came on the line. "This is Agent Burton. Can I help you?"

My heart hammered so hard, it hurt. "It's me, Jazz. What's wrong? Is Sammy OK?"

"Sammy again? Why wouldn't he be?" He paused. "I thought you'd like to know, in case you hadn't heard the news. Sam Maceo's right-hand man turned up dead early this morning. You might remember him: Rico Giovanni."

"Holly's Rico?" I let out a sigh of relief. "What happened?"

"His body was riddled with bullets, and dumped off in front of the Kit Kat Club late last night. The police suspect he was killed by a rival in the Downtown Gang."

"Do they have any suspects? Any evidence?" I began to breathe easy. Sammy was alive and well and Rico, Holly's abusive beau, was dead. Now the world seemed shiny and bright.

"The police aren't naming any names, yet, but I have a different theory." He lowered his voice. "You and I both witnessed what happened in the hospital yesterday."

"What do you mean?" I played dumb. "We saw Holly, half-dead from that beating Rico gave her. As far as I'm concerned, that lowlife got what he deserved."

"Don't you remember what Nathan said? Those threats he made against Rico?"

"So? He was just letting off steam." I held my breath, afraid of what he'd say next.

"Sorry, Jasmine, but I have to ask you and Nathan to come downtown for questioning. We both heard what Nathan said, clear as day." He cleared his throat. "Unless we can prove otherwise, Nathan is a prime suspect in Rico Giovanni's murder."

CHAPTER TWENTY-SIX

"Nathan? A suspect?" I gasped into the phone. Burton had some nerve, accusing him of murder. "You're all wet! Nathan wouldn't hurt a fly, much less gun down a gangster."

Or would he? I recalled his reaction at seeing Holly in the hospital, the way his fists clenched in fury. I knew for a fact he owned a gun, but could he really murder a man in cold blood?

"It's just a theory, but we have to consider all possibilities," Burton said drily. "We can't take threats like that lightly, especially when the victim turns up dead the next day."

"Serves him right, after what he did to Holly..." I took a deep breath, trying to control my anger. "Why are you even working this case? I thought you didn't cover homicides."

"I volunteered. Since Rico was smuggling booze, that could provide a valid motive for murder. Besides, I couldn't withhold vital information in a murder investigation." His voice was so monotone, so flat, I knew he still held a grudge.

"You volunteered? How big of you." Was Burton trying to incriminate Nathan out of spite or was he getting back at me?

"Nathan isn't a killer," I fumed. "Do you have any actual evidence or proof that places Nathan at the Kit Kat Club? Or is it all speculation?" I'd eavesdropped on enough of Mack's conversations to ask the right questions.

"We're working on it." He paused. "Any idea where Nathan was last night?"

"He was visiting Holly in the hospital," I said, hoping that was a good enough alibi. "He left after he dropped me and Amanda off at the Oasis after eight o'clock."

"How late was he there?"

"I don't know. Why don't you ask him yourself?"

"That's why I'm calling you. I stopped by earlier, but he seems to have disappeared."

"Disappeared?" Was Nathan in hiding? With a Fed agent on his tail, accusing him of killing a Beach Gang goon, who could blame him? "I'm sure he's on an assignment, that's all."

"Let me know when he comes in," Burton said coldly, as if we *both* were suspects.

"Instead of hounding Nathan, you should be questioning Johnny Jack since Rico's body was found in the Downtown Gang's area." Then I blurted out, "Why don't you interrogate Rico's partner, Colin? He had a lot more motive than Nathan."

"You mean Colin Ferris? How do you know him? What motives?" Burton sounded wary.

"I kind of met him last night, at the Oasis," I stammered.

"He was at the Oasis? Seems to be your favorite juice joint, doesn't it, Jasmine?" Even over the phone, I could hear his frustration. "Maybe I should ask your pal Sammy about Colin. I'd like to know why a Beach Gang thug was on a rival gang's turf."

Me and my big mouth. "What for? Sammy's not involved."

"You sure? We'll see what Homicide digs up. Thanks for the tip." With that, he hung up.

I sat there, head in my hands. Instead of taking the heat off Nathan by mentioning Colin, I'd managed to get Sammy in hot water. Obviously Burton was still mad at me, but did he have to take it out on my two favorite fellas?

Mrs. Harper signaled me over, but I returned to my desk, pretending not to notice. I was in no mood to talk about debutantes and dances, or fabricate a romance with Burton for her amusement. Clearly Burton and I were no longer friends, but definitely foes.

As I sat at my desk, trying to figure out what to do next without actually working, I heard voices at the entrance.

Surprise: In walked Mack with Nathan right behind, their excited voices carrying over the newsroom. I jumped up to greet them. "Mack! Nathan, where were you?"

Nathan unloaded his camera equipment on my desk, slapping his knee. "What a scoop! Did you hear? Rico turned up dead, full of bullets, smack dab in front of the Kit Kat Club. Got some good photos too. He had so many holes in him, he looked like a colander."

I cringed at the image. "You were there with Mack?"

He nodded. "Good old Mack called me in the middle of the night about a mob hit. Boy, was I glad it turned out to be Rico." This time he slapped my desk. "Serves the bastard right, after the way he worked over Holly. Now she's finally free of that bully, for good."

"Thank God." I could almost hear his heart beating on his sleeve. "How's Holly doing?"

"A lot better. I doubt she knows that Rico is dead yet, and I'm not sure how to break the news." His face fell. "To be honest, I don't know if she'll be glad or upset."

"Probably a little of both. After that beating he gave her, I'd think she'd be relieved." For a fleeting moment, I wondered if Nathan could be guilty, but kept my trap shut. "Hey, I'm sorry to burst your bubble, but Agent Burton is looking for you."

"Agent Burton? Why?" Did he already forget the threats he'd made yesterday at the hospital?

I couldn't sugar-coat it: "He wants us both to go downtown for questioning in Rico's murder."

"Oh yeah?" Nathan blanched. "That's bunk!" He rushed around the office, grabbing files and papers. "I don't have time to talk to him or the cops. I'm taking Holly to Houston to recuperate."

"What's the rush?"

"Don't you see? Holly's in danger. What if Rico's killer goes after her and tries to punish her too? They may assume she's his accomplice since she hid Maceo's booze in her hotel room."

What could I say to make him change his mind? "Are you sure that's a good idea? Think of how guilty you'll look to the cops. They'll think you kidnapped Holly and tried to run."

"Who cares what the cops think? You know I'm no killer." No use trying to talk any sense into Nathan when he was gripped by some romantic fantasy, starring himself as Rudolph Valentino and Holly as the damsel in distress in "The Sheik."

"Hold your horses, Nate. Did Mr. Thomas give you time off?"

He flashed me a panicked look. "Mack will make up something. I'm running out of time. Maybe you can sweet-talk Burton, stall him for a day or two."

Sweet-talk Burton? Fat chance. "I doubt Burton will listen to anything I have to say."

"Don't worry, I'll be back before Splash Day." He gave me a mischievous grin. "I wouldn't miss watching the bathing beauty contest for the world."

"I'll bet." I smiled at his eager expression. "How will you convince the nurses to let Holly leave the hospital with you?"

He looked smug. "I already figured that out. Last night, I told them I was her brother."

"Did they buy it?" I took in his sandy hair, rumpled shirt and worn cowboy boots. In a word, you'd describe him as disheveled, a far cry from Holly's dainty, dark-haired good looks. "Wait, Nate. Before you go, what about my bathing beauty photos? I need them for my profiles."

He disappeared into the darkroom, and returned with a stack of folders. "Here, you can use these. Keep them safe. And don't forget my photo credits!"

I heard a commotion at the door and looked up to see two uniformed cops standing by the entrance. Nathan peered around the corner, still as a mime.

Mack ambled over, holding his cigar. "How can I help you, sirs?" He sounded as casual as if he was entertaining guests at home.

"We're looking for Nathan Cooper," a young mustachioed cop said. Luckily, Mrs. Page, the busybody receptionist, was gone for the day, or she'd point straight at Nathan.

Mack turned around, pretending to survey the newsroom, and gave us a quick wink. Shaking his head, he stuck his elbows out, his burly frame blocking the cops' view. "Nathan Cooper? I believe he's out of the office, on assignment."

Thank goodness Mack came to the rescue once again.

"Go out the back way," I mouthed to Nathan, pointing to the exit. "Hurry, get out. Now!"

Nathan gave me a grateful look before he tiptoed out the back door. I just hoped Burton wasn't waiting outside, ready to nab Nathan before he could make his escape with Holly.

CHAPTER TWENTY-SEVEN

My heart heavy, I watched Nathan sneak out the back exit while Mack stalled for time, giving the cops a bunch of false leads. I hoped Nathan and Holly would make it to Houston before Burton and the cops realized he'd skipped town. I assumed Nathan was innocent, but heading for Houston with Holly right after Rico's murder made him appear guilty as hell.

The cops seemed skeptical, scanning the newsroom, firing off questions, until Mack had to practically push them out the door. After they left, I checked to make sure Nathan was gone, then made a beeline for Mack.

"What was that all about? Tell me what happened with Rico?"

"Hello to you too, little lady." Mack made a show of tipping his hat. "Got a call from a source about a body in front of the Kit Kat. So I called Nathan right away to get a jump on the other news rags. You should've seen the look on his face when he saw the victim. Pure joy."

"I can imagine. But how did he recognize Rico in the dark, especially if he was all shot up?"

Mack puffed on his cigar, the sweet scent of cherry tobacco wafting my way. "The shooter left the face alone. Rico was positioned right in front, under a gas lamp with the light shining on him, bright as a spotlight. Maybe the killer was sending a message?"

"You're the expert on Galveston gangs. What message?"

"Stay off my turf and out of my way. Or else."

I mulled it over. Could Colin kill his own partner? And why? Were they fighting over the stash of booze, or jockeying for a position of power in the Beach Gang? I recalled how he threatened Sammy, his vicious tone. Obviously it didn't take much for Colin to blow his stack.

Too bad I couldn't examine Nathan's photos of Rico, but they were still undeveloped. Did he see something unusual at the scene, a clue perhaps? What was the real reason Nathan needed to leave town in such a hurry? I wanted to ask Mack, but I doubted he'd tell me the truth. What if I was completely wrong and it *was* an enemy in the Downtown Gang?

"Let me ask you a question." Mack rubbed his chin. "Did Nathan know this guy? They seemed to have some sort of history, the way he was chortling over his murder. Kinda morbid, if you ask me. Laughing over a dead guy's body. You'd think Nathan was in a rival gang."

"As far as I know, they'd never met." I glanced around the newsroom to make sure no one was listening. "Perhaps they were interested in the same woman?"

Mack nodded knowingly. "Well, I'll be. Nathan's in love with a gangster's moll."

"I wouldn't call her that exactly," I began, then bit my tongue. Boy, would Nathan get a razzing from the newshounds now.

Mack raised his brows. "So you've met her? What's she like?"

"She's a wonderful gal, and I hope they're very happy together," I recited.

"You make it sound like they're eloping," Mack snorted.

"Says you." I returned to my desk, hoping Mack wouldn't ask me any more questions. Good thing Nathan was leaving town or he would've killed *me* for blabbing.

Mrs. Harper shot me her get-to-work-now look. Yes, ma'am!

I began sifting through Nathan's photos of the bathing beauties, trying to get inspired to write up more profiles. Then I remembered the old file on the pageant history, and pulled it out to compare articles and photos.

Head down, I tried to concentrate on my interview notes, weeding out the sob stories that might depress our readers—not exactly the light, sunny fare fit for the society section of our family-oriented paper. A couple of hours later, I'd banged out at least two or three stories I thought Mrs. Harper might actually approve. I handed her my rough drafts and waited while she perused my stories, marking them up with a red pen like a nitpicky schoolteacher.

"Not bad, Jasmine, but you've got a few holes here and there. If you get these questions answered, you might have at least one we can use for tomorrow's paper."

Only one? Swell. By now it was after five, too late to go to rehearsals. I could try to catch the girls at the Hotel Galvez, before they went off to dinner or more likely, the bars on the Strand or Market Street. Without Mrs. Wembley hovering around, I hoped they'd give me more candid answers.

That evening at the boarding house, I told Amanda the good news. My Egyptian maiden perfume lamp cast flickering lights and a rose scent, providing the perfect backdrop.

"Guess what? We don't have to worry about Rico anymore. He was gunned down last night on the Downtown Gang's turf."

"You don't say!" she gasped, eyes big as saucers. "I heard some thug was killed, but I had no idea it was Holly's fella. Doesn't Nathan have a crush on her? You don't think …?"

I shook my head. "Still, it doesn't help his case by fleeing with Holly to Houston."

"You never know what a man will do for love," Amanda sighed. Even in an emergency, she was a hopeless romantic.

"Say, I'm heading to the Hotel Galvez tonight if you want to come along. You can talk to the girls while I do some follow-up interviews with the contestants."

"I'd like to, but I'm working at Star Drugstore tonight. I hate for you to go alone." She looked worried. "Just be careful."

After sprucing up, I took the trolley down to the Galvez, pencil and notepad tucked in my bag, hoping to catch the beauties off guard. I still needed to put the final touches on my profiles of Delysia and Antonia, and flesh out Miss California

I wandered around the lobby, expecting to run into a few girls, but they were nowhere in sight. Disappointed, I went to the front desk, asking the clerk, "Are the bathing beauties here tonight?"

The reed-thin dandy looked me up and down. "I believe they had to make an appearance at some night spot, maybe the Surf Club or the Grotto. Are you supposed to join them?"

"Yes," I fibbed. "Can you double-check the location, please?"

As I waited, I surveyed the restaurant, wondering if the girls were dining with love-struck fellas. I thought I recognized a familiar face, and moved closer for a better look: Colin Ferris was dining with Beach Gang leader Ollie Quinn and two middle-aged men, talking and laughing as if they hadn't a care in the world. From their fancy duds, I couldn't tell if the men were bootleggers or out-of-town businessmen. Considering Rico had just been murdered, Colin sure wasn't showing a bit of remorse or sorrow for his dead partner.

What were those two hoods doing here in public, when they had their pick of Beach Gang hideaways? Was it a coincidence or were they looking for Holly or Jo Beth or the stash of Johnnie Walker Black? Slowly I inched away from the front desk, wanting to make a mad dash for the exit, but trying not to attract attention.

I pulled my floppy hat down over my face and made my way toward the second floor. Upstairs, I fled down the hall, looking for Jo Beth's room and rapped on her door, hoping to hide. When she didn't answer, I turned the knob and it opened without a hitch. Strange. I studied the keyhole and noticed the door frame was nicked and scratched where someone had forced the lock.

Had the gangsters broken in here earlier? I tiptoed inside, noting that the room looked neat and organized, nothing seemed out of place. Quickly, I checked under the bed: The suitcase was still there, so I squatted down and pulled it out without any effort. No doubt they'd already cleared out the booze, probably the same liquor Colin had tried to pawn off on Sammy.

Still, something was rattling inside, but it sounded muffled. Using a handy bobby pin, I jiggled the locks and managed to pry it open: A hotel towel was wrapped around a heavy, bulky object.

Hands shaking, I pulled off the towel, jumping back when I saw the handgun inside.

CHAPTER TWENTY-EIGHT

Was it the murder weapon? Whose gun was it and why was it hidden here? Was it still loaded? My heart dropped. Now I really felt sorry for Jo Beth: Not only had Rico and Colin used the hotel room as their own personal dumping ground, she could be arrested as an accomplice if the cops found this handgun here.

What should I do, take it with me as evidence or leave it behind? Frankly, I was scared to pick it up, afraid it might go off. I stared at it closely, trying to memorize the details, looking for any numbers that might help identify the weapon, but I knew nothing about guns.

A crazy idea crossed my mind: Could Jo Beth be working with Colin? Maybe he came by to get the booze, and coerced her into hiding the gun? Then a more onerous thought hit me: Could Nathan have hidden the gun here, using Holly's key? Was Rico's death a crime of passion or revenge? Is that why they were on the run?

Hold your horses, Jazz. How could I doubt my friends? I was beginning to sound like my aunt's favorite radio show, *Mystery House*.

I shoved the suitcase under the bed, trying to think of a way out of this dilemma. But for now, I had to sneak out of the hotel without getting caught by Colin or Quinn or anyone else I knew.

Feeling like a cat burglar, I shut the door quietly, and tiptoed down the stairs. The lobby was filled with tourists and guests checking in, laden down with bags. After all, the Pageant of Pulchritude was only a few days away.

Craning my neck around a creamy white column, I surveyed the restaurant: Thank goodness Colin and Ollie Quinn were gone. Was it safe to leave now?

Then I thought of what Sammy said at the Oasis: Colin could be waiting for me, this time outside the hotel. All I'd done was hurt his male pride, but with his temper, I didn't want to take any chances.

Since Nathan was on his way to Houston, I didn't know who to call. It was too dangerous for Sammy to show up here and I was still persona non grata with Burton. Hiding behind the column, I waited for the lobby to quiet down and approached the front desk again.

"Where'd you go?" The snippy clerk frowned. "I thought you were going to the Grotto?"

"I was visiting a friend here." I smiled, trying to soften him up. "For now, may I use your phone?"

"Our phones are reserved for *paying* guests." He sniffed and straightened his yellow bow tie, appraising my casual attire.

"I'm a friend of Jo Beth Walton. You can put it on her tab."

I smiled to myself. Wouldn't Jo Beth be miffed when she saw her final bill?

"Miss Dallas?" He nodded with approval. "Very well, young lady. Follow me." We went to a small room behind the desk where operators were talking non-stop into headphones, plugging their wires in and out of the switchboards. Amanda had worked as a switchboard operator for a while, but she told me the constant chatter made her daffy.

"Who do you wish to call?" The clerk raised his brows. "I hope it's not long-distance."

"The police department, please." Burton was my last hope.

The clerk stared at me in alarm, beady eyes blinking. "You want to call the cops? Why?"

"My fella is working the night shift," I fibbed. "Just checking to make sure he's OK."

The dandy relaxed his stance and pointed to a phone on a shabby desk in the corner. Such a contrast from the luxurious lobby and restaurant out front. After the operator connected me, I left a message for Agent Burton, knowing he wouldn't be there at this hour, but hoping they could reach him right away.

"I'll be at the Galvez, waiting in the lobby, in case he gets this message soon," I told the cop on duty. "Tell him it's an emergency."

Before I left, the clerk gave me a quizzical look. "Agent Burton, huh? He's your fella?"

What a Nosy Nellie! I gave him a sly smile and rushed out into the lobby, praying he wasn't the gossipy type.

After settling in a plush sofa, I studied the crowd, enjoying the variety of people on parade: Young and old, foreigners and locals, all had gathered in anticipation of the world-famous Miss Universe Pageant. Men wore wide-brimmed straw boaters and seersucker suits, while women displayed embellished hats and pastel summer frocks. Several guests arrived in native garb representing their homeland, from rich embroidered dresses to bright Indian saris, supporting the pride and joy of their countries.

The comfortable couch made me sleepy, so I shut my eyes a moment. Then I felt a hand clasp my shoulder. Burton? Turning around, I froze when I saw Colin Ferris and Ollie Quinn, grinning at me like crazy circus clowns.

"Fancy seeing you here, Jazz," Colin said, all smiles and good looks. "Remember me? You still owe me a dance, darling."

Then he took my hand and kissed it, pretending to be a perfect gentleman. His green eyes seemed to sparkle under the chandeliers, but up close they appeared ice-cold, like fake emeralds.

I was too shocked to speak, pulling away. What did he want? Why the faux British "Lord of the Manor" act?

"You haven't introduced me to your lovely lady friend, Colin." The roly-poly Ollie Quinn gave a slight bow. "Are you one of our bathing beauties come to our fair shore?"

Blushing, I stood up, in case I needed to make a run for the exit.

"I'm a society reporter." I emphasized the word *society* so they knew I was harmless.

"I thought you looked familiar." Quinn eyed me and nodded.

Oh no. Did he recognize me from the infamous photos taken at the Surf Club? He smiled and shook my trembling hand, his grip firm. How many men had he killed with those strong hands? Were they behind Rico's murder?

"Nice to meet you." I faked a smile and stepped back, my poor hand limp after that death grip.

"Say, anytime you want to come by one of our nightclubs, just mention my name. I'm sure you've been to the Surf Club? The Hollywood Dinner Club?" Quinn held out an oversized business card, embossed in gold letters. Was he razzing me?

"Thanks." I wanted to throw the card away, but then again, it might come in handy one day.

Quinn turned to Colin, giving him a wink. "I'll leave you two alone while I get the car." He tipped his hat. "Hope to see you again soon. Don't be a stranger, Miss Cross."

Wait, how in hell did the Beach Gang leader know my name? Did Colin mention me?

In the background, I heard the desk clerk say, "I've already asked the valet to bring your car around to the front, Mr. Quinn."

Figured the daffodil would kowtow to wealthy gangsters.

After Quinn left, Colin sidled up to me, standing uncomfortably close. "Glad I ran into you, Jazz. I wanted to apologize for the other night. Sorry I got carried away."

"There's no need." I tried to act nonchalant, avoiding his intense gaze. "We both got a little plastered."

"I'll say." He leaned forward, his breath hot on my neck. "When I find a woman so attractive, I just can't help myself."

What a lounge lizard! He sounded more like Douglas Fairbanks than a hot-under-the-collar hood. How to get rid of him?

"Thanks, but I'm already taken," I fibbed, backing away.

"I don't see any ring on your finger." He reached for my hand, and held it up as proof, eyes narrowed. "So how's your pal Sammy? He's not your fella, is he?"

"No, we're just friends. Why?" Was that a veiled threat?

"Good." Colin smiled as if he meant it. "Maybe you'll give me another chance."

Was he nuts? "A chance at what?" I played dumb, not sure how to react. Did he really think I'd be interested in a common criminal— and a possible killer to boot?

"Take a wild guess." He pretended to admire my dangly earrings, then reached over and kissed me on the cheek, his stubble rough on my skin, smelling of cigarettes and scotch.

Damn it, wouldn't you know?

That's the moment I saw Agent Burton stride through the front entrance, heading right toward me and Colin.

CHAPTER TWENTY-NINE

"Jasmine, I got your message." Agent Burton's eyes darted back and forth between me and Colin. "But please, continue. Don't let me interrupt your private party."

"Colin was just leaving," I said, my face flaming. "Thanks for stopping by."

"So what's he doing here?" Burton glared at Colin whose smug smile faded.

"It's a free country, ain't it, Fed?" His green eyes darkened as he scowled at Burton. "You know this guy?"

"Sure, it's my job. I need to keep up with all the movers and shakers in town." I pasted on a sunny smile like a nervous society hostess. "I take it you two have met?"

"You could say that." Burton eyed Colin. "Sorry to hear about your pal, Rico. Shouldn't you be planning his funeral?"

Suddenly Colin was in gangster mode, puffing out his brawny chest. "That's none of your beeswax." He moved toward Burton, only inches from his face, but Burton didn't flinch. "Mind your own business, Fed." Except for their tailored suits and natty hats, the men looked like they were facing off in a street fight.

"Hoodlums like you are my business," Burton snapped. "Give my regards to Ollie. I saw him waiting out front. What is he, your errand boy now?"

"Funny guy." Colin raised his fist, but Burton grabbed his wrist, forcing his arm down.

The skinny clerk gasped and fluttered across the lobby, no doubt worried about a showdown in front of his rich guests. "Oh, my! Gentlemen, let's keep it civil, please."

"I need some fresh air," Colin scowled. "This place is getting crowded. See you later, doll face." He gave me a tight-lipped smile, and tipped his hat as he left.

"Doll face?" Burton frowned. "Don't you know who he is? He's a torpedo for the Beach Gang. A cold-blooded killer. Why didn't you tell him to go to hell?"

"I tried to brush him off, but he wouldn't let me go." My words tumbled out in a rush. "Colin threatened Sammy that night at the Oasis. I didn't want to make matters worse."

Luckily, Burton seemed so distracted by Colin, he'd forgotten about questioning Nathan, at least for now.

"I don't get you, Jasmine." He shook his head. "Every time I see you, you're with a different guy. Nathan, Sammy and now Colin?"

"I'm not *with* anyone. They're all just friends."

"You and Colin are friends now? A hit man?"

"Applesauce! You know what I meant."

"So why'd you call me tonight? I didn't mean to break up your little fling."

"What fling?" I rolled my eyes at his jab. "I was afraid Colin and Ollie might try to corner me, follow me home. Believe me, I was scared to death." I motioned toward the hotel rooms. "If you want, I'll show you the real reason I called."

"By all means." We took the stairs and I led him down the hall to Jo Beth's room. As I opened the door, Burton warned me, "Careful, I could report you for breaking and entering."

"The lock was already broken when I entered. Please watch the door, will you?" Again I squatted down, pulled out the suitcase and undid the locks, loose after all the tampering.

"What are you doing?" He frowned. "Didn't Colin and Quinn already take the bottles?"

"You need to see this." Hands shaking, I removed the towel, exposing the gun. "I wonder if it's the gun they used to kill Rico?"

Burton edged closer. "What in hell?" He wrapped the towel around the handle and carefully picked up the gun, squinting at the barrel, checking the chamber. "How'd you know it was here?" His eyes narrowed. "Did Nathan ask you and Jo Beth to hide it for him?"

"You're all wet. I was looking for Jo Beth, and found this in here by accident," I bristled.

"Oh yeah? I'd better take this downtown for evidence, find out if it's been fired recently."

"Careful with that thing! It may be loaded." I covered my face, as if that would help.

"Don't worry. The chamber is empty. Whoever used this already fired off all six rounds." Burton glanced at the gun again before he wrapped it in the towel, then held it out to me.

"No, thanks." I stepped back, alarmed. "What do you want *me* to do with it?"

"Hide it in your purse. I'll have the experts examine it and dust it for fingerprints, then try to match the bullets. If it *is* the murder weapon, we can find out who gunned down Rico."

"In my purse?" Oh, swell. First, Ollie Quinn's card and maybe a murder weapon, too. "Why don't *you* carry it out of the hotel?"

"They may think I'm stealing towels." He smiled. "Besides, I'm already armed."

Unfortunately, I was in no position to argue with a Fed agent holding a gun. "Sure it's safe to take it now? What if the gangsters come after Jo Beth? I don't want to put her in any more danger."

"She's already in danger. I can tell the lab to rush the forensics, and return it before anyone notices it's gone."

Seeing my hesitation, he grabbed my purse and stuffed the weapon inside. Now it looked like a pregnant football. I tucked my now-bulging bag under my arm, praying I wouldn't run into any of the bathing beauties.

As we left the Galvez, the coast was clear—no gangsters or bathing beauties—even the beach activity had died down. I felt a blast of warm, salty sea air as we walked outside to his car. This time, Burton didn't hold the door open for me, but slammed his car door, staring straight ahead as he drove. What a difference from our previous dates, or rather outings, since we weren't dating and probably never would go out again.

"Thanks for coming to my rescue," I said, to break the ice.

"Did I have a choice? The cops made it sound urgent." He blew out a frustrated sigh. "Then I walk in and see you necking with Colin Ferris, a Beach Gang goon?"

"Necking? What do you think I am, a vamp?" I was beyond insulted. "He forced himself on me, just like he did at the Oasis."

"Says you. I didn't see you fighting him off."

"I didn't want to make a scene in public. How would that look if I screamed bloody murder in the Galvez lobby?" I bristled, raising my voice. "I needed your help. I wanted to show you the gun."

"Next time you need help, call your friend Nathan." He hit the steering wheel. "Oh, that's right. He skipped town with his beauty pageant girlfriend. You lied to me, Jasmine. You knew exactly where he was but you kept quiet."

"What do you expect? You practically accused him of murder. Trust me, Nathan blows a lot of hot air, but he's no hit man."

"Unlike your boyfriend Colin," he said, frowning as he pulled up in front of the police station.

"Well, now you have some evidence to prove it wasn't Nathan."

"We'll have to wait and see." Burton got out of the car, and leaned over my door.

"If you don't mind, I'll stay in the car."

"Suit yourself." He snatched my purse and went inside the building. I couldn't help but smile at seeing such a masculine guy carrying my bag, holding it out like a dead skunk.

A night guard met him at the door, and did a double-take when he saw me sitting in Burton's car. I took a few deep breaths, trying to calm down. What had gone wrong? I replayed the evening's events, from the time I spied Colin and Quinn to Burton's tirade. The only good news was that I'd found the gun, and possibly the murder weapon, that might save Nathan's neck.

Burton emerged a few minutes later, and handed me my purse. "We'll get the results by morning. Then I'll find a way to return the gun to Jo Beth's hotel room."

"Great. The sooner, the better."

Starting the car, he squinted at me, blue eyes frosty. "Jasmine, before I take you home, I have to ask: Why is Ollie Quinn's business card in your purse?"

CHAPTER THIRTY

Swell. I'd overlooked that minor detail. "Ollie Quinn gave it to me, said I could use it to get into his nightclubs," I told Burton, getting defensive. "What was I going to do, tear it up in his face?"

"You're a riot." Burton glared at me. "Imagine my surprise when I pull out the gun and Ollie Quinn's business card falls out of your purse. The cops on duty saw it, too. Quinn may consider you a welcome guest, now that you're consorting with criminals like Colin."

"I am *not* consorting with criminals. I had no idea Colin was in the Beach Gang."

"What if he wasn't? He's still a gangster." Then he brightened. "Say, why don't I hold onto this card for now? We can compare the fingerprints on the gun with the ones on his card."

"Don't forget, my prints are on the card too."

"You didn't touch the gun, did you?"

"Of course not. I thought it was loaded." I made a face.

"Then everything's jake." He slowed down, heading toward the beach. "You know, it might be smart to stay on Quinn's good side. You may want to call in a favor one day."

"Oh really? What kind of favor?"

"Who knows? You may need to bail out your jailbird friends."

"You slay me." I frowned. Did he mean Nathan or Sammy, or himself? Tired of trading barbs, I watched young couples strolling along the Seawall, their hair and clothes blowing in the muggy breeze.

In the distance, the Crystal Palace glowed in the dark, Galveston's version of the Taj Mahal. I wished I could join the carefree crowd milling about or sitting on the beach, eating ice cream, enjoying the fresh seaside air. Not long ago, Burton and I had taken a romantic stroll here, getting to know each other, but tonight was different. Now I felt trapped inside a pressure cooker.

Trying to change the subject, I asked, "What about Jo Beth? Should I tell her about the gun?"

"No, it's best if she doesn't know. Suggest that for her own safety, she should change hotel rooms, especially in light of Rico's death. But tell her to leave the suitcase under the bed."

I nodded in agreement. "You're right. I'd feel responsible if anything happened to her. Why don't I call her tonight?"

"Good idea." With a pang of guilt, I realized that the contestants' dance at the Hollywood Dinner Club was only two days away. So far I'd failed to convince Burton to raid the club and, after tonight's fiasco with Colin, this wasn't the best time to bring up the subject. All Sammy could do was wait and see what Johnny Jack might dish out as punishment.

Burton parked in front of the boarding house, making no attempt to walk me to the door. Figured.

As I got out, he warned, "Be careful, Jasmine. We've had our eye on Colin Ferris for a while. We haven't been able to pin anything on him yet, and given his background with Rico, he may be our prime suspect. You may think this is fun and games, but he's armed and very dangerous."

I whirled around, leaning over his Roadster. "In case you didn't get the telegram, I'm not interested in Colin. We're not an item, and we're not friends. You should know by now that I'd never date a gangster, especially a murder suspect."

"I know that, Jasmine." Burton nodded, working his jaw. "But he seems to have a crush on you. Hard-boiled hoods like him consider nice girls like you a challenge."

Was he right? I stood there on the walkway, watching him drive off in the dark. Seems Sammy and Burton weren't the only ones who had to worry about getting tailed by gangsters.

By now, it was almost ten o'clock and I needed to call Jo Beth at the Hotel Galvez before the switchboard closed. Luckily Aunt Eva wasn't downstairs, so I used the private telephone in the parlor.

When Jo Beth answered, she naturally sounded surprised to hear from me late at night. "We just got in from a performance at a really ritzy place, I think it was the Surf Club?" she said, sounding breathless. "We didn't make too many mistakes, so I think we're ready for the Hollywood Dinner Club Friday night."

After I told her about Rico's murder, she practically cheered. "What a relief! I almost jumped for joy when I heard the news! That bastard got what he deserved."

My sentiments exactly. "You may want to change hotel rooms right away, just in case his partner or some gangster comes back, looking for the suitcase."

"Rico had a partner? Holly and I always assumed he was acting alone so his boss wouldn't find out," she said, upset. "Are you sure?"

"Remember the first day of rehearsals, when Sam Maceo came in with Rico and a second bodyguard? We think he was Rico's partner, Colin Ferris."

"Colin? Green eyes with auburn hair and dimples?" she asked. "That's the same guy we met tonight at the Surf Club. He's too cute to be a gangster!"

"Colin was there? Tonight?" Such a lounge lizard. I admit, he also had me fooled at first.

"He came in late. After the dance ended, he introduced himself to all the girls." She sighed. "What a sheik!"

"Be careful, Jo Beth. Colin is dangerous. Did you know he's in the Beach Gang?"

"How dangerous? I told him my room number so he can call me. Now I've got the shakes." She inhaled. "OK, I'll sleep in a different room tonight, then move in the morning."

"Be sure to leave the suitcase there under the bed, just in case he comes looking for it." I paused, thinking of my already-past deadline. "Say, can you do me a favor? I need to interview a couple of girls, confirm a few things before I turn in my stories. I tried to stop by tonight, but everyone was out." I hoped the dandy wouldn't blab about my (her) phone tab or my run-in with Colin and Burton.

"I'll be glad to. After all, I owe you. Thanks, Jazz." For once, she seemed sincere.

That night, I stayed up late to finish my profiles, handwriting them by the lamp in the parlor. Since I still needed to type and edit them in the morning, I'd have to try for the evening edition.

Thursday

I'd fallen asleep on the sofa and woke up by dawn, before anyone was awake. Rushing upstairs, I got ready in a jiffy and took the early morning trolley, arriving to work by seven o'clock. Boy, wouldn't Mrs. Harper be surprised when she saw my neatly typed stories on her desk, ready for her edits.

Besides the receptionist and Mr. Thomas, I was the first reporter to arrive. No surprise since most of the reporters stumbled in by nine, usually hung-over and half asleep. Mr. Thomas raised his brows when he saw me. "Morning, Jazz. Is everything alright?"

"It's all jake. Why do you ask?" When he didn't reply, I added, "Need to finish my stories soon." I glanced over my notes, trying to decipher my late-night handwriting, and managed to pound out a couple of stories. Mrs. Harper smiled with approval as she settled in at her desk.

Exhausted, I took a break when Mack showed up at work after nine o'clock.

"Any word from Nathan?" I asked him, worried.

"Not yet, but that's a good sign," Mack said. "My sources would tell me if the cops caught him leaving town with Holly. I'm sure they wanted to question her too."

"That's a relief." I wondered if I should mention the gun we found at the Galvez, but decided to keep quiet, knowing he'd call his cop buddies and snoop around. "I was afraid they'd arrest him on some trumped-up charges."

"They've been known to do worse." Mack nodded. "But I'm sure Nathan can talk his way out of anything."

"I hope so." Nathan's quick wit had gotten him out of more than one tight spot, but dealing with cops took a different skill, usually involving cash. "Say, have your sources found any connection between the two dead girls?"

"Those hookers? The main similarities were their ages and the fact both were killed elsewhere and dumped off later. Apparently both were beaten and then strangled to death." Mack pulled out a cigar and lit it, blowing fat puffs of smoke to the ceiling. "So it appears to be the same M.O."

"That's all? No one claimed the bodies? No identifying marks? Any witnesses?"

"I did ask my pal about the second victim, and he confirmed that she didn't have any special markings or tattoos. Maybe she was a new recruit and didn't measure up?" He leaned back, waving his cigar. "Sorry to disappoint you, Jazz, but we can't investigate either case until Splash Day weekend is over."

My face fell. "By then, it's yesterday's news. No one will care or remember."

"That's the idea." Mack cocked his head toward Mr. Thomas' office. "Even the head honcho told me to put these stories on the back burner."

Big surprise. "Speaking of stories, would you mind looking over my bathing beauty profiles? They're due by noon."

"I'd rather stare at the photos, but sure, I'll give them a quick read." He made a few scribbles before handing the pages back to me. "Tough assignment. Let me know if you need help with any more *interviews*," he said with a sly grin.

What a card. Wish I'd never asked for his input. Now I had to re-type each story again. After I made the changes, I handed Mrs. Harper not two, but three, fresh-off-the-typewriter stories with the photos attached, barely making my deadline.

"Good job, Jasmine," said Mrs. Harper, pleased for once. "We'll run these in the evening edition."

Finally my stories met her approval. "Great! Say, can I take an early lunch? I'm so hungry, I could eat my hat."

"Yes, of course." She leaned forward, and lifted her spectacles. "But be careful, Jasmine. I heard you were keeping company with Ollie Quinn and his sidekick at the Hotel Galvez last night. Anything I should know about?"

CHAPTER THIRTY-ONE

Why was I so surprised? Mrs. Harper's spies were everywhere.

"I wasn't quite keeping company with Mr. Quinn or his sidekick, but I *was* at the Galvez last night. How did you know?"

"I've got my sources." She gave me a smug Cheshire-cat smile.

I suspected her snitch was the skinny dandy who watched us like a hawk from his perfect vantage point behind the front desk.

I smiled sweetly. "Well, your source got it wrong. Quinn just introduced himself and shook my hand, that's all."

"Oh really? I also heard there was a row between Agent Burton and Quinn's bodyguard." She raised her brows and smiled. "Didn't Burton protect you?"

The newsroom quieted and the reporters grinned like hyenas. Now I wanted to find that gossipy tattle-tale at the Galvez and wring his scrawny neck.

"Thank goodness it didn't turn into a fistfight!" I cut her off.

No use denying anything, or she'd keep blabbing the whole story to the nosy staff. Flustered, I checked my watch, saying, "Time for lunch!" I gathered up my things, trying to make my escape before she kept talking. "Can I get you a sandwich?"

"I'm going out, but I'll return soon." She waved a gloved hand in my direction. "I'm warning you, be careful. Watch your step."

Face flushed, I rushed outside, needing some fresh air. Between Mrs. Harper's spies and Mack's cherry cigar, I felt suffocated.

Golliwog came out of hiding and followed me down to the street vendor, where I ordered a chicken salad sandwich, mostly for her, and a cold bottle of Dr. Pepper.

Golly followed me to a small park, where we shared my sandwich. She circled my ankles, showing her appreciation, her jet-black fur warm and silky.

To treat myself, I wanted to stop by Eiband's and admire their latest offerings of vanity cases, perfumes and mesh purses. I needed some color, some visual stimulation to break up the monotony of black on white, the lines of ink on paper. Even Golly looked monochromatic with her solid black fur. One day I hoped to dignify her with a collar to show she was an adopted pet, if she ever let me get close enough.

As I strode into the elegant department store, I felt a rush of cool air, a stir of excitement. Sparkling crystal chandeliers hung from high ceilings, twinkling like hundreds of tiny bright rainbows. Instantly, I was swept into a color catalogue come to life, filled with earthly delights and objets d'art: racks of gossamer beaded frocks and sleek evening gowns, Oriental silk robes with embroidered cranes hung on padded hangers, calling my name like beguiling sirens.

In the vanity department, glass shelves boasted fine ceramic powder jars and perfume lamps from Germany and France shaped like exotic animals, fanciful ladies, peacocks and parrots, even wizened old men. Why would anyone select a fat Buddha powder jar or wrinkled rug merchant figural over a lovely Japanese geisha or Egyptian maiden or ball-gowned dancer?

Across the counter, displays of dazzling perfume bottles lined the shelves, in cut crystal geometric shapes with ornate stoppers or tinted glass in shades of pale peach and pink, adorned with shiny embossed labels or gilded bottles with silky tasseled atomizers.

Tempting, but I kept walking toward the stunning displays with rows upon rows of bright enameled mesh purses, and glittering handmade French cut-steel beaded bags.

This time, I had my eye on a fine guilloche vanity case, preferably a tango compact with a lipstick, made by Finberg or Foster Brothers or Ripley & Gowen or the Thomae Company. Naturally I knew all the top compact makers by heart. I stopped to admire the beautiful sterling compacts with intricate details, including romantic bucolic scenes and floral designs. After checking the price tags, I decided to pass on these stunners until I was flush with cash.

Feeling like Jasmine in Wonderland, I made my way over to a colorful display of dainty chrome enameled vanity cases with whimsical scenes: knights in shining armor, an Oriental maiden, a frisky terrier, bright birds, lovely ladies. Not only was the price within my budget, these tiny treasures made me smile. Lately I'd almost forgotten how to smile.

"May I help you, dear?" And how! The sales clerk, a sweet older woman, her henna-dyed hair in a bun, smiled at my eager expression.

"Yes, please," I cooed, pointing to a few fun compacts. She set out half a dozen little beauties on a black velvet tray, attached with chains and finger rings or lipstick holders. Inside most contained tiny lipsticks, fitted powder and rouge containers with powder puffs. So many choices, so little cash! Finally I settled on two dancers with their legs outstretched against a sunray of pink, green, orange and blue, reminding me of the bathing beauties.

What a splurge! Didn't I deserve it after all my hard work? I reached into my handbag and pulled out a five-dollar bill, my last bit of dough until pay day Friday. "It's the berries!" I sighed as the clerk handed me my treasure.

For once, I didn't have to put my purchase on lay-away, and even got a dollar and some change in return. Tucking my handbag under my arm, I held the vanity case by its finger ring, admiring the way the enamel glistened in the sun. As I trotted down the street, I pretended I was Helen Kane or Louise Brooks window-shopping along Fifth Avenue or Hollywood Boulevard.

On my way back to the *Gazette*, I waved to the Italian jeweler who had seen the gold charm I'd found at the crime scene. The longer I held onto it, the guiltier I felt. Was it wrong to keep it as possible evidence? If I turned it over to the cops now, wouldn't they get suspicious? Or worse, would they try to get rid of it?

"Come in, come in, pretty lady," he called out, motioning me toward the shop entrance. "I have something to show you."

"What is it?" Why did he think I could even afford his pricey baubles? In my simple chiffon dress, I certainly didn't look like a wealthy debutante or socialite.

I wrapped my new vanity case in tissue and tucked it in my purse pocket, next to the gold charm. He opened the door as I stepped inside the chic shop, and glanced inside the glass display case.

"Look what I just got!" the jeweler said proudly. With a flourish, he reached into the showcase and held up a beautiful gold charm bracelet, shimmering under the lights, missing one charm.

Was it the P.O. victim's charm bracelet? I held my breath, studying the dangling charms, suspiciously similar to the gold charm hidden in my purse.

"You got the charm?" the shopkeeper asked eagerly.

"It's in my bag." I pulled it out to compare and held my breath: It appeared to be a perfect match, similar in gold content, period and style. "Where'd you get this?" I tried to act casual, wishing I could compare the bracelet with Nathan's photos of the crime scene.

He shrugged, looking away. "Two guys come in soon after you, wanna pawn the bracelet, say they need jack fast. I don't ask any questions. None of my business."

"Who were they? What did they look like?" Were they cops or gangsters, I wondered? Who had access to the victim between the time she was found and taken to the morgue? The jeweler fingered the bracelet, ignoring my questions, so I changed my approach.

"This bracelet looks a lot like the one that belonged to my sister, but the charm fell off a while ago. I think her ex-boyfriend took the bracelet after they broke up."

"I see," he nodded, hopeful. "You maybe wanna show this to your sister, buy it back for her?"

Was he kidding—on my pauper's salary? "I'd like to, but I want it to be a surprise. How much is it?"

"Five-hundred dollars. Solid gold. A bargain."

A bargain? Oh brother, that girl was some pricey prostitute. I'd have to work years to pay off such an extravagance.

Then I had a brainstorm. "Maybe her new fella will buy it for her as a gift? I can bring him by later to show it to him."

Who could I ask to play the part? Had Burton or Nathan gotten a good look at the bracelet?

"Yes, yes! Later today?" His smile returned, his gold tooth gleaming like the charms.

"Maybe tomorrow?" I paused. "Do you know their names? What did they look like? I wonder if it *was* her ex-boyfriend."

"Young guys." He shrugged. "One light, one dark like me. No names or papers, a cash-only deal."

Did he mean Colin and Rico? If so, how did they get their hands on this bracelet? And why did they need so much cash, and fast?

"Thanks. My sister will be so surprised!"

Walking back to the *Gazette*, I mulled over the jeweler's words. Did Rico or Colin steal the bracelet off the victim—if so, how? Perhaps it was a dirty cop or even a medic or the coroner who took it, and asked the thugs to fence the bracelet. Were they paid off to mishandle the case, accidentally on purpose? The gangsters were up to their necks in dirty tricks.

Whoever swiped the bracelet knew it could help ID the dead girl and wanted to keep it under wraps. I began to wonder: Were they trying to frame the jeweler? My instincts told me he was innocent, a patsy unwittingly drawn into the crime. If he *was* involved, why would he flash around the victim's bracelet?

Deep in thought, I felt someone roughly bump me from behind. Startled, I turned around—crying out, "Watch it!"—when a man in a fisherman's cap yanked my purse away, and raced down the street, clutching my bag full of treasures in his hot little hand.

What a coincidence. Why wasn't I paying attention?

"Give me back my bag!" I called out, following the purse snatcher as fast as I could. Damn it, I was going to get that vanity case and gold charm back if it killed me. My feet pounded the pavement in my flimsy shoes as I ran after the robber screaming, "Help! Stop that thief!"

CHAPTER THIRTY-TWO

Panicking, I raced after the purse snatcher, yelling at the top of my lungs, "Help! Stop that thief! He stole my handbag!"

I wished some Good Samaritan would intervene, but people moved out of our way, watching transfixed, as if we were Olympic sprinters in a relay race.

Heart pounding, I dashed down the street, frantic with worry, hoping one of the reporters would hear me and help catch the thief. Almost all my essentials were in that purse, including my new vanity, gold charm and my last dollar.

Out of breath, I stopped when a lady with a baby carriage blocked my path, while the robber ran ahead. Talk about bad timing *and* bad luck.

I was still a block away when a newsie in front of the *Gazette* building charged at the thief, tripping him up, laughing as he fell flat on his back. The boy tugged on my bag, pulling it from the man's grip as he tried to scramble to his feet.

"Beat it!" the newsie shouted, giving the robber a hard kick before the jerk took off running. I craned my neck to catch a glimpse, but he shot off down the street before I saw his face.

When I caught up, breathing hard, the newsie handed me my bag. "Looking for this, ma'am?" I recognized my hero at once: It was Finn, smiling with his gap-toothed grin.

"You're a peach!" I hugged the youth and almost kissed his freckled cheeks, but he pulled away, clearly embarrassed. "Thanks, Finn! You saved the day!"

"Aw, you don't have to do that," he told me, blushing. "Just part of my job, watching out for you ladies."

I checked inside my purse and luckily, nothing appeared to be stolen. The charm and vanity were undamaged and intact. What a relief! Grateful, I stuck out my hand. "I'm Jazz. Jasmine Cross."

He wiped his hands on his pants, then shook mine. "Nice meetin' ya, ma'am."

Ma'am? Guess I seemed like a mummy to him. "Call me Jazz. Say, did you get a good look at the thief? Have you ever seen him before?" I was so shaken up, I never really noticed his face.

"Naw, all these hoodlums look the same to me." Finn shrugged, shuffling his feet.

By now, a handful of people and a few reporters stood on the sidewalk, wondering what caused the commotion. I turned to the small crowd, asking, "Did anyone happen to see the purse snatcher? Do you know who he is?"

Murmurs went around, but no one spoke up. Guess they were too busy to notice or care.

"What happened?" Mack bustled down the steps, waving his cigar. "What'd I miss?"

"Finn stopped a purse snatcher in his tracks." I patted his back, giving him another hug. "My hero!" This time he turned beet-red, staring at his scuffed shoes. "The least I can do is give you a reward."

Finally Finn brightened and held out his grubby hand, smeared from fresh newsprint. "It's my last dollar, but you're worth every cent." I placed the bill in his small hand.

"Hot dog!" he beamed. "Thanks, Jazz! Anytime you need help, you can call on me!"

A few folks applauded and even tough-guy Mack had to smile at the boy's bravado.

After the ruckus died down, I sat at my desk, trying to catch my breath, my legs still wobbly. I rubbed my shoulder, still sore from the attack. Was it a random robbery or did the thief see me leave the jeweler? Worse, did the shop owner send the mugger after me to swipe the gold charm?

A few reporters gathered around, pelting me with questions. Still winded, I related a brief version of the story, leaving out the hour that I spent shopping at Eiband's and the victim's gold charm bracelet. Was I being punished for my guilty pleasure?

"Sure you're OK, Jazz?" Pete asked.

"Why don't you file a police report?" Chuck suggested.

"No need, thanks." Did I really want to alert the police? The cops probably thought I was a gangster's moll after seeing Quinn's card in my bag last night.

Worse, Burton might hear about the attempted robbery and try to interfere. But then again, I doubt he'd even care.

"I'm glad you're alright, Jasmine," Mrs. Harper sighed. "Those horrid hooligans sneak up on you when you least expect it. Can you imagine, trying to mug a young gal in broad daylight?"

I nodded. "Finn really saved the day. If he hadn't tripped the thief at that moment, then he'd have gotten away with my purse and all my valuables."

Hank, the cranky sportswriter, said, "What do you expect? I'll bet muggers wait around by fancy shops for dames like you to rob. They think you've got dough coming out of your ears."

"What do you mean, dames like me?" I shot him a dirty look. "You're screwy. What dough?"

"Hoity-toity, with the nice clothes and hair. Smooth hands, clean nails. You look like you've never done a hard day's work in your life," he snorted.

"Oh yeah?" I challenged him. "I'll have you know I helped my family plenty at the boarding house and my dad's grocery store."

"That's right," Mr. Thomas chimed in, giving me a friendly wink. "I saw her at the Camel Stop a lot when she was younger, helping out her pops."

"Hank, if I didn't know any better, I'd think you were giving Jasmine a compliment." Mrs. Harper raised her brows. "A society reporter needs to appear hoity-toity, as you say."

What? Was I hearing right? Were my bosses defending me? And praising me as well?

"All I'm saying is you don't look like a scrubwoman," he scowled, returning to his desk.

"Gee, thanks, Hank." I batted my lashes at him. "Didn't know you felt that way."

"Felt what way?" I heard a familiar voice and looked up to see Nathan walking through the front entrance, all loaded down with camera equipment, grinning from ear to ear.

CHAPTER THIRTY-THREE

"Nathan!" I jumped up, wanting to ask him a million questions, but decided it wasn't the right time or place with the whole staff watching and listening.

"Glad you made it back in one piece." Mack grinned around his cigar. "I heard the cops were hot on your trail."

Everyone knew he liked to exaggerate, a bad habit left over from his days of yellow journalism and scandal sheets.

"How was your trip? How's Holly?" I asked, helping him with his equipment.

"She's OK." Nathan forced a smile. "Naturally she's disappointed about missing this year's pageant, but she wants to try again next year, if they bend the rules a little."

"Good for her." I lowered my voice. "So what else happened? Tell me everything!"

"Well, I can't tell you *everything*," Nathan said slyly, "but it was an adventure." He leaned forward, his voice low. "Let's talk later without an audience. How about a ride home?"

"Sure, I'd love one, especially after I almost got mugged today."

"What? What happened?" Nathan pulled up a banker's chair by my desk. After I filled him in about the purse snatcher, he frowned. "I'll be glad to help you confront the jeweler. Do you think he sent that thug after you to swipe the charm?"

"The thought crossed my mind. Still, I need to give him the benefit of the doubt." I took a deep breath. "To be honest, I still have the shakes."

"This time, you'll have me along for protection." He thumped his chest. "If you want, we can stop by after work."

"Today?" Did I really need to get mugged twice in one day?

Mrs. Harper handed me a few articles to proof, including my profiles of the bathing beauties. I couldn't wait to show them to the girls later. I knew Sammy and Dino would like to see the photos, especially the shots of Antonia. "Thanks!"

She patted my back in a rare motherly gesture. "We gals have to stick together. We're rather outnumbered here in the newsroom."

"I'll say." Maybe she was just being nice because of the mugging, but I was still so rattled, I felt grateful for any show of sympathy.

I buried myself in work, the attack fresh in my mind. Was it just a coincidence I got robbed right after leaving the jeweler? Or had some robber followed me from Eiband's, figuring I had money to burn? What a laugh.

After a few hours, Nathan came by and asked, "Ready to go?"

"Sure. Can't wait to hear about your trip." I raised my brows.

As we were leaving, Mrs. Page called out, "Jasmine, phone call for you!"

I hurried over to her desk, mouthing, "Who is it?"

She covered the receiver with her dainty manicured hand. "Agent Burton."

I shook my head no, putting a finger to my lips, whispering, "Tell him I already left!" Now what did he want? Had he heard about the mugging or did he know Nathan was back in town? It was impossible to keep anything quiet in gossipy Galveston.

"Who was on the phone?" Nathan sounded worried.

"Agent Burton. Don't worry, I told Mrs. Page to tell him I had already left."

"Great. He's the last person I want to see," he groaned. "Even if I'm not a suspect, he'll probably accuse me of kidnapping Holly, a prime lead." Knowing Burton, he was probably right.

Outside, I waved good-bye to Finn as we got into Nathan's Model T. "So how did Holly take the news about Rico?"

"Holly cried half the way home, but by the time we got to Pasadena, she was feeling better," he said. "She told me the whole sob story: how they met when she was in high school and he was in a tough Houston gang, how she wanted to help save him from a life of crime, but he refused to listen. You know, the same old gangster-meets-good girl routine."

Nathan stopped at the corner of Market and L Street to let a fancy horse and buggy pass by. "In a way, I think she realizes that Rico's death was for the best. She told me she didn't have the courage to leave him otherwise, especially with a baby on the way. Now she's finally free of that bastard."

"Poor thing," I sympathized. "Will you keep in touch with her?"

"I'll try, but she may not be ready for anything romantic, yet."

"What about later?" I teased him. "What else did she say?"

"You know me, always got my ear to the ground. Maybe I've learned a few things from you and Mack." He grinned. "But she made me promise not to spill the beans."

"Please, spill!" I squeezed his arm. "Is it about the gangs? The bathing beauties?"

"Nothing like that." He shook his head. "She was pals with all the girls, including Jo Beth. Sure, things got sticky with Rico around, but Jo Beth pretended everything was peachy."

"Is that all?" I hoped for some good gossip, maybe a cat fight or two backstage. "So what's the scoop? Is it about the Beach Gang? The Maceos? I promise, mum's the word."

Luckily, it didn't take much coaxing to get Nathan to talk.

"You know those rumors about friction within the Beach Gang? Apparently, they're all true. Turns out Ollie Quinn and the Maceo brothers are feuding over the brothels on Post Office Street."

"You don't say!" I was all ears.

"The Maceos want to shut them all down and get out of the prostitution racket, but Ollie Quinn wants a bigger piece of the pie. He already controls Mrs. Templeton's, and now he wants to take over the Downtown Gang's whorehouses."

"Could their feud somehow be connected to both prostitutes' deaths?" I suggested.

"I wouldn't be surprised if Rico killed both girls himself," Nathan fumed. "Holly did tell me that Rico sided with Ollie Quinn, not the Maceos. I think he stole some of Sam Maceo's private stash as a final blow, in case the gang leaders parted ways. Rico figured he had nothing to lose with Quinn on his side."

"Very interesting. You think that's why Rico was killed?"

"She didn't know, but I'll bet Rico was killed for a number of reasons." Nathan blew out a breath of air, clearly frustrated. "Rico wasn't a very nice guy. Whatever she saw in that loser is beyond me."

"I wonder whose side Colin is on?" I mused out loud. "He's supposed to be Rico's partner, but I suspect he's the one who carried out the hit."

"Colin, who's Colin?"

"He works for the Beach Gang. I forgot to tell you the news. You were in Houston with Holly. Where'd you stay, by the way?"

"Her parents put me in the guest bedroom. Why?"

I enjoyed watching his face turn pink.

"Just curious." I shrugged, trying to hide my smile. Then with a start, I realized we were stopped in front of the jewelry store. "Can you park down the block? I don't want the jeweler to see me yet."

"Yes, ma'am." He parked by the millinery shop two doors down, and held out a hand. "So what's the gag? Shouldn't we rehearse this?"

"Let's say you're my sister's rich fiancé, wanting to buy back her long-lost bracelet as a surprise." I tensed up, getting the jitters all over again. "But I'm having second thoughts about seeing the jeweler so soon. Is it OK if I don't go inside? When you ask to see the bracelet, tell me how he reacts. And watch out for a thug in a fisherman's cap."

"Got it," Nathan said with a nod.

As I waited in the car, clutching my bag to my chest, I mentally replayed the mugging all over again. Really, it had happened so fast that I was still in shock. I'd never forget the acute feeling of surprise and loss of control, coupled with the fear of being a witless victim.

If it weren't for Finn's quick thinking, this day would have been ruined. From now on, I needed to be more cautious, but not afraid to walk down this street, or any street, alone.

Lost in thought, I jumped when I heard a knock on my window.

Nathan stood there with a puzzled frown. "The shop's closed, but the sign said it's open till six." He glanced at his wristwatch. "It's only five-fifteen now. Wonder why he left so early?"

"Good question," I said, secretly relieved. "You know how these mom and pop shops are. They keep their own hours, close at a moment's notice." Then I began to worry: What if the jeweler *was* behind the attempted robbery?

"Come on, Nate. Step on the gas." I looked around nervously. Was the thief watching us now?

"We can go back later tomorrow," Nathan offered. "You were saying…who's Colin?"

"Remember that goon who came to the Opera House with Sam Maceo and Rico?" I told him an abbreviated version of the night at the Oasis and the Galvez, leaving out some choice details. "I ran into Colin at the Hotel Galvez after Rico was shot and called Agent Burton. After I showed Burton the gun under the bed, he took it to the police station as evidence later that night. They're supposed to dust it for fingerprints."

"I bet Burton hopes that my fingerprints are all over the gun," Nathan snorted.

"Burton became really suspicious when you took off with Holly to Houston," I reminded him. "But after seeing Colin at the Hotel Galvez, I suspect he's the real killer."

Nathan slowed down as he approached the boarding house. "Well, speak of the devil. Look who's here."

Agent Burton leaned against his Roadster, arms crossed. Nathan and I traded worried glances while he parked in front.

"I've been looking for you." Burton tipped his hat in greeting, and ambled over to Nathan's Model T. "Both of you."

CHAPTER THIRTY-FOUR

"Should I make a run for it?" Nathan eyed Burton, gripping the steering wheel.

"You sound like a gangster. Running will make you look even more guilty." I studied Burton, trying to assess his demeanor. "Let's find out what he wants."

I got out of the car, smiling at Burton as if it was a social call. "Hello, stranger."

"You two are hard to track down." He frowned. "I tried to call the paper, but they said you'd gone for the day. I have some news for you both."

"Good news, I hope?" I motioned for Nathan, but he stayed in his Model T, ready to flee.

Burton walked over to Nathan's car. "This involves you, too. But I don't want to stand here on the street discussing police business. Is there somewhere else we can go?"

Nathan refused to move, watching Burton warily. Where could we talk, besides the boarding house? I didn't want to involve my Aunt Eva, especially if any of her gossipy church friends were around. Those Nosy Nellies were worse than reporters.

"How about Star Drugstore?" I suggested. "It's quiet now after the lunch rush, but too early for supper." And it didn't hurt that Amanda was working there today.

"Perfect." Burton nodded. "Jasmine, you can ride with me. Nathan, you coming?"

I held onto my hat as he raced down the street. "What's this all about? I doubt you came all this way just to talk about the weather."

"Remember the gun from the Galvez? We got the results back from forensics."

"Already?" I held my breath, dying to know: "Whose gun was it? Did you arrest anyone?"

"Not yet. I need to talk to Nathan first, find out what Holly told him, what he knows."

Why was he stalling? "Nathan doesn't know anything," I said in his defense, looking back to make sure he was still following us, but he'd slowed down to a crawl.

Trying to distract Burton, I decided to tell him about the gold charm, the attempted mugging, the bracelet. "We tried to stop by the jewelry store after work, but it had closed early. What should I do with the charm, turn it over to the police?"

"Why didn't you tell me this before?" Burton demanded.

"I wanted to check it out first," I said, my face getting hot. "Besides you, I didn't know who to trust on the force."

"Jasmine, as long as you have that charm, you're not safe. Someone may be trying to cover up that girl's death, and make sure she remains a Jane Doe. The charm is a loose end."

I sucked in my breath. "You think the mugging was planned?"

"I think the jeweler, or someone connected to him, knows that the charm bracelet could help identify the victim and eventually lead to the killer." He honked his horn at some children on bicycles who veered too close to his Roadster. "I don't know if the jeweler is responsible, but obviously they're watching his shop. They may be looking for you right now. Do you still have the charm with you?"

"Yes, it's in my purse, thanks to Finn." I smiled at the memory. "What I want to know is: How'd the victim's bracelet end up at the jewelry shop?"

"That's the thousand-dollar question. Only a few people saw the gold bracelet on the dead girl's wrist at the crime scene, mainly the police and the press," Burton said.

"You think it's a bad cop or the gangs?"

"Could be both. Say, someone on the inside tried to get rid of the bracelet, gave it to some thugs to fence. Obviously, they didn't know its value until they took it to the jeweler."

I fingered the gold charm, noting the fine engraving. "What should I do with this?"

"You were right not to turn it over to the cops." Burton parked in front of Star Drugstore, and held out his hand. "Let me take a look." As he studied the charm, his face grew grim. "No wonder they wanted this gem. It looks like real gold, engraved in Latin." He placed it gently in my hand. "For now, keep it safe, maybe at home, not in your handbag."

"It was dark, so I bet the killer forgot the bracelet was on her wrist." I placed the charm back in my purse. "I assumed it was worthless, but I didn't see it up close since the cops wouldn't let us near the victim."

Burton's mouth twitched. "I wouldn't say these palookas know their jewelry. They were in a hurry, dumped the body late at night, and forgot about the bracelet until the next day."

I mulled it over. "So they tried to steal it, realizing it's evidence."

After we got out of the car, Nathan walked over to Burton, sticking out his arms like a wanted criminal. "If you're going to arrest me, you may as well do it now," he said dramatically.

Burton held open the drugstore door, motioning for us to go inside. "First I need to interrogate you in front of witnesses."

Was he joking or serious? Hard to tell with Burton.

"Here, in public?" Nathan blanched, hands in his pockets.

As we walked in, Amanda waved from across the empty diner. Only one old coot sat at the horseshoe counter, nursing a cup of coffee, clearly hung-over.

"My favorite customers! Sit wherever you'd like." She pulled me aside. "What are you doing here with Burton *and* Nathan?"

"I think he wants to rake Nathan over the coals." I gave her a gentle nudge. "Stick around and we'll both find out."

We settled in a corner booth in back and Amanda came by our table, making small talk, taking her time. "What do y'all want?" she asked, a gleam in her eye.

After we ordered, Burton sat across from us, fiddling with some change. Luckily the music box blared out, "Let's Misbehave," covering up our conversation. Very apropos.

Burton eyed Nathan, and got right to the point. "So, tell me why you left town with Holly in such a hurry?"

"I was afraid she was in danger." Nathan shifted in his seat. "She was a sitting duck in the hospital. What if Rico's killer came back and tried to bump her off, too?" He faced off with Burton. "You'd do the same thing if it was your girl."

"Your girl? You sure move fast." Burton looked amused. "So did your girl have anything interesting to say about Rico or his bootlegging operation?"

"Not really," he mumbled. "She was so upset about Rico, she was in no state to talk."

"Nothing about his sideline booze business or Ollie Quinn or the Maceos?"

Nathan remained poker-faced, moving around in the booth.

Amanda returned with our orders, asking Nathan, "Sure you don't want anything?" She hovered, raising her brows as I sipped on my lemonade and Burton dug into his key lime pie.

"I'm not hungry." He fidgeted with the salt and pepper shakers. After she left, he turned to Burton. "So what's this all about? Why'd you want to talk to me?"

Burton savored his pie, then set down his fork. "I'm sure Jasmine told you about the piece of evidence we found at the Galvez? You may want to know the results."

We leaned forward in anticipation. "Was it Colin?" I had to ask.

"Your boyfriend?" Burton shot me a cold look. "I'm sorry to say, no. Turns out the gun belongs to Rose Maceo. His fingerprints were all over the handle."

CHAPTER THIRTY-FIVE

"Rose Maceo killed Rico?" I stared at Burton in shock. "Positive? I assumed it was Colin all along." Finally the truth, or was it? Stunned, I sank back against the worn red leather booth, taking in the information. Was Colin just following Quinn's orders, planting the gun to incriminate Rose Maceo, or was *he* guilty?

"We think so." Burton nodded. "The bullets match the ones we found at the crime scene."

"That makes sense." Nathan breathed a sigh of relief. "I heard there was a rivalry between the Maceos and Ollie, but obviously Rico sided with Quinn."

"Colin must also be siding with Quinn, since I saw them dining at the Galvez with two men," I added. "I bet he planted the gun there that night. If you ask me, it wasn't the best hiding place."

"I think they wanted the gun to be found. Let's say someone tipped off Rose Maceo about Rico's sideline booze biz." Burton frowned. "So why haven't they killed Colin yet?"

Was he really asking for our opinion?

"Isn't it possible someone from the Downtown Gang killed Rico? Johnny Jack is still furious that the Beach Gang burned down his headquarters, the Lotus. After all, Rico was left at the Kit Kat, the Downtown Gang's new club," I pointed out.

"True." Burton nodded. "But let's say the killer wanted to frame Rose Maceo. So he used Maceo's gun, but wore gloves to hide his own prints. Question is, how'd he get hold of his gun?"

"So it had to be someone in the Beach Gang." A mental bulb flashed as I recalled Colin's meeting with Sammy at the Oasis, and the threats he made.

"What if Colin is double-crossing the Maceos and playing both sides?" I suggested. "When I met him at the Oasis, he was trying to sell Sammy some of Maceo's stolen liquor."

"I wouldn't be surprised. Rats like him can't be trusted." Burton gave me a warning look.

"Booze is only half the story." Nathan spoke up. "Holly told me there's a big feud going on in the Beach Gang between Ollie Quinn and the Maceos over their prostitution racket."

"So Holly *did* talk after all." Burton raised his brows at Nathan. "What else did she say?"

Nathan's face flushed, but he continued. "Seems Quinn wants to expand their business, open up more cathouses, even take over the Downtown Gang's turf. But the Maceos are dead set against it and want to shut down the whole operation. Bad blood all around."

"I've heard the Maceos don't allow prostitutes into their clubs, even as customers." Burton nodded, fiddling with some change. "But it all comes down to money."

"More bang for the buck," Nathan said with a grin. "Literally."

"You slay me." I rolled my eyes. Nathan was back to his old self, making tasteless jokes, treating me like one of the fellas.

Burton scowled. "Please. There's a lady present." He handed Nathan a nickel, as if trying to get rid of a naughty child. "Why don't you make yourself scarce and go pick out a song?"

"Thanks." I smiled at Burton. "Nathan acts like a pesky little brother sometimes."

"A little brother with a dirty mouth."

"Ain't We Got Fun?" came on the music box, hardly the right song for the occasion. Nathan returned, snapping his suspenders, his mood now jovial. "Now that I'm no longer a suspect, I can take a hike, leave you two alone."

I blushed at his implication, glad to see Nathan go.

After he left, I asked Burton, "So why haven't they arrested Rose Maceo for Rico's murder, if there's concrete proof?"

"You know why. How would it look if one of the pageant's top sponsors was arrested for murder right before Splash Day?" He shrugged. "Yes, we found the murder weapon, but all we have is circumstantial evidence. Without a credible witness or confession, we can't be positive Rose Maceo is the killer. And I doubt the top brass wants to investigate the case anytime soon."

"Politics as usual." I leaned forward, trying to work up my nerve, drumming my nails on the table. "By the way, have you changed your mind about...you know, the raid?"

"Why would I?" Burton frowned, his mouth tight. "You really expect me to raid the Hollywood Dinner Club and single-handedly try to bring down the Maceos, just to appease a rival gang leader? What chance do I have going up against the Maceos and their goons? The Beach Gang won't think twice about killing me, while the city looks the other way."

"What about Sammy? I'm just trying to help him out of a jam."

Burton noticed my mood darken. "I'm sorry, Jasmine. My hands are tied. I took an oath to uphold the law, and I'd never compromise my principles."

"Even if it meant life or death?" I persisted.

"Don't you get it? If the Maceos think I'm doing Johnny Jack's bidding, that will only trigger more gang wars. I'm trying to prevent more senseless deaths, including my own." He slapped the table. "Gangsters are taking advantage of the public, profiting off Prohibition. They think nothing of harming or killing off decent citizens just to line their pockets."

Sure, I admired his Honest Abe speech, but to me, he sounded more like a damn Boy Scout. "So you're going to do nothing for Sammy." I glared at him.

"What else can I do?" Burton sounded sincere. "Raids can be unpredictable. The Maceos may fight back, and then the whole event will turn into a Wild West shoot-out."

"Of course you're right." I heaved a sigh. "But Sammy's running out of options. I suggested he leave town for a while, even change his name, but he won't listen." Johnny Jack had made an impossible demand, assuming Burton would never go along, setting up Sammy to take the fall. Damned if you do, damned if you don't.

"Can't you convince Sammy it's a no-win situation?" he said.

"Worth a try, if you take me to the Oasis now. I'll try to talk some sense into Sammy, explain that even if you raided the place, innocent people may be killed—including the bathing beauties."

I called Amanda over, and she rushed up, looking anxious. "Was the lemonade too tart? You sure have a sour look on your face."

Normally I'd laugh, but she knew I was serious. "Can you get off work early to see Sammy? You always cheer him up."

"What's wrong?" She frowned at Burton, taking off her apron. "It's quiet now so they won't mind. I'll say it's an emergency."

I nodded. "It *is* an emergency. Sammy's life is on the line."

OK, so I was being a tad melodramatic but I'd seen first-hand what the gangs could do, especially if they considered one of their own a traitor or worse, a stool pigeon.

Before we left, Burton handed Amanda a few bucks and she stuffed them in her pocket without bothering to ring up our bill, clearly distracted. I knew Amanda was worried about Sammy, and just as upset with Burton.

Outside Star Diner, a newsie yelled: "Bathing Beauty Pageant and Parade! Lots of pretty girls for Splash Day! Read all about it!"

The evening edition was out! I couldn't help but feel a sense of pride as I scanned my articles on Antonia, Miss Italy; Michelle, Miss France; Delysia, Miss San Antonio; and Jo Beth, Miss Dallas, next to Nathan's crisp photos. I even got my own bylines, as Mr. Thomas had promised. Smiling, I gave the newsie a dime for two copies, and told him to keep the change. I knew Sammy and Dino couldn't wait to get their hands on a copy so they could ogle the gorgeous gals.

Now I showed Burton the paper, pointing to the pictures.

"I wouldn't want these girls to get hurt. They're my friends."

"I know. Tell Sammy a raid will only create more problems, not solve them. Besides, aren't the Maceos also his friends?"

How did Burton know that?

"True." I dreaded facing Sammy, but did he really expect Burton to be one of Johnny Jack's hired thugs?

After we piled into his Roadster, Amanda and I skimmed the paper, admiring the photos, chattering while Burton drove. "This is your stop, ladies." He parked half a block from the Oasis, and as we got out, he caught my hand, his face softening. "Be careful, Jazz. You know I don't want anything to happen to Sammy...or to you."

Touched, I dug into my purse, and handed him the gold charm. "Here, maybe you should hold onto this for me. Just in case."

He seemed puzzled. "In case, what?"

"For good luck." I had to admit, Burton was a rare commodity: A straight arrow in a crooked profession. Sad to say, honest Treasury agents rarely lasted long in Galveston.

CHAPTER THIRTY-SIX

"How's Sammy going to get out of this mess?" Amanda asked me, her face pale, as we headed to the Oasis.

"Wish I knew." I sighed. "Got any bright ideas?"

"Why doesn't he quit the booze biz for good? It's so risky!"

"Believe me, I've tried to persuade him. He wants to stick it out long enough to make some serious money, then open a nice place like the Hollywood Club."

"Wouldn't that be swell? I'd love to see the bathing beauties dance there Friday night." Her face lit up. "Hope he asks me to go!"

By now, twilight was taking over the sky, a soft palette of peach, rose and pink. Since it was still early, Market Street seemed quiet, even peaceful. A balmy breeze blew the palm trees, swaying in time to the jazz echoing out of the speakeasies lining the street.

At the Oasis, I held the newspaper over the small door slot so Dino could get a preview of Antonia's glamour girl shot. The door flew open and Dino greeted me with a big smile. "Get a load of her! What a spicy tomato!"

"Thanks for helping with Antonia's profile." I'd called Dino a few times for clarification, and he was happy to oblige, though I had to clean up his Italian translations. "Is Sammy here?"

"He's getting ready for a big crowd this weekend. If we're still open." He eyed me, then returned to the paper with a grin.

"Tell Antonia I'll see her this weekend. Can't wait!"

Downstairs, the Oasis looked nice and neat, and even our mascot Doria, hovering above the bar, looked spiffy with a new coat of polish. Fresh carnations and daisies adorned the tables, courtesy of the flower shop on the corner. The owners, older widows with a knack for design, always offered Sammy a good discount on end-of-day bouquets and leftovers. Plus it gave them an excuse to flirt with their handsome neighbor. A few sad sacks slumped over the counter and watched us with dull eyes, drinks glued to their hands.

Frank gave us a nod from behind the bar, wiping cocktail glasses and stacking them in a pyramid. Sammy came over to welcome us, circling his arms around me and Amanda in one big bear hug. "How are my two favorite flappers? What brings you ladies here?"

I stared at him in surprise. Sammy seemed relaxed, even cheerful for a change. "I wanted to show you my articles on the bathing beauties." I stalled handing him the *Gazette*. "Remember these girls?"

Sammy motioned to a nearby table, pulling out our chairs. "Do I!" He grinned, flipping through the pages. "Did you show this to Dino? He'll get a kick out of seeing Antonia in the paper, looking like a movie star."

I smiled, recalling Dino's reaction. "Sure, I gave him his own copy to drool over."

"He'll probably sleep with it under his pillow." Sammy whistled as he studied the photos.

"Don't get too excited." Amanda huffed, elbowing him in the ribs. "Those girls are too young for you. They're practically jailbait."

Sammy blinked, giving her the once-over. "How old are *you*?"

"Old enough," she purred, flashing him a suggestive smile.

"Good to know." Sammy gave Amanda a squeeze. "Say, your picture should be in the paper, too. If you were in the pageant, you'd win the whole shebang." He was laying it on thick, all right, and Amanda ate it up with a silver ladle.

"Why, Sammy, flattery will get you everywhere—and anything." She batted her lashes like a love-struck loon.

Oh, brother. I didn't want to watch these two make goo-goo eyes at each other all night. Flustered, I tried to change the subject. "Sammy, we need to talk. Want to go to your office?"

"Why the long face? Go ahead, spill it." He leaned forward, not bothering to dismiss Amanda.

"Have you had a chance to reason with Johnny Jack? Did he change his mind about Agent Burton raiding the Hollywood Dinner Club Friday night?"

"Not yet." Sammy shook his head, clamming up when Buzz appeared to take our drink order. Poor kid had already seen one raid too many. "How about a round of Cokes, sport?"

After Buzz left, I told Sammy, "I tried to convince Burton to raid the Hollywood, but he's afraid it could turn into a big gunfight, and end up hurting innocent bystanders."

Sammy nodded. "Knowing Rose and his goons, he's probably right. After I thought it over, I realized one raid wouldn't stop Johnny Jack. He'd keep pushing us around, giving us orders, till we all got ourselves killed."

"You said it." So he finally figured out it was a losing battle.

Still, I was annoyed that Sammy had asked me to stick my neck out and risk my relationship with Burton—all that drama and trauma for nothing! Worse, now Burton didn't seem to trust me, practically calling me a floozy and treating me like some gangster's moll.

Buzz returned and set down our bottles of Coca-Cola, giving us a lopsided grin. I stared at the worn table, carved with initials and scribbles. "Have you given any thought to leaving town, waiting until after Splash Day? That'll give Johnny Jack time to cool off."

"Why should I miss out on all the fun? Lots of dough pouring into Galveston this week." Sammy pulled out a Camel and lit it, taking a few lazy puffs. He sure seemed cavalier for a man whose life was in jeopardy.

"What happened? Did Johnny Jack back off?" I asked, hopeful.

"Nothing like that." He brightened. "But I think I found a solution to my problems."

"What kind of solution?" Amanda and I pulled up our chairs.

"I decided to partner up with an ally, fight fire with fire."

"What do you mean?" I sat up, gripping his wrist, trying not to think the worst. "Are you planning to burn down one of his clubs?"

"That's nuts!" Amanda said as we exchanged worried looks across the table.

"Don't be daffy. Who said anything about a fire?" Sammy leaned back in his chair with an easy grin. "You've heard the expression: The enemy of my enemy is my friend."

"Sure, but who do you mean?" I swallowed. "Rose Maceo? Ollie Quinn? George Musey?"

Suddenly Sammy stood up, forcing a smile, his arms outstretched. "Well, look who's here! You're just in time to celebrate our good fortune. My new partner in crime."

My heart dropped as I turned around to see Colin Ferris, the Beach Gang's enforcer, walk over and shake Sammy's hand.

CHAPTER THIRTY-SEVEN

Watching Sammy and Colin act like new best buddies made my stomach twist in knots, as if my own brother just punched me in the gut. How could he join forces with Colin, make a deal with the devil?

Now I assumed he'd have to switch sides, leave the Downtown Gang's turf and form a new alliance with the Beach Gang.

"Colin's here to discuss business," Sammy said formally, as if Colin was an investment banker.

"Fancy seeing you here again, Jasmine." His expression implied we had some sort of private joke.

"Colin, why don't you grab a drink at the bar?" Sammy told him. "I'll be right there."

Colin gave me a smug smile as he passed, running his hand along my chair. "See you later, doll face."

Why me? I turned to make sure Colin was out of earshot before I flared up. "Sammy, how in hell can you partner with Colin? Don't you remember he threatened your life? You can't trust a dirty double-crosser like him. He'll smile in your face, then stab you in the back."

Sammy frowned. "How do you know so much about Colin?"

"Didn't you hear? His partner, Rico, was gunned down two days ago, dumped off at the Kit Kat Club." Sammy didn't need to know about my *rendezvous* with Colin at the Galvez. Not yet.

"That doesn't mean Colin did it. No one's been arrested." Sammy avoided my gaze, puffing on his Camel.

"Not yet. But he's not exactly in mourning. I'd say he's a likely suspect." For now, I decided to keep quiet about Rose Maceo's gun and fingerprints. I took a deep breath, trying to calm down. "OK, tell me the truth. Why'd you decide to join forces with Colin?"

"Let's just say I didn't have much choice," Sammy admitted. "Colin came back the next day with some big baboon, but Dino was able to warn me in time. I did some fast-talking, told him we had lots in common. I agreed to take the booze off his hands, and he agreed to back me up."

What a surprise. Naturally, it all came down to cash. What else? Sure, I was glad Sammy had help fighting off Johnny Jack, but did it have to be Colin Ferris, Ollie Quinn's right-hand man?

"Did he try to hurt you, Sammy?" Amanda searched his face for signs of a beating.

"Don't worry, toots, we're no slouches in that department. Dino and I can handle ourselves." Sammy puffed out his chest.

How could I talk some sense into his thick skull? "What if the Maceos find out you're siding with Colin? Aren't they feuding with Ollie Quinn?"

"They'd be the first in line to help us fight Johnny Jack."

"Wouldn't it be better if you tried to smooth things over with Johnny Jack?" I persisted.

"It's a done deal." Sammy patted my hand. "Hey, everything will work out. I needed more stock for Splash Day anyway."

He looked over my shoulder, his eyes following Colin, who strode over to our table.

"How about a round of drinks for these lovely ladies?" Colin acted like he owned the bar.

"We were just leaving." My heart started racing as I stood up, my chair scraping on the uneven wood floor, ignoring his outstretched hand. "See you later, Sammy. Coming, Amanda?"

"Amanda, is it?" Colin tipped his hat at her. "I haven't had the pleasure of meeting your pretty friend."

Oh no. I didn't want Amanda to get involved in this fiasco. Upset, I turned on my heel, darting toward the exit. For all I knew, Colin was the mugger who tried to swipe the gold charm.

After I reached the stairs, I felt a tapping on my shoulder. "Amanda?" Yet Colin stood there instead, smirking. Figured she'd stay seated next to Sammy, oblivious to my predicament.

"What's the rush, doll?" He licked his lips suggestively. "Why don't we have a drink?"

"I'm tired. I need to get home." I avoided his intense gaze, staring at Sammy, hoping he'd intervene.

"I'll be glad to take you home." His bright green eyes lit up. "It must not be far."

Damn, the last thing I wanted was for this two-bit thug to know where I lived. "Thanks, I've got a ride." I tried to signal Amanda and Sammy, but they were too engrossed in each other to notice.

"Too bad." He leaned forward, taking off his hat. "Say, got any plans for Friday night? I hear the bathing beauties are dancing at the Hollywood. Should be quite a show. I caught a preview at the Surf Club one night and boy, those hoofers can really kick up their heels."

Was he serious or was he baiting me? Did he think I'd be caught dead with the likes of him? Caught dead was right. But I kept my lips zipped, for Sammy's sake.

"Friday night? Don't you need to be here, in case Johnny Jack sends his goons?" This time, I looked him straight in the eye.

"Don't you worry, doll. I've got eyes and ears on this place." He flashed me a smug smile. "But it's always nice to see and be seen with a pretty lady in public. Get my drift?"

I got his drift, all right. He wanted an alibi in case something happened to Johnny Jack or Sammy.

"So how about it, Jazz? You and me hit the town, make some whoopee, just us two."

"Thanks, but I've made other plans," I told him, fumbling for an excuse. "I've got a date." Great. A big fat fib. Who could I recruit for this mission of mercy, Nathan?

"A date? Is it that Fed agent?" He scowled, his green eyes flashing. "What's his name, Burton?"

Why not play along? I nodded, hoping Burton was free Friday night. "Yes, as a matter of fact, we're going together."

I clutched my bag to my chest like a shield, hoping he'd get the telegram and leave me alone. "Thanks anyway."

A bullet dodged, a problem averted, at least for now.

"Oh yeah? You'd rather go with that wet blanket?" Colin looked disappointed as he slunk away.

Now I had to make sure Burton agreed to be my fake date.

"What were you two jawing about?" Amanda finally made an appearance, her cheeks flushed red, her lipstick smeared.

"The pageant." I pasted on a smile, and grabbed her wrist, dragging her upstairs and past the line outside the door, not even bothering to say good night to Buzz or Dino.

On the trolley, Amanda beamed at me. "Guess what? Sammy invited me to the bathing beauties performance at the Hollywood! The Maceos gave him great seats, right by the stage!"

"That's swell." I suspected Amanda had nudged Sammy more than once. "Glad Sammy is taking a night off from work. He must feel confident about partnering with Colin."

"I'll say! He told me it would seem more suspicious if he *didn't* attend. After all, only Galveston's elite is invited."

Elite or eclectic? Splash Day events provided nouveau riche gangsters and gamblers an excuse to rub shoulders with Galveston's old money set. I, for one, couldn't wait to watch all the action, on and off-stage.

"Colin invited me to go, too. As if I would really go out with a gangster." I could imagine the editors' reaction if I turned up at the Hollywood with a Beach Gang hood. "He practically admitted he needed me to be his alibi. Of all the nerve!"

"He must think he's a big cheese." She frowned. "Why does he need an alibi?"

"Who knows?" I held on tight as the trolley bounced along, hitting every rut in the road. "If Johnny Jack finds out Sammy is siding with Colin and the Beach Gang, then either way he's a goner."

Friday

The next morning I hurried to work, looking over my shoulder, expecting to see a mugger leap out of the bushes or from a dark alley. Galveston was full of narrow alleys sandwiched between tall brick Victorian buildings, perfect hiding places for thieves, rapists and killers. Don't be a scaredy-cat, afraid of your own shadow, I thought. What happened to my moxie?

I threw back my shoulders, held my head high and charged forward down the street. My etiquette teacher would be delighted: She always nagged us to improve our posture, instructing us to balance a book on our heads and walk around in circles. I usually started giggling during these demonstrations, so she always made me do it over and over, until she was convinced I had perfect posture. What a laugh.

Outside the *Gazette*, I tipped Finn an extra nickel for two more papers. "Holding down the fort?" I teased, watching him blush.

Finn nodded and handed me the papers with a shy grin.

"Nice job on the bathing beauties!" Mr. Thomas called out from his office, waving the paper. "And the articles aren't bad either." Even old Mr. Thomas acted like a peeping Tom, ogling the girls.

I was pleased to see they'd reprinted my profiles in today's edition. Miraculously, the photos appeared enlarged while my stories had somehow shrunk. Oh well, my words couldn't compete with the girls' gams anyway.

You could feel the excitement in the air, crackling like electricity during a hurricane. Not only was today payday, but Splash Day weekend had finally arrived. Anyone and everyone in town was looking forward to the parades and pageants. The whole staff was even getting off early to attend the weekend festivities, whether for business or pleasure.

Naturally Mrs. Harper got to cover the juiciest feature stories, complete with front-row seats to all events. Still, she asked me to take notes, to see who was wearing or doing what, for filler material and sidebars. At least I got the coveted invitations.

Mr. Thomas handed out our paychecks one by one, acting as if he was the Easter Bunny passing out *Fabergé* eggs. Wouldn't that be swell? After collecting our checks, Nathan and I decided to go to Lone Star Bank to get some cash and deposit the rest.

"Let's stop by the jeweler on the way," he suggested. "Take a look at the bracelet."

"Sure," I agreed. "I'm so broke, I've got nothing to steal but a comb and a lipstick."

As we approached the shop, the jeweler stepped out onto the sidewalk, waving us inside. "Come in, come in!" he beamed.

"We want to see the pretty gold bracelet." I squared my shoulders, refusing to be afraid or intimidated. The jeweler appeared unfazed, unaware that I'd almost gotten robbed outside his shop.

"Yes, yes, of course." He gestured to Nathan. "Is this the lucky fella? The fiancé?"

"That's me," Nathan gave me a friendly wink, placing his elbows on the case. "Ready to settle down and get married."

"No, no." The jeweler frowned and waved Nathan away from the glass, vigorously wiping away any smudges with a white cloth. "Let me show it to you. You got the charm?"

"No, sorry, I forgot it," I told him, glad I'd given it to Burton for safekeeping.

"Too bad." The jeweler scowled and placed the bracelet on a black velvet pad.

Nathan's eyes widened as he studied the charms, and he gave me a slight nudge with his foot. "Very pretty," he said. "How much?" As he fingered each charm, I could tell he was trying to memorize the different shapes and symbols.

"Five-hundred," the jeweler boasted. "Best piece in shop."

"That's a lot of clams." Nathan whistled, eyes wide. "Too rich for my blood *and* my wallet."

The jeweler's face fell, so I gently elbowed him in the ribs. "My sister would love it!"

"Maybe I can put it on lay-away?" Nathan forced a smile, adding, "Anything for my pumpkin."

Pumpkin? No girl wanted to be called a pumpkin, even by a fictitious fiancé.

"So what do you think? Is it the same bracelet?" I asked Nathan when we were safely outside.

"Sure looks like the one on the dead girl's wrist." He nodded. "But I need to examine my crime scene photos. I still have them somewhere, even though the story was killed, along with the girl." He smiled at his own pun. "I wonder how it ended up there, of all places. You'd think those palookas would hock it out of town, not on a busy street in plain sight."

"True," I agreed, wondering if it really was Rico and Colin.

As we walked to the bank, I filled Nathan in on last night's events and Colin's invitation to the bathing beauties' performance at the Hollywood. "Now I have to ask Burton to go with me like it's Sadie Hawkins Day," I grumbled. "What a dumb Dora!"

"Forget about Burton. I thought we were all going together, you, me and Amanda."

"Sammy invited her to go. I'm sure she'd rather sit at his front-row table, not some crummy spot in back with the press. Say, what if I asked Burton to meet us there, so it's not a real date?"

"Suit yourself." Nathan shrugged, clearly disappointed. "You really want to bring that flat tire?"

Back at the office, I wondered how I could bring up the subject to Burton. We weren't exactly sweethearts, calling each other on the hour, whispering sweet nothings. Nor were we friends, but we weren't enemies either. So what were we then?

I waited until the newsroom was empty, then before I chickened out, I asked the operator to dial the police department. After the connection, I cleared my throat and said, in my best reporter's voice, "Agent Burton, please."

"One moment. Who's calling?" came the operator's tinny voice.

"A friend." What would I tell him—that I needed protection from a Beach Gang hood? He was already mad at me for badgering him about Sammy. Wouldn't he feel insulted if I asked him on a last-minute date?

I almost hung up the phone before the operator returned. "I'm afraid Agent Burton is out. May I take a message?"

"No, thanks," I mumbled and hung up, relieved. Guess I'd have to take my chances with Nathan. I figured Colin would be too distracted by the sexy shebas on stage to notice that my actual date *wasn't* Agent Burton.

CHAPTER THIRTY-EIGHT

That evening, Amanda and I chattered nonstop as we got ready for the bathing beauties dance routine, aptly called *High Kicks and High-Jinks at the Hollywood*. I couldn't wait to see the final show Mrs. Wembley created to impress not only the paying patrons, but Sam Maceo, the mayor and all the muckety-mucks in town.

Amanda's excitement was contagious. I slipped on a tea-length floral chiffon gown of teal, lilac, gold and plum, with cap sleeves and a handkerchief hem, and slid on a beaded headband with a peacock eye feather. For effect, I added some gold eye shadow and rimmed my eyes with kohl. Who did I think I was, Cleopatra? I wish!

I admit, I was disappointed Burton hadn't invited me to be his date tonight, but after my *faux pas*, I wouldn't blame him for staying far away from me *and* the Hollywood Dinner Club.

My face burned as I recalled his indignation when I asked him to raid the Hollywood tonight, how I'd hurt his pride, and questioned his morals. Adding insult to injury, Sammy decided to team up with Colin, not needing my help after all. Frankly, I didn't know who was a worse threat: Colin or Johnny Jack?

Too bad I couldn't share my resentment with Amanda. She was over the moon tonight, excited about her first real date with Sammy, and I didn't want to be a wet blanket.

"Let's give those bathing beauties a run for their money," Amanda said, dusting fine gold powder on her bare arms, neck and chest. "This glitter is the latest thing. Want some?"

"Sure, I'll try it." A sprinkle of gold dust accented the peacock feather perfectly. What I really needed was a sprinkle of fairy dust, not glitter, if I wanted to get through the evening.

Nathan and I planned to arrive early to give the beauties copies of the *Gazette*. His flattering photos of the contestants rivaled any glamour shots of Hollywood starlets.

As we added our final touches, Amanda said, "We'll look for you tonight at the show. I wonder if we can share a table, like a double-date?"

"Nathan's just a pal. We're sitting at a table out in the boonies, reserved for journalists. Sammy snagged a table up front since he's best buddies with the Maceos. Besides, wouldn't you two lovebirds rather be alone?" I teased.

To be honest, I wasn't sure how comfortable I'd be on a double-date with Amanda and my half-brother anyway.

"Yeah, we'll be alone with about two-hundred other people!" She slid a pale blue garter over her thigh, a cute lacy one that matched her teal-blue silk bias-cut gown.

I smiled in approval. "That dress is gorgeous on you. Makes your blue eyes sparkle."

"Well, you don't look so bad yourself, sister!" She smiled, straightening my headband. "Just making sure you look perfect in case you see the Fed agent. Let him eat his heart out! What's going on with you two anyway?"

"Who knows?" I sighed. "He's all business these days. It's better that I go with Nathan since we both have to work." Still, I felt a pang of jealousy, wondering: Would Burton show up with a date?

Nathan picked me up promptly at seven, so we'd be there in plenty of time before the floor show started at eight. "What a sight for sore eyes! You're the bees' knees in that get-up!"

"Thanks, Nathan. You sure clean up nice," I teased. His hands were usually covered in some sort of chemicals or dye from processing photos.

Aunt Eva came downstairs, inspecting me as if I was a contestant myself. "How lovely!"

"I wish you could join us tonight, Eva," I said and meant it.

"Jazz, frankly, I wouldn't dare go to any of those gangsters' nightclubs. But I know that you have a job to do, so I hope you enjoy yourself. Maybe I'll stroll over to the Seawall tomorrow, if it's not too crowded? I'd rather not be in the midst of all that pushing and shoving."

"That'd be swell," I told her as we said good-night. "Hope to see you there."

Tonight Nathan was driving his father's Packard, shined and polished for the occasion.

"I couldn't show up at the Hollywood Club in my old jalopy," he explained, proudly holding open the car door. "Plush leather seats and everything. We deserve to come in through the front door for a change, not just as working stiffs."

"And how!" I agreed, smoothing out my frock. Nathan drove west down Seawall Boulevard over to 61st Street, miles away from the hustle and bustle of the beach: the Crystal Palace, Murdoch's, the row of speakeasies facing the ocean.

You could tell the tourists from the locals strolling about by their fine buttoned-up clothes and elaborate hats, an easy target for hustlers. Except for the big wheels in town, many Galveston natives tended to dress down for special events, or stay away from the crowds altogether.

I turned to Nathan, imagining the Seawall lined with bathing beauties tomorrow, hoping for their big chance. "I wish Holly could attend the pageant this weekend since she can't compete."

"I do too, but she's too self-conscious about her looks. After all, she's still Miss Houston and wants to keep up the image. She'd rather not show her face in public until it's all healed."

"Poor thing." I shook my head. "It's not fair. If she was still in the contest, she'd win hands down!"

"You said it." Nathan nodded. "But it's safer if she stays in Houston, away from the Beach Gang, and Rico's killer. I find it hard to believe it was Rose Maceo."

"He probably was framed, like Burton said."

"I wouldn't be surprised. Lots of folks want revenge against Papa Rose. I'll bet the list is a mile long."

The Hollywood Dinner Club appeared like an oasis in the desert, the first nightspot in the country to offer air-conditioning along with drinks, dancing and a five-star floor show, featuring world-famous stars and performers.

Bright searchlights crisscrossed the darkening sky, beckoning the privileged crowd. Cops and bouncers guarded the entrance like it was Buckingham Palace, shutting out the unfortunates who didn't possess that special piece of paper allowing entrée into a magical castle.

A valet held open the Packard door for me, and I felt like Daisy in *The Great Gatsby*, stepping out of a long limo. Outside, I recognized a few bold-faced types who I only read about in the papers: the Moodys, the Sealys and the Kempners. How exciting to cross paths with Galveston's high and mighty, even from a distance.

In reality, the Hollywood Dinner Club was a sophisticated saloon, casino and dance hall, and even the local snobs found the lavish décor and entertainment more than socially acceptable—never mind that it was run by gangsters. Charming businessmen in public, but hoodlums behind closed doors.

We showed our invitation to the dolled-up dame at the Hollywood's entrance, stepping into a fantasy jungle playground, featuring a lavish tropical theme: lush flowers, potted plants and colorful murals of wild animals.

A giant stuffed grizzly bear greeted us by the entrance. Zebra skins covered the circular booths, and a delicate orchid sat in crystal bud vases on each table. Exotic stuffed wildlife posed in corners, ready to pounce: a lion, a tiger, even a gorilla, lending a masculine yet eerie air of elegance. Personally, I pitied these proud beasts, ending up as mere decorations in this opulent showplace. The effect was dramatic, if not overwhelming.

Scanning the sea of rich and prominent locals, I couldn't help but wonder: Would Johnny Jack dare make an appearance tonight? He loved a good party as much as he loved beautiful women.

Still, would he risk venturing into enemy territory just to make a statement? Was he still expecting Burton to raid the club on demand? Despite the danger of a real showdown between Johnny Jack and the Maceos, I wanted to watch the fireworks first-hand.

During Splash Day weekend, I knew city officials hoped to keep the peace, declaring a temporary truce between the Beach Gang and Downtown Gang. Still, trying to get Johnny Jack and Ollie Quinn to mend fences was like asking them to dance the Charleston together.

We pushed past the ushers and attendants, heading backstage to see the girls. Nathan handed me the extra newspapers, waiting outside while I slipped into the dressing rooms.

"Hi Jazz!" a few gals called out. I waved to the bathing beauties I'd come to know and like in spite of my initial resistance. The girls were in various stages of undress, some in full regalia, while others frantically applied their face paint and dabbed on pale powder with big fluffy puffs.

With a smile, I handed out extra copies of the paper to all the featured beauties, giving hugs to Antonia and Michelle, Delysia, Sara and Jo Beth.

"You're a peach!" squealed Jo Beth.

"Merci beaucoup," said Michelle.

"I will treasure this always," said Sara, Miss New Orleans.

"I know you ladies are busy, but I wanted to say good luck and break a leg!"

"Break a leg? Why do we break our legs?" Michelle looked confused while the girls giggled.

"It's just a showbiz saying," I explained, smiling at her.

"Guess what?" Jo Beth pulled me aside, talking fast as she buttoned up her navy blue sailor's top and tap pants. "A talent scout is supposed to be in the audience tonight. She told us she represents agencies in Hollywood. Los Angeles, the real place, not this club. They saw our pictures in the paper and want us to audition, maybe as models or even for the moving pictures."

"Jo Beth, that's swell!" I said, noting her shining eyes and bright smile. "How thrilling! Who's the talent scout? Which agency?"

She shrugged, pulling out curlers from her long hair. "I've got her card somewhere. This guy at the Galvez told me she was looking for fresh young faces. Your articles and Nathan's pics did the trick!"

"Great," I told her, delighted. "Good luck!"

"Gee, thanks!" The light in her eyes dimmed. "I just wish Holly could share all this excitement with us. She's like a sister to me."

"Holly will be here in spirit, cheering you on," I consoled her. "Maybe she can compete next.year?"

"Yes, but it won't be the same. What if she misses a chance to go to Hollywood?" Jo Beth turned to go, her happy face in place. "Now I'd better shake, not break, a leg!"

Mrs. Wembley appeared out of the shadows and walked toward me. Nervous that I'd been caught backstage, I started to rush off when she stopped me, holding out my articles like an olive branch.

"These are some fine pieces of journalism." She nodded, patting my back. "You made my girls so proud, especially the foreign contestants. Your interviews made them feel special, that they're more than a shapely pair of legs or a pretty face."

"Thanks so much. I'm flattered." I blushed, recalling my initial impression of the beauty queens. "I'm looking forward to the show."

"You'll be surprised to see how much they've improved. Like night and day!" She beamed. "Before you go, Jasmine, please tell that nice young man his photos made all the girls look like movie stars. Tasteful and not tacky."

Was I hearing things? "Gladly. Nathan will be so pleased."

I returned to Nathan's side and as we took our seats at a small table by the aisle, I whispered, "Guess who's your biggest fan? Mrs. Wembley!"

"Oh yeah?" He frowned, skeptical. "That old biddy?"

"I'm serious. She gave us both nice compliments on the articles, especially your photos."

"You don't say." He smiled. "Tell her I'll be glad to take as many pictures as she wants."

"Tell her yourself. You're the ace shutterbug."

"Thanks. Say, that reminds me. I need to take a few more shots before the show starts."

"Of the girls?"

"I wish." He tilted his head toward the stage and I saw the Maceos glad-handing a bunch of stuffed shirts, including Mayor Hodgkins and a few other bigwigs who looked familiar. "You know, the usual muckety-mucks and cluckety-clucks. The Maceos and their cronies: the mayor, councilmen, senators, gangsters."

"Cluckety-clucks?" I smiled at his pained expression. "I'll go freshen up in the powder room. Be back soon."

As I made my way to the ladies' room, I noticed Mrs. Harper at a ringside seat with Mr. Thomas, along with Mack and Dave Nelson, the managing editor, and gave a slight wave. All the *Gazette*'s head honchos sat at one large well-placed table. How convenient. I wanted to walk over to say hello, but didn't have much time.

I entered a side hall where a few flappers had gathered outside the bathroom, waiting their turn. While I stood there, I listened to the gossip, fingering my long pearl necklace, but I'd heard it all before. Being a society reporter does have a few perks.

Finally I was able to take a quick peek in the mirror, powder my nose and adjust my headband. The lights were starting to dim while I headed down the hall to my table, and the curtains slowly began to draw open.

Suddenly it was pitch-black, the moments right before a show starts, when the orchestra gears up to play. Without warning, I felt an arm grip my waist, a hand grab me roughly from behind in the dark.

"Who are you? Let go of me!" I hissed, trying to yank away, but the attacker's grip tightened. Struggling to get free, I whirled around and in the dim stage lights, I saw Colin grinning at me with those devilish green eyes.

His lips tickled my ear, strong hands gripped my shoulders, his breath hot, his voice raspy. "So we meet again."

CHAPTER THIRTY-NINE

"Where's your Fed fella, Jazz?" Colin hissed, pulling me to him in the dark. Where did he come from?

"Leave me alone!" I squirmed, trying to wriggle out of his tight grasp. "Get your grubby paws off me!"

Taking my shoulders, Colin kissed me hard on the mouth, his breath reeking of whiskey and cigarettes.

I admit, I'd never been kissed that way before, but it was more of a sneak attack than a real kiss. Reeling back in shock, I managed to shove Colin away with both hands. "How dare you!"

"You smell like flowers." Colin gave me a smug smile and tipped his hat, polite as a stranger on the street, before he walked off like nothing happened. "Have fun tonight."

Fun? Was assaulting me in the dark fun to him? My head spinning, I rushed back to the ladies' room to catch my breath. Disoriented, I sat in the lounge, my arms and legs shaking, afraid to go back out.

When I heard the orchestra start tuning up, I freshened my lipstick and combed my tousled hair. After I made sure Colin was gone, I hurried to my table, glancing at the magic act in progress, a warm-up to the main attraction.

Settling in my chair, I pasted on a sunny smile, smoothing out my frock to keep my hands and legs from trembling. After all, the show must go on.

"What took you so long?" Nathan looked worried.

"Colin." I avoided his gaze. "Nothing I couldn't handle."

Nathan jerked up, angry blue eyes darting around the club, ready for a fight, but I waved him away as if everything was jake. Sure, I'd managed to fend off Colin this time, but I wondered why he kept targeting me for his surprise attacks. Was he stalking me—if so, why? Did Ollie Quinn put him up to it? Did he want the gold charm? He had some nerve, forcing a kiss on me, knowing I had no interest.

With the safety of the crowd and gaiety of the performances, finally I was able to relax. A cocktail waitress in skimpy tap pants and a halter top kept buzzing around, batting her lashes at Nathan. He ordered us a couple of rounds of Manhattans, enjoying the view.

The orchestra played a lively Gershwin number, then quieted when Sam Maceo, looking debonair in a dark, double-breasted suit and Panama hat, took the stage as the master of ceremonies.

"Ladies and gentleman, these beautiful girls have arrived from all over the world to grace us with their lovely presence. Please join me in welcoming these fair maidens as they demonstrate in a modern dance that not only do they deserve their beauty titles, they have true talent as well." Sam Maceo could moonlight as a carnie at the county fair and easily reel in the crowd.

One by one, the girls all walked onstage, wearing their sashes over cute sailor outfits, beaming brightly and waving to the crowd like pageant pros. Even the shy girls like Antonia, Miss Italy, and Sara, Miss New Orleans, looked happy and proud, a far cry from the timid wallflowers I'd met a week ago. I doubted they could see me in the audience, but I smiled back, feeling a rush of joy and anticipation.

Then the beauties broke into a lively number that involved lots of marching and kicking. The true troupers tap-danced in front, no doubt distracting the crowd from the less-talented hoofers who paraded around and saluted in back. Such a sly sleight-of-hand.

I had to give it to Mrs. Wembley, who managed to choreograph the bevy of belles. She knew the mostly-male audience didn't really care about perfect performances with so many lovely ladies on stage.

Nathan elbowed me, his bright blue eyes big as pancakes. "Get a load of those gams!"

"How can I miss them?" I replied, amused at his kid-in-a-candy-store expression.

Scanning the crowd, I spied Amanda and Sammy near the front. Naturally he stared transfixed at the stage with the same goofy grin as Nathan. All men are lotharios, I decided, lusting after new and shiny dames. As I sipped my drink, I caught Amanda's eye and we both shook our heads in sisterly sympathy.

"Where's Burton?" She mouthed across the room, but I signaled that I didn't know. I was surprised he wasn't on security duty or at least watching the performance for fun. After all, his badge granted him entrée into all sorts of hot spots. Would his presence have kept Colin at bay?

The curtains closed and the orchestra played loudly while the crew set the stage. For the next number, the beauties wore sheer gowns tied with gold rope belts, and gold ballet slippers. As the dance started I recognized a modified *Dance of the Fairies* from their first rehearsal. In the center, two girls sporting butterfly wings spun on their toes as the chorus fluttered by. To Mrs. Wembley's credit, this routine was a fresh, modern version with faster twirls and spins, and less leaping and running around in circles.

I leaned forward, whispering, "Look familiar?"

Nathan nodded. "Either the gals have gotten better or I'm too zozzled to care."

"Lay off the booze. The editors are here."

"So what? Don't be a spoilsport. They've had their share of hooch." He grinned and picked up his camera. "Guess I'd better get to work. If you call this work." I watched him position his camera in the far right aisle, away from the tables.

Afterwards, the crowd broke into thunderous applause and even Mrs. Wembley came out to take a bow. Good for her, not letting Sam Maceo steal her thunder after all of her hard work.

Looking around, I wondered if Johnny Jack and his goons were waiting in the audience, expecting Burton to appear and shut down the club. I tensed up, wondering where he was. I glanced over at Amanda and Sammy, but he didn't act very worried about the Oasis. If Colin really had eyes and ears on the place as he'd said, who was minding the bar? Seems Dino remained behind, and I felt sorry for him, being stuck at the Oasis while Antonia made her dance debut.

"We'll take a short break before we continue with our next routine," Mrs. Wembley told the crowd over the orchestra.

Nathan returned to the table, and set down his camera equipment on his chair. "Why don't we mingle?" I suggested, standing up. "We need to give our regards to the editors. Without them, we'd never have gotten past the front door."

"Count me out." He groaned. "What a bunch of party poopers."

"Chin up!" I grabbed his arm and we pushed a path through the crowd, smiling to a few familiar faces. Quickly I scanned the audience, but saw no sign of Burton. Was Colin still here?

As we made our way around the club, I admired the flashy flappers and debutantes dressed in the latest Paris fashions, sleek bias-cut gowns with bugle beads or sequins sparkling like stars, or rows of long fringe, dripping off the silk in waves, with hemlines skimming the knees. How scandalous! In contrast, the society matrons belonged in the Edwardian era with their high collars, bustles and bows—and stuffy expressions to match.

At the editors' table, I noticed Mrs. Harper and Mr. Thomas acting chummy, leaning on each other, smiling in unison. My boss was dolled up in a floppy floral hat and ruffled pale peach chiffon dress with a low neckline sporting ample cleavage that I tried hard to ignore. What was going on? Were they just hooched up or actually having a fling? So what if they were? Both editors were divorced, middle-aged and available.

Still, I shook the thought out of my head. Office romances were tricky enough, and frankly, I didn't want to see my two senior bosses flirting across the newsroom. Very unprofessional, not to mention uncomfortable *and* distracting.

"You two look nice." Mrs. Harper smiled. "Hope you're taking lots of good photos, Nathan. One of our debutantes broke off her engagement, so there's a big hole in the society section. We'll need lots of extra pictures for tomorrow."

Mr. Thomas piped up. "Beautiful girls sell newspapers!"

"Happy to help." Nathan grinned as the men nudged each other.

My boss motioned me over. "Anything exciting so far? Any juicy scoops?"

"Not yet, but I'll keep a look-out," I told her. What did she expect, a catfight? Backstage sabotage? A hair-pulling contest?

"Sorry your girlfriend couldn't make it. What's her name? Holly?" Mack said to Nathan sincerely, chomping on his cigar. "Say, Jazz, where's that Fed agent fella? Isn't he stuck on you?"

All eyes focused on me. You'd think they'd be more fascinated by the half-nude bathing beauties than my lackluster love life. Had they seen me with Colin?

"Too bad he had to work," I said to shut Mack up. Why was it any of his beeswax? To change the subject, I added, "Looks like it'll be a nice day for the parade tomorrow."

"I hope so." Mr. Thomas nodded. "Splash Day events depend on good weather. Lots of work to do this weekend, people!"

"I don't mind mixing business with pleasure. Thanks, boss!" Mack grinned, elbowing Mr. Thomas. Boys will be boys.

After we made small talk, I turned to go, saying, "Enjoy the show." I wanted to chat with Sammy and Amanda before the next performance, but the lights flickered on and off so we headed back to our seats. Nathan resumed his stance behind the camera.

When the orchestra started to play a few jazzy Cole Porter tunes, the girls marched out in sparkly silver sequined outfits, topped with smart caps and feathers, a spitting image of the Ziegfeld Follies. Arms linked, they formed a chorus line, doing a series of high kicks, their legs long and lean, dazzling the crowd. Wolf-whistles and applause filled the nightclub.

Next the dancers formed two rows, smoothly breaking into groups of four. If you used your imagination, they could almost pass for half-dressed can-can girls at the *Moulin Rouge*. Nathan snapped his pics as fast as possible, trying to time his shots with the high kicks.

Impressed, I applauded along with the crowd until my hands hurt. What a difference from the motley bunch of amateurs we watched less than a week ago.

Suddenly the lights went dark a moment and I heard a loud scream onstage. The beauties stopped dancing and the club quieted down. What was wrong? Then the lights turned on and a gaggle of gals started running from the stage, screaming, and jumping like they were walking on hot coals. Without thinking, Nathan and I rushed to the front to see the commotion.

My heart stopped and I jumped back, paralyzed with fear.

A huge copperhead slithered across the stage, its scales glistening in the spotlight, stretching to its full length of six feet.

CHAPTER FORTY

"Snake! There's a snake on the stage!" A few girls squealed as they bolted off the stage toward the exit.

They weren't the only ones screaming their heads off. "Help! Please do something!" I yelled. "Copperheads are poisonous!"

Whose bright idea was it to unleash a dangerous snake onstage?

Talk about pandemonium! Scraping back chairs, the musicians grabbed their instruments and cases, and gingerly made their way down the stairs and out the door.

A violinist picked up his chair and held it by its legs, poking the chair at the copperhead like a timid lion tamer. But when the snake lunged at him, he dropped the chair and ran off with a loud yelp.

"Let's go!" I screamed bloody murder and grabbed Nathan's arm, but he was too busy trying to take photos in the midst of chaos.

"I can't leave now. These pictures are priceless. Let's stick around, see what happens. We are journalists, after all. We don't get fazed by snakes and spiders."

"Speak for yourself!" I told him, trembling. "I'm terrified of all creepy-crawly things, including rats and bats. Copperheads are poisonous, lethal in fact."

Shaking, I make a mad dash for the exit, but I was stuck behind dozens of other patrons, panicking as if we were sinking on the Titanic. Keeping my distance, I watched the snake slither around the stage, looking for a victim, oblivious to the commotion it caused.

Then I heard Sam Maceo's voice booming across the nightclub. "Folks, please return to your seats. We've got this all under control."

Maceo stood next to an older American Indian man in full regalia, with long black braids and a profile right off a Buffalo nickel.

Holding a long knife, the Indian climbed onto the stage, circling the copperhead, staring it down like a snake charmer. A small crowd gathered to watch on the sidelines, mouths open, exchanging confused glances. They must have thought this was the "High Jinks" portion of the evening.

By now, most people had fled, including the beauties, probably going to the Galvez or speakeasies or anywhere they felt safe from snakes. Who could blame them? During the 1600s, Galveston had the not-so-honorable distinction of being known as the "Island of Snakes," and various reptiles still roamed the beach town.

I suspected Johnny Jack was behind all this hoopla, determined to disgrace and humiliate his rivals, the Maceos and Ollie Quinn. Surely the snake hadn't shown up on its own to steal the spotlight.

How in the world do you sneak a six-foot long snake into a well-secured nightclub like the Hollywood? Did Johnny Jack have a plant, a spy inside the Beach Gang? Probably he'd paid some errand boy or goon to sneak into the back, turn off the lights, then release the unwelcome visitor onstage. Maybe he'd coerced a musician to carry it inside an instrument case or valet or suitcase? Frankly I'd rather leave an investigation of snakes to the cops.

Chanting in a deep voice, the Indian continued to circle the copperhead, its cold eyes fixated on him. As he tiptoed around the stage, arms out, the snake followed his every move, poised to strike. Then in a flash, the Indian attacked: He stomped on the snake with his boot, and cut off its head while the body writhed and wriggled.

Shuddering, I hated to think how close the girls came to getting bitten by the venomous snake. With a dramatic flair, the Indian picked up both pieces of the huge copperhead, the body still twisting and turning. Then he held the pieces above his head like a champion prizefighter in victory.

A young boy brought out a big tub and the Indian threw the snake inside, sealing the lid with his fists. What was he planning to do with it, I wondered? I'd read that Indians used every part of an animal or reptile they killed, wasting nothing. Did that apply to deadly copperheads as well?

The small crowd broke into loud applause while the Indian bowed and smiled. You'd think he was the star of the show. No doubt, he'd earned every penny the Maceos paid him.

Nathan and I stared at the Indian, then each other, dumbstruck.

"Best floor show I've ever seen," Nathan cracked. "And it's hard to top half-naked girls."

"Glad you got your money's worth." I knew the snake was supposed to disrupt the performance, but Smooth Sam managed to turn a fiasco into live entertainment.

Across the club, I spied Amanda and Sammy, jaunty in a light linen suit and bowler hat, and hurried over. Amanda hung on Sammy's arm, as elegant as any star couple in *Photoplay*. "Did you see that Indian chop the giant snake in two?" she gasped. "I swear, I had the heebie-jeebies. That snake could've killed someone!"

"I'll say!" I turned to Sammy. "You think Johnny Jack was behind this spectacle?"

"I'd bet on it." Sammy nodded. "He must be desperate to pull such a stupid stunt. Believe me, he can act like a five-year-old if he doesn't get his way."

"It was stupid, all right, but it worked," said Nathan, arms extended. "Look at this place. It's half-empty. Why don't we sit a spell, rest our dogs? This may be the first and last time I ever get an invite to such a swanky spot."

"I can get you in anytime you want." Sammy thumped his chest. "But now I need to get back to the Oasis, and find out if the Downtown Gang's goons paid me a visit tonight."

Outwardly he appeared calm, but I could tell he was worried, the way he kept jangling his keys.

"I thought Colin had it covered? He seemed pretty confident the other night." I wondered if Sammy knew Colin was in the crowd.

"Who knows?" Sammy shrugged. "He talks big, but I don't trust his mug. Like I said, he gave me no other choice but to hire him."

At last, the truth. "You mean pay him off? Protection money?" I looked around at the stragglers milling around the almost empty club. "By the way, I saw him here tonight."

"What happened?" Sammy's head snapped toward me. "Did he talk to you?"

Did I really want to spell it out? "He tried to get fresh, but I gave him the cold shoulder."

"Did he touch you?" Sammy balled up his fist. "If he tries anything, so help me God…"

I'd seen up close what Sammy's fists could do to an enemy, and I didn't want to cause a rift between Sammy and Colin, now that they were so-called allies.

"I'm fine, really. I told him to take a hike. He got the telegram." But did he? Seemed the more I resisted, the more he persisted. "Besides, don't you two have an agreement?"

"I don't give a damn about our agreement." Sammy's face darkened. "If he was here, then he's not holding up his end of the bargain. Besides, Johnny Jack already had his fun tonight. He's waiting to strike when I'm not paying attention, just like that slimy snake onstage."

Sam Maceo came up the aisle, all smiles as if nothing unusual had happened, and slapped Sammy on the back. "Hey, sport! How'd you enjoy the evening?"

"Big Sam!" Sammy towered over the dapper Italian, patting his shoulders. "You should keep that Injun in your act. He and the snake stole the show."

"Good idea. I hear he knows how to use a knife," he joked. "Thank God he volunteered to help." Sam Maceo let out a laugh, and I began to wonder if the snake was actually part of the performance. Then he grabbed Sammy by the elbow and I heard him ask, "All kidding aside, any idea who let the snake out on stage?"

"One guess," Sammy said. "Your old pal Johnny Jack."

Big Sam's dark eyes narrowed. "I thought so. Well, give Johnny Jack a message for me, will you? Tell him I'm coming for him, when he least expects it."

"You and me both." Sammy nodded, his jaw working.

Then Sam Maceo's mood brightened, his public face again in place. "Are you all going to the parade tomorrow?"

"You bet!" Nathan exclaimed. "We're covering the story for the *Gazette*." He put his arm around me. "I'm the shutterbug, she's the reporter. Don't worry, we'll be there bright and early."

Maceo stared at us with a twinkle in his eye, and I instantly knew why he was called the "Velvet Glove." His dark eyes were warm and inviting, making you feel as if you were the only person in the room. "You two kids did those stories? Keep up the good work." He shook our hands, cupping mine warmly, smiling his approval.

Kids? He was probably in his early thirties, about Sammy's age, but his charm and sophisticated manner made him appear older and wiser. "Thanks. Nice to meet you, Mr. Maceo." I blushed, flattered. Even if he was a gangster, Sam Maceo liked my articles!

"Call me Sam, or Big Sam if you prefer." He grinned at Sammy, a half-foot taller, then handed us a business card. "Feel free to contact me if you ever need anything."

Great, so now I was pals with both Ollie Quinn and Sam Maceo, notorious Beach Gang overlords. What would Burton think if he saw me making small talk with Big Shot Sam?

"Excuse me, sir. If you ever need an extra dancer for your floor shows, let me know." Amanda stuck out her dainty hand and Maceo kissed it like a proper gentleman. "My name's Amanda. If you want, you can reach me through Sammy." She patted Sammy's shoulder for emphasis. My pal Amanda had moxie to spare.

Maceo sized her up with a glance and winked. "I'll do that, doll. My pal Sammy's sure got good taste in women."

Snapping his fingers, Maceo summoned a cocktail waitress, who appeared instantly. "Stay a while. Have a round of drinks on me. Whatever you want." Even Agent Burton couldn't complain, since the drinks were on the house.

A man with a handlebar moustache tapped Maceo on the shoulder and he turned around and shook his hand, easily moving in and out of conversations. He looked familiar, but I figured he was part of the old money crowd, or was it the nouveau riche set?

"Duty calls." Maceo tipped his hat and nodded to us as he walked away. "Better go make the rounds. Enjoy the evening."

After he left, we sat there in stunned silence. Only Sammy was nonplussed, lighting up a Camel and leaning back in his chair, relaxed for a change.

"I can't believe we just talked to Sam Maceo," Amanda piped up, breathless. "He's such a big wheel! He knows all these famous people!" You'd think she'd just seen the ghost of Rudolph Valentino come to life. True, in these parts, Maceo was a local legend.

"Big Sam is a good egg." Sammy blew smoke rings over his head. "Let's say he and Johnny Jack do business in different ways."

Despite his charm, I couldn't help but wonder if Sam Maceo had ordered the hit on Rico. Did Rose Maceo gun Rico down himself, or was he being framed? Still, this wasn't the right time or place to discuss Rico's death, especially on the Beach Gang's home turf.

The cocktail waitress, a cute redhead with freckles, returned with our drinks, setting her tray on the table. Nathan and Sammy looked her up and down in appreciation, and Sammy handed her a five dollar bill. She squeezed Sammy's arm while Amanda flashed her icy blue daggers. "No need to pay, good-looking. Drinks are on the house. Courtesy of Big Sam."

A familiar voice said: "How generous."

I almost jumped when I saw Agent Burton standing over the table, looking disheveled, an unusual departure from his Brooks Brothers attire of a pressed suit and polished shoes. Stone-faced, he flashed his badge at the unsuspecting cocktail waitress.

"As you may know, the Volstead Act prohibits the sale, transportation and manufacture of alcohol."

Panicked, she dropped her tray on our table and scurried off, without looking back.

"So we've heard. Luckily we're not guilty of any of those things." Sammy glared at Burton, and blew a burst of smoke in his direction. "Sorry you just missed Sam Maceo. You could recite the Volstead Act to him."

"Where were you? I assumed you were working," I told him, my heart thudding. "The show's over. You missed all the excitement."

"What excitement? This place looks deserted. Yes, I was working, but I'm off duty now." Burton pulled up a chair, squeezing in between me and Nathan. "Where's that waitress?"

He snapped his fingers in the air, signaling for a drink. "Time to celebrate. Didn't you hear the news? The Kit Kat Club got raided tonight. Johnny Jack is right where he belongs—in jail."

CHAPTER FORTY-ONE

"What the hell? You raided the Kit Kat? No bullshit?" Sammy shot up so fast he almost tipped over the table, cocktails and all. "Johnny Jack is in jail? This I have to see to believe."

"Be my guest." Agent Burton gave him a sly smile. "I can take you there right now. But I doubt he'll be happy to see you considering he's the one behind bars."

Sammy studied Burton, his expression a mix of skepticism and relief. "What happened? How'd you get in? The Kit Kat has guards posted at every door."

"Let's just say I have my ways. Johnny Jack needed to learn his lesson." Burton looked smug. "Now he knows I'm no pushover."

"Wish I'd been there to see his face." Sammy whistled. "You got some balls on you, for a rookie. Now we're both on his hit list."

I swear, he almost went to hug Burton, but stayed put, still staring at him in surprise.

Amanda squealed, reaching over and squeezing Sammy's neck. "Sammy, that's swell! You're off the hook. Johnny Jack can't hurt you now."

"Won't Johnny Jack try to buy his way out of jail?" I wondered, still in shock.

"Sure, it's possible." Burton nodded. "But he's made enemies on both sides of the law, and no judge will hear his case till Monday. Too bad he'll miss all the fun this weekend."

"Well, I'll be damned." Sammy's smile lit up his handsome features like a marquee. "For once I don't have to worry about Johnny Jack on my back." He walked over and shook Burton's hand. "I owe you one, sport. Let me know how I can repay the favor."

Burton winked at me. "How about a bottle of Champagne, since Sam Maceo is picking up the tab? A fancy French one, the type Jasmine likes." He had some nerve, all right. First, the Kit-Kat Club raid, then the Champagne.

"My pleasure." Sammy ordered the snootiest Champagne he could pronounce, on the house, so we weren't technically breaking the law. The bottle arrived in minutes and Sammy popped the cork with the flourish of a magician pulling a rabbit from a hat.

As we sipped our Champagne, we filled Burton in on the show, saving the deadly snake for last.

"I don't know which snake is worse. Johnny Jack or the copperhead," Sammy cracked. "They're both reptiles."

"You said it!" I agreed, enjoying the cool bubbly.

"I could get used to this—and how!" Amanda held her glass askew, her face flushed, and leaned on Sammy's shoulder.

"To wine, women and song!" Nathan made a toast, then refilled his glass.

"I'll drink to that." Burton grinned at me, and took a sip.

He certainly was in a playful mood, his eyes bright, drinking fine Champagne in public. Still, I wondered if our celebration was a bit premature. Once Johnny Jack was sprung from jail, I assumed he'd try to get his revenge.

After we'd made toasts all around and drained the bottle, Burton stood up and stretched, looking my way. "It's been a long night. Anyone need a ride?"

"Do you mind?" I glanced at Nathan, feeling guilty. I was always taught to "dance with the one who brung you," but I was dying to talk to Burton alone. Since this fiasco finally seemed settled, at least for now, I hoped we could make amends, start over as friends. But then what?

"Not at all. I want to look for Jo Beth and the girls anyway, take a few more photos," Nathan said. "Then I need to go by the *Gazette*, develop them in time for tomorrow's paper."

We said our good-byes and I turned to admire the Hollywood as we stood outside, waiting for the valet to bring around Burton's Roadster. Would I ever get a chance to come back?

When his car appeared, Burton tipped the valet, then held the door open for me. "How about taking the scenic route, down Seawall Boulevard?" I suggested. "Tomorrow the area will be packed during the parade."

"Sounds good. Did I mention I have to work parade duty in the morning?"

"Poor you. Forced to guard all those beautiful dames. What a tough job," I razzed him.

"Someone has to volunteer." He smiled. "Besides, don't you think I deserve a reward after tonight?"

"And how! I'm so relieved you didn't get hurt. Was there any gunfire at the Kit Kat Club?"

"That's not Johnny Jack's style. As Sammy said, he's a sneaky snake kind of guy who prefers to catch you off-guard."

"Like tonight. Those poor girls. Everyone was scared to death, including me."

"Sorry I missed all the excitement." Burton rubbed his chin. "Say, I was surprised to see Sammy tonight, all dressed up in his glad rags, with Amanda on his arm, like a regular fella. I thought he was more of a mole, who stays burrowed underground."

I smiled at his double entendre. Didn't Burton rely on moles, or informants, as a Fed agent? "True, Sammy has a tendency to work too much, like most men I know." I eyed him. "He's looked forward to this for weeks. Plus the Maceos gave him front-row seats."

"Must be nice. Too bad some of us had jobs to do." He pretended to grumble.

"Thanks for saving Sammy's neck." Grateful, I squeezed his arm. "You managed to do the impossible: Put Johnny Jack behind bars. Hope he stays there a long time."

Burton smiled in the dark, pleased. "I didn't do it for Sammy. Sure, I like the guy, but I want Johnny Jack to know he's not the top dog in town. The gangs don't control Galveston, no matter what they think or how hard they try." His knee brushed mine as we drove, and this time I didn't pull away.

I had to admire his bravado. "How in the world did you pull off that stunt?"

"Call it a surprise attack. Off the record, right?" He glanced at me, slowing down as we approached Murdoch's to let a few people cross over to the Seawall. "We got a tip that Johnny Jack was storing surplus bootleg at the Kit Kat Club. The place was nearly empty, so we were able to search the whole bar."

I sat up, wanting to hear every detail. "I think half the town was trying to crash the party at the Hollywood Dinner Club. So how did Johnny Jack react? Wish I'd been there!" Or maybe not.

"He had a smirk on his face, almost daring us to arrest him, like he didn't believe we'd actually do it. The only time he got nervous was when we tried to enter the back room. He said I needed a search warrant, and got his guards to block the door, sticking guns in our faces." Burton looked smug. "So I called his bluff, and pulled out my warrant. I came prepared."

I shivered, picturing the face-off between the goons and the good guys. "What'd he do?"

"Johnny Jack had no choice but to let us in. Some high-rollers were playing poker so we broke up their game. Not only did we catch them gambling, the place was filled with crates of booze." Burton smiled, enjoying my reaction. "Imagine my surprise when the first crate we opened was filled with Johnnie Walker Black."

"You don't say." I was stunned. "Was it from Sam Maceo's stolen stash?"

He nodded. "I suspect Rico or your Beach Gang buddy Colin sold it to Johnny Jack right under Big Sam's nose."

My face felt hot, recalling Colin's kiss, feeling like I'd somehow cheated on Burton. But it wasn't a real kiss and Burton wasn't my real beau. So far we were two friends who kept crossing paths. A lot.

"If Sam Maceo ever found out his rival got his prize stock, all hell might break loose." I shook my head, staring at the Crystal Palace, all lit up like a giant birthday cake. "Such a bloody business. What's the point? Risking your life for a drink?"

Burton parked by the Hotel Galvez, facing the beach, his face half-lit by the bright moon. "You know it involves more than drinking. To the public, it's like forbidden fruit, a way to rebel. For the gangs, it's not only about the money, but power. Control. Respect. Bootlegging pays the bills for many immigrants fresh off the boat. They feel their options are limited so they turn to crime."

"There are easier ways to make a living. Rum-running should be a last resort." I thought of Sammy, appreciating the irony. As a bar owner, he was clearly breaking the law, so I suppose that made him a criminal. Luckily, in Galveston, no one seemed to care.

"Yes, but take the Maceos. They'd never make this kind of dough as barbers," Burton noted. "By selling booze and operating casinos, these gangsters can live like royalty without a formal education or work experience. Who knows what they might accomplish if they went straight?"

Did he also mean Sammy? "Good point. After all, the gangs do run their various rackets like businesses. No wonder they call it organized crime."

I had a thought. "Are you sure that's the whole story? Rico was Maceo's right-hand man, so he might have been involved in their other rackets. Maybe he wanted to move up in the Beach Gang, and Rose Maceo put him in his place."

"Yeah, six feet under," Burton cracked. "We may never know the real truth." Glancing at his watch, he started the car. "Guess I'd better take you home, Cinderella. Your Aunt Eva may think you turned into a pumpkin."

How nice that he remembered her name, after only meeting her once or twice. His gold watch caught the light, reminding me of the charm bracelet. "By the way, do you still have the charm? I was surprised to see a Saint Jude charm on a prostitute's bracelet."

Burton dug into his pockets. "Maybe it wasn't hers. She could have borrowed it or stolen it. Could be a gift from a john, or an ex-boyfriend. You never know with these types of girls." He gave me the charm, his hand lingering. "Hold onto this for now. Since there's no official investigation, I didn't turn it in as evidence. Just be careful not to flash it around any jewelers or gangsters."

"I'm more worried about *you*," I admitted. "Aren't you afraid Johnny Jack will retaliate?"

Burton stopped in front of the boarding house, resting his arm across my car seat. "Sure, but as long as he's locked up, I'm safe. His thugs won't make a move without his consent." His face clouded. "But keeping him in jail is the problem. If he pays off the right people, he could be out in no time. Then I'm a sitting duck."

CHAPTER FORTY-TWO

I shivered, despite the muggy breeze, seriously worried about Burton. In many ways, his job was like being in a gang, and twice as dangerous. He'd risked his life to uphold the Volstead Act, a nonsensical law both the cops and the public ignored. Trouble was, he didn't have the support of a gang, or even the police force, to protect him.

"At least the gangs know you can't be bribed or bought," I told him. "But that won't stop them from trying."

"Even if they manage to get rid of me, someone else will take my place, as long as Prohibition is in effect. I hope I live long enough to see it abolished."

"Don't say that!" My stomach clenched. "Nothing will happen to you, if you're careful."

"I'm always careful." He started to lean forward, then seemed to change his mind.

I admit, I was both disappointed and relieved. What if he'd detected Colin's whiskey and cigarettes on my breath?

Burton walked me up the brick path to the boarding house, jingling his change. "Say, are you busy Sunday night? Want to go to the beauty pageant with me?"

I was so pleased, I turned into a silly Southern belle on the spot. All this talk of doom and gloom could wait until after the Bathing Girl Revue. "Why Agent Burton, I thought you'd never ask."

"I wouldn't blame you if you changed your mind. After all, I've got a target on my back." Burton frowned.

"Are you trying to talk me out of going with you?"

"Hogwash!" Was that a blush under his bronzed tan? "Shall we make it seven? We can stop by Gaido's or the Hollywood Dinner Club first for a bite to eat."

"I'd love that." I nodded, beaming. For once, we were going on a real date. No pretense, no fake romance, no secret agenda. He gave me a quick peck on the lips and rushed down the walkway, a spring in his step. "See you tomorrow at the parade!" I called after him.

Eva met me at the door, looking around the porch. "Was that Agent Burton? I thought you went out with Nathan? My, my. Hard to juggle two fellas in one night," she teased.

"Eva, you know I'm no vamp! Nathan had to work tonight so James drove me home."

"How nice of him. So tell me about your adventures! How was the bathing beauties' dance routine?"

"We all had a swell time," I told her, failing to mention the snake or the raid. "Say, are you going to the parade tomorrow?"

"You know I don't condone women flaunting their bodies for public amusement," she sniffed. "But it may be nice to get out of the house and enjoy the festivities."

Please, not another lecture from Aunt Eva atop her high horse. Sure, I was all for women's emancipation, but after meeting the bathing beauties, I didn't want to be so quick to judge or criticize anyone who wanted to improve their lot in life. Clearly, good looks was no guarantee of happiness or a charmed existence.

"Is Amanda home yet?" I hoped Sammy was a gentleman and wouldn't try to take advantage of her tipsy state, but knowing Amanda, she'd be the one manhandling *him*.

"Not yet, but I expect her home by midnight. If not, I'll have to give Sammy a piece of my mind!"

Oh boy, that was a scene I didn't want to miss.

In my room, I got ready for bed but couldn't relax, worrying about Burton. I got up and turned on my cockatoo perfume lamp, hoping the cool citrus scent would lull me to sleep.

When I finally nodded off, I dreamt that I was dancing with Agent Burton at the Hollywood, the club as sparkly as a planetarium. Just as we were leaving, a black Ford drove by and Colin leaned out the window, aiming a Tommy gun right at Burton.

Before he could shoot, I let out a blood-curdling scream, and woke up in a cold sweat. Did anyone hear me cry out? Not exactly a good start to Splash Day.

Saturday

Saturday morning loomed crisp and clear, perfect parade weather. I couldn't wait to watch the bathing beauties, and I was looking forward to seeing Burton.

Amanda was still asleep, after her big night on the town, so I quietly got dressed in a two-piece peach shorts and top outfit and went downstairs. Aunt Eva was in the kitchen making scrambled eggs, when we heard a pounding on the door.

Nathan stood outside, a handful of photos in his hand, a stricken look on his face. "Nathan! What are you doing here so early? Is something wrong?"

"I'll say!" He nodded. "I wanted to catch you before you went to the parade. Where can we talk in private? I need to show you something."

Nathan rarely showed up unannounced, so I knew it had to be important. "How about the parlor?" As we passed the kitchen, I told Eva, "Nathan's here so we're going to visit a few minutes. If you want, he can drive us to the parade."

Eva wiped her hands on a gingham towel. "I've got breakfast to make for my boarders. You're welcome to join us, if you want. I can go later with a friend from church."

"Thanks, maybe another time?"

Nathan followed me to the parlor and plopped down on the pink velvet couch, carefully spreading out the photos across the sagging cushions. Then he handed me the photos, one by one, showing the bathing beauties in various poses, at rehearsals, at the Hollywood, applying make-up backstage.

"Recognize anyone?" he asked, stone-faced.

Was this a pop quiz? "Sure, here's Jo Beth, and Miss California and Antonia..." I put the photos on my lap, watching Nathan's expression. "These are all wonderful pictures. Mrs. Harper will be glad to use any of them. So what's the matter?"

He picked up a photo and handed it to me. "Look at this one, taken on the first day of rehearsals. See the pretty brunette with her arm extended during the high kicks, her face in shadows? I don't remember her, do you?"

"Everything was a blur the first couple of days," I admitted. "So much to take in, it was overwhelming. I couldn't keep up with names or titles or dances."

I held the photo under the bridge lamp for a better view, squinting while I examined it closely. Then my heart stopped for a moment and I pointed to an outstretched arm. "Looks like one of the girls is wearing a gold charm bracelet!"

Realization sunk in as I studied the black-and-white image. Clutching the photo, I stared at Nathan in shock.

"That poor dead girl on Post Office Street wasn't a prostitute at all. She was a bathing beauty!"

CHAPTER FORTY-THREE

"How in the world did a bathing beauty end up in the red-light district?" I asked Nathan, still reeling from the surprise. I jumped off the couch, ready to call the cops. But would they cover it up, just like everything else?

"Good question." He frowned. "I wonder if she was even reported missing?"

"I bet she was, and the city probably buried it." I shook my head. "No wonder we didn't hear a word. We're the *last* people they'd tell. They don't want reporters snooping around. What a scandal! A bathing beauty found dead in the red-light district?"

"If we did try to report it, they'd just kill the story. And the gangs may kill us as well."

"Let's not get too carried away," I said, trying to calm down. "You know what I think? I suspect she was a foreigner who didn't speak English, and she lost her way, literally. It's so unfair."

"What's unfair is her killer is still out there. We can't let him get away with murder." Nathan was breathing hard, punching the sofa cushions. "I wish I could find the bastard and choke the life out of him, like he did to that poor girl."

"I wish you could, too." I had to agree. "She came here with high expectations, and ended up losing her life."

Aunt Eva rapped on the door and poked her head in the room. Nathan and I exchanged worried looks, hoping she hadn't heard. "Hello, Nathan. How about some breakfast? I've got eggs, hotcakes, sausage and fresh-squeezed orange juice."

"Thanks, ma'am, but we're late for the parade. Next time?"

Nathan rarely turned down any offers of free food, but we'd both lost our appetites. "Please tell Amanda we had to go to the parade early," I told Eva before we left.

Nathan drove to the Seawall like he was racing in the Indy 500, getting stuck in bumper-to-bumper traffic. "Wait. I have an idea."

He gave me a mischievous grin, then took a sharp turn and maneuvered his Model T across the busy boulevard. Somehow he managed to squeeze in between two cars and putter down the middle lane. Throngs of well-heeled tourists stood on the sidelines, waiting for the parade to start.

A cop stopped us, crossing his arms. "Where do you think you're going, buster?"

"I'm the official pageant photographer," Nathan said, pointing to his equipment in back. "They'll raise Cain if I'm late. You know how ladies hate to be kept waiting!"

"You said it. I've got three daughters," the cop said, winking. "Go ahead, sport. You can park by the Galvez." Lucky for us, he blocked the oncoming traffic and directed us to the hotel.

"Quick thinking," I told Nathan as we parked, impressed that his white lie worked. "Let's try to find Jo Beth or one of the beauties before the parade starts."

"How will you bring up the missing beauty queen?" Nathan asked me, lugging his camera equipment on his back.

"We'll just ask them to identify the gals in the photos. Watch how they react." I tapped his shoulder. "What made you dig those photos up anyway?"

He shrugged. "When Mrs. Harper said she needed extra photos, I thought it'd be fun to include some earlier shots of the rehearsals, sort of a before and after spread. I don't even remember seeing the brunette, since she was cut off in the pics. Never noticed the bracelet either, but I wasn't looking at their arms." Figured he was ogling their figures.

As we waited for the parade to start, a throng of people started gathering on both sides of Seawall Boulevard. Nathan set up his camera by one end, and I stood in front so no one could block his shots. I looked around at the crowds, but it was so packed I didn't see anyone I knew. Where was Agent Burton?

The Ball High Marching Band started off the parade with a few patriotic numbers, though July Fourth was a month away. Finally the mayor gave a short speech about Galveston's history and the town's reconstruction after the Great 1900 Storm.

"The Seawall is a symbol of our can-do spirit, our resolve to recover and rebuild our town. Like Lazarus, we rose up from the depths of death and destruction, determined to survive and thrive again." Yes, that was a sappy speech by anyone's standards, yet the crowd went wild, cheering, "Galveston! Galveston!"

Triumphant, the mayor climbed into a regal Rolls Royce and the hayburner proceeded slowly down Beach Boulevard. The bathing beauties formed a line along the Seawall, awaiting their chariots.

I marveled at the wide array of bathing costumes in Easter egg colors, long and short, with ruffles or bows and matching bandanas or scarves, floppy hats or elaborate headbands, some wearing long flowing capes.

Nervously I watched the contestants climb into different cars, standing on the back seat, holding on to nothing more than flimsy ribbon straps or ropes. One daredevil actually stood on the roof of a fancy Bentley, her heels sliding along the slick top. To me, she was risking her neck, positioned precariously without any railings or support. Hundreds of gawking people milled around, walking between cars, causing them to stop and start. Didn't anyone realize how dangerous it was for the girls?

With one hand waving at the crowd and the other holding on for dear life, the beauties were in a perilous position, somehow managing to maintain their balance in a moving car. A few held onto colorful parasols, twirling them as they passed.

Anxious, I prayed none of the cars would suddenly brake and send a girl crashing into the windshield or worse, the street. How they kept their poise and composure, in high heels no less, was beyond me. Yikes!

When I saw Antonia, dressed in a modest red two-piece outfit, baring her arms and knees, I waved and called out to her. Then I heard a deep male voice yelling her name, and saw Dino across the boulevard, vigorously clapping and whistling.

Even from a distance, I saw Antonia blushing, waving back at him with a big smile. I'd never seen the baby grand grin so broadly at anyone or anything. I rarely saw Dino out in public, except when he had to stock the shop or, as he liked to say, "go see a man about a dog." Nice of Sammy to release him from his post for such a special occasion. Dino stood near Sammy and Amanda, who watched the parade side by side.

Next in line were Delysia and Sara dressed in form-fitting one-piece wools suits. You couldn't miss Jo Beth, who wore a skimpy shorts and tank top outfit with a cowboy hat over her long blond hair in ringlets, a rope in her hand. When the car stopped, she pretended to lasso some folks on the sidelines, while the crowd burst into applause, calling out "Dallas! Dallas!" Leave it to Jo Beth to ham it up for the crowd's benefit.

A few floats adorned with flowers and streamers promoting local businesses filled in the gaps between the star attractions. Michelle looked chic in a silky ruffled shift and matching cloche, blowing kisses to the crowd. Miss Hawaii ended the pageant, wearing a floral sarong and a lei of oleanders around her neck, not exactly the Hawaiian island's native flower. I admired her resourcefulness, guessing that she'd made it herself the night before.

The onlookers broke into enthusiastic applause, rushing toward the girls while they exited the vehicles, the cops failing to stop the stampede. Frankly, I was worried the bathing beauties might get trampled by the crowd. According to the agenda, the girls were supposed to change at the Hotel Galvez in preparation for the upcoming sportswear portion of the parade.

"I'll go look for Jo Beth," I told Nathan. "Maybe she'll recognize the girl in the photo." Gritting my teeth, I carved a path as I made my way down the line of cars. I elbowed my way along the boulevard, hoping to catch one of the girls before the next parade started. Unfortunately, it seemed they'd already been whisked away to prepare for the next parade.

I returned to Nathan's side. "Sorry, I couldn't find Jo Beth. Did you get any good shots?"

"A few." He grinned. "But from this angle, the photos look like they belong in girlie magazines."

"I doubt the editors will approve. Why not move around, try different shots? Just do your best. We can talk to Jo Beth later."

The noon sun beat down on us as we waited for the second parade to start. Impatient, I fanned myself with my floppy wide-brimmed straw hat while Nathan repositioned his camera.

"What's the hold-up?" he grumbled, tapping his foot.

Once again, the mayor took the podium, trying to calm down the excited crowd. "Ladies and gentleman, glad you could join us today," his voice boomed. "Please be patient as our beauties change into their sporty looks. I guarantee you won't be disappointed when you see these lovely ladies modeling the latest sportswear fashions from all over the world."

Soon the parade started again, but this time Miss New York was in front, wearing a ruffled polka dot outfit with a glittery star headband. Miss California came next, in a smart shorts set, and Miss Florida followed in bloomers and matching top, both with kerchiefs tied around their cropped hair.

Jo Beth appeared wearing blue jeans and a red-checked shirt with suspenders, looking like a farmer's daughter. As the parade of beauties showed off their tennis and golf and polo outfits, the crowd oohed and aahed in appreciation. Who played polo in Galveston?

Next came a few gals in jaunty jodhpurs, riding breeches and yachting fashions, posing like athletes. Trailing the parade, I scanned the length of cars, but didn't spot Antonia or Michelle in the line-up.

I rushed back to alert Nathan. "I don't see Miss Italy or Miss France anywhere!"

"Maybe they're still getting ready or the cars got stuck in traffic," he said with a shrug. "Or they knocked off early to get ready for the main event."

Perhaps the sponsors asked them to perform other pageant duties, or make a separate appearance elsewhere. Would Jo Beth know where they were? I had to elbow the eager gawkers out of the way as I made a beeline for Jo Beth's car, and tried to catch her eye. At first, she ignored me, continuing to wave as if she'd already won the whole contest.

Finally the car came to a stop and I called out to her, "Where's Michelle and Antonia?"

She cupped her hand. "They didn't make this parade? All I know is we were supposed to meet at the Galvez after both parades and take some photos for that talent scout."

"Who was it?" I yelled. "The same lady?" People may have assumed I was part of the procession, I stuck so close to her car.

A cop came up and yanked on my arm to pull me away. "Move along, miss!" he snapped. "You're slowing down the parade."

Ignoring him, I shrugged off his grip, jumping out of his reach. "Which talent scout?" I shouted at Jo Beth. "What's her name? What does she look like?"

"Like a big gypsy. She wears lots of make-up and scarves."

Alarm bells went off in my mind. "Did she give you her name?" I persisted, following alongside her car as it crept forward.

Jo Beth struck a pose for a pushy photographer, who got in front of me, but I shoved him right back into the crowd. Not very ladylike, but I was starting to worry.

"Now I remember." Jo Beth crinkled her nose. "Mrs. Temple or something? She told us she has a photography studio or talent agency near the post office."

I stopped in my tracks, staring at Jo Beth in alarm. Did she mean Mrs. Templeton's whorehouse on Post Office Street?

CHAPTER FORTY-FOUR

"You mean Mrs. Templeton's place?" I asked Jo Beth, starting to panic. "Is that her name?"

"Maybe." She shrugged, a pageant smile plastered on her face. "Can we talk later, Jazz? In case you haven't noticed, I'm in the middle of a parade."

I managed to keep pace with the car, despite the irritated driver who kept trying to shoo me away. "Jo Beth, tell me. Who took them? What happened?"

"Miss Templeton met us at the hotel, told us we'd make a lot of money if they took photos of us in our bathing suits. We were supposed to go after both parades, not now. Ask the fairy at the Galvez. He set it all up."

"You mean the prissy clerk in the lobby?" Did *he* work for Mrs. Templeton as well?

Jo Beth stopped waving and turned to me, her expression now serious. "Oh no! You think something's wrong? She seemed so nice, like a funny old grandma."

"Don't worry," I told her, though I was plenty worried. "We'll find them, bring them back in time for tonight's event." I turned to go just as two burly cops approached me, holding clubs.

"You're slowing down the parade, miss. Get out of the way!" They tried to follow me as I pushed a path through the crowd, elbows out, until I lost them.

Luckily I managed to get to Nathan just as the parade was ending. "I found out the missing beauties are at Mrs. Templeton's cathouse, posing for pictures. We've got to go over there right away."

"Girlie pictures?" His eyes widened. "Is that all?"

"All I know is they're in trouble." I heaved a sigh. "I'm going to ask Sammy for help. I'll meet you back at the car in a jiffy."

"Bring Dino along, too. We'll need all the muscle we can get if we're going to pry those poor girls loose from the gang's clutches."

"You said it." As the parade ended, I found Sammy standing by Amanda and Dino.

"Where's Antonia? Why wasn't she in this parade?" Dino looked like a kid who got lumps of coal for Christmas.

"I've got some bad news." I pulled them aside. "You've heard of Mrs. Templeton's place? She duped the girls by posing as a Hollywood talent scout and, and offered to take their photos. I think Antonia and Michelle are there now."

"The whorehouse on Post Office?" Dino yelled, his face twisted in fury. "What in hell?"

A few tourists turned to stare at us with a frown.

"Pipe down," I hushed him.

Sammy crossed his arms, his head tilted. "How could they fall for that bunch of bull?"

"Remember these girls are foreigners," I pointed out. "Their English skills are limited at best. They have no idea who or what Mrs. Templeton really is."

Sammy looked upset. "We gotta get them out of there."

"And pronto," Dino said, eyes bulging. "God help anyone who touches Antonia!"

"I have an idea that may work," I told them. "Why don't you and Dino pretend to be new clients, and take a look around? Then we'll find a way to distract them so you can nab the girls."

"OK by me," Sammy said, breathing hard. "We can't go barging in like gangbusters. If they saw this freight train coming at full speed, they'd run away."

He elbowed Dino, whose eyes were bugging out by now. "Calm down, big guy. We'll find her. Lucky for us, I carry a gun."

"You don't plan to use that thing, do you?" I eyed the gun. "What if the girls get hurt by accident?"

"Last resort. Let's hope Mrs. Templeton doesn't give us any lip." Sammy shook his finger at me and Amanda. "You two be careful. Don't do anything stupid."

"I'm no dumb Dora and neither is Amanda," I said, miffed. "We can handle ourselves."

"I'm coming with you, Sammy," Amanda insisted. "I know how to improvise on the spot."

"Nathan and I will meet you there. Wait for us!" I called out, but they'd already vanished in the crowd. Carefully, I tried to cross Beach Boulevard, but a heavyset matron shoved a huge picnic basket at me, and I almost fell onto the pavement.

Holding tight to my hat and purse, I rushed toward the Galvez, dodging pedestrians and traffic, and found Nathan loading his camera equipment into the back seat of his Model T.

"Do you know how hard it is to carry this monstrosity through a huge crowd of people and cars without breaking anything?" he griped. "So what's the plan?"

"Sammy and Dino are going ahead. They'll pose as clients to get inside, and try to grab the girls. Amanda's coming, too."

Sounded simple in theory.

"Swell." Nathan rolled his eyes. "How are we going to sneak the girls out? We may as well hold our own parade and strike up the marching band."

"Got any better ideas?" I scanned the crowd once more, trying not to worry. "I wonder what happened to Agent Burton? He was supposed to be working the parade today."

What if he was ambushed by the Downtown Gang?

"I doubt he wanted to miss an assignment like this!" Nathan howled. "Getting paid to protect bathing beauties?" When I glared at him, he added, "I'm sure he's fine."

"I hope so. Do you know how to get to Mrs. Templeton's house? I was there once with Burton. On business."

"Every hot-blooded male within a fifty-mile radius knows where it is." Nathan grinned and gunned his engine, racing toward Post Office Street.

"I hope they don't start snapping nude photos of the girls. At their age, those photos will ruin their reputations, and haunt them for the rest of their lives."

"Could be worse." Nathan gunned his motor. "What kind of sickos want to take advantage of innocent girls, especially foreigners?" His face looked pale, sweaty, his knuckles white on the steering wheel.

"Hope we get there in time before Mrs. Templeton tries anything else." I shook my head, breathing hard. "By the way, have you ever been to a bordello?" I blurted out. "What's it like?"

"I refuse to answer on the grounds it may incriminate me." Nathan blanched, avoiding my gaze. "Why do you want to know?"

"I need to be prepared, just in case. We'll call it research."

"OK, you asked." Nathan stared ahead, his face and ears turning pink. "Depends on the brothel. Some look like five-star hotels, while others resemble flophouses. They're similar to a department store with a variety of different wares and price tags, in assorted shapes and sizes. Merchandise that you can sample, but not take home."

I blushed at his analogy. "Well put, but it'll never get printed in the *Gazette*."

After Nathan parked, I spotted Sammy's car in front. We got out and peered in his car and found Amanda hiding in the back seat. She jumped when I tapped the window. "Sammy and Dino went inside already. Did you see anything yet?"

"Not yet. We can't just loiter on the streets, doing nothing. They're bound to get suspicious." I turned to Nathan, pointing to the house. "Why don't you pretend to be a student looking for some action or whatever you drugstore cowboys call it?"

Nathan suppressed a smile. "I can't believe you actually said that out loud. But that's not a bad idea. I can distract the call girls and give the fellas time to find the bathing beauties."

After he left, Amanda pouted. "What are we supposed to do? Just sit on the sidelines while they rescue the damsels in distress?"

"Got any better ideas?" I asked, eyeing the cotton-candy pink bordello.

"Maybe." I could see a gleam in her eye. "What do you suppose is going on in there? You don't think they're *with* anyone?"

"Sammy and Dino? Hogwash! I'm sure Mrs. Templeton is giving them the ten-cent tour. Say, why don't we go around the side and try to peek in the windows?"

"Jazz! They'll think we're peeping tomatoes." She acted shocked, but she gave me a smile. "Let's go. We can't sit around forever. What's the worst that can happen?"

As we tiptoed across the yard, we kept an eye out for passing cars but the neighborhood seemed fairly quiet. I tried to glance in the windows, but all I saw were lacy curtains fluttering in the warm breeze. Even the working girls must have been at the parade today.

We crept toward the backyard, where I heard voices coming from one of the side windows. I recognized Mrs. Templeton's melodious voice carrying across the quiet street.

"I can tell that gentlemen like yourselves want something special, so I've saved the best for last. We happen to have two fresh-faced bathing beauties all the way from Europe, ready to entertain you, if the price is right. Are you interested?"

My heart stopped. Were they offering up Miss Italy and Miss France to Dino and Sammy as prostitutes? I exchanged horrified looks with Amanda. Nude photos were bad enough but this was the worst-case scenario.

"That does it! We're going inside." Amanda grabbed my arm, whispering, "Follow my lead."

"What are you going to do?" I stared at her, terrified for Antonia and Michelle.

"Watch me." Amanda took the front stairs two at a time, and burst through the double stained glass front doors, crying out, "Where is my good-for-nothing louse of a husband? I swear, if he's here, then he can forget about coming home tonight or any night!"

Talk about making a grand entrance.

The bordello looked like a genteel old hotel with chandeliers hanging from the high ceilings, walnut Victorian furniture, and several plush Oriental carpets on the hardwood floors.

"What's the ruckus?" Mrs. Templeton rushed into the hallway, hands on her generous hips, a long scarf wrapping her head. "Why are you ladies in here, making all this racket?"

Heads popped out of upstairs bedrooms, and a few girls in lingerie stood outside their rooms to watch the commotion. Sammy appeared behind the madam, giving us a sly wink.

As if on cue, Amanda flung herself at Sammy. "You scoundrel! What in God's name are you doing here, you bum? In this whorehouse, of all places?"

Sammy played along. "I wasn't doing anything, honest, sugar!"

"Not yet! You think I was born yesterday?" she cried out.

That's when Dino emerged from the bedroom, cradling Antonia in his bulky arms like a sleeping beauty, her bathing costume loose on her petite frame. Seizing his chance, he shoved Mrs. Templeton aside and made a beeline for the door.

"Where do you think you're going, buster? What are you doing with my girl?" Mrs. Templeton barged after him, but Sammy blocked her way, fending her off with his elbows.

"Your girl? She belongs to Italy!" Dino sputtered, shaking with anger. "If you touched one hair on her head, I'm coming for you!"

I held back, opening the front door for Dino. "Thank God! Where's Michelle?"

"Still inside the room," he panted, rushing out the door. "Hurry, grab her, before these assholes get to her."

By now, Amanda was pounding Sammy's chest, doing a first-rate job of acting like the wronged woman. While the madam tried to intervene, I slipped behind them into the room, gasping when I saw Michelle passed out on the bed. What had the girls been given? Opium? Hooch? Cocaine?

Professional camera equipment was set up in a corner with lights and props, including colorful paper parasols, blankets and beach balls. A black leather lion tamer's outfit was also laid out on the bed, complete with accessories: a lace-up bustier, tiny tap pants, top hat and a whip. I hoped the girls were too doped up to pose or perform or whatever they expected, praying we'd gotten there in time.

When I tried to get Michelle to stand up, she collapsed on the bed. Clearly I needed Sammy's help, so I went out into the hallway to get his attention.

"Calm down, honey," I told Amanda in my best Southern drawl, signaling my brother. "He's not worth your time or your tears." Sammy took the cue and snuck off into the bedroom.

"You said it!" Amanda sobbed, covering her face. "That good-for-nothing palooka!"

I hugged her heaving shoulders like a good friend. "Who needs that two-timing loser?"

While we performed our act, Sammy rushed out carrying Michelle, limp as a bed doll, trying to dodge Mrs. Templeton. "Wait a minute! You can't just waltz out of here with the bathing beauties!"

She lunged for his shirt tail, yanking him back. We flanked her hefty frame, holding onto her fleshy arms.

"These girls aren't your property." I faced her. "Let them go!"

"Times are tough, honey." She looked at me with sad, dark eyes. "Every fella in town wants to sleep with a bathing beauty. I'm just providing a service, giving the public what they want. Those foreign girls bring top dollar!"

"You think it's OK to dope up innocent girls and sell them to the highest bidder?" I fumed.

"It's only for the weekend. They won't know what hit 'em." Then she stuck her finger in my face, bracelets jangling on her arm. "Say, don't I know you from somewhere?"

"I came here looking for my cousin." I faked a smile. "Thanks for finding her!"

"Your cousin is a bathing beauty? Why didn't you say so?" Skeptical, she looked me up and down. "Well, if we can't have the real thing, you two prissy missies will have to do."

Catching me off-guard, she twisted my arm behind my back until I cried out, "Stop, you're hurting me!" She pulled on Amanda's long locks, trying to drag her into the bedroom.

Did the old battering ram really think she stood a chance against two flappers one-third her age? We twisted out of her grasp and tried to pin her to the wall, but she lashed out like a cornered wildcat. Frantic, she clawed at our clothes and faces, her long red nails sharp as talons. I hated to attack someone's grandmother, but this was no sweet little old lady. When that didn't work, she tried to stomp on our toes and kick at our shins. Ouch—she weighed a ton!

Then she seemed to relax, no longer resisting. What was wrong? Suddenly I felt cold steel pressed against my back. I whirled around to see Colin, aiming his gun at me.

CHAPTER FORTY-FIVE

"Hello, Jazz." Colin moved toward me, too close for comfort. "We meet again."

"What are you doing here?" I sucked in my breath.

"I can ask you the same question." His green eyes narrowed. "What are two nice girls like you doing in a place like this?"

"Is this one of the Beach Gang's brothels?" I demanded. "Did *you* kidnap the bathing beauties, and bring them here?"

"You ask too many questions," he scowled.

"Goes with the job," I snapped. "Journalist, not prostitute."

With a huff, Mrs. Templeton smoothed out her clothing and fluffed her hair, then stomped over to Colin. "These damn busybodies took away my bathing beauties! Two big fellas carried them right out the front door! Don't just stand there, do something!"

"Lucky for us, we have two lookers to take their place. In the dark, no one can tell the difference," Colin replied, smirking.

What a sickening thought, that they considered us mere merchandise, playthings for men of means. Where were Sammy and Dino and Nathan when we needed them?

Colin led us into the back bedroom with all the props, poking us with his gun like a cattle prod. I noticed Amanda's terrified expression, and felt guilty for dragging her into this mess. Colin followed us into the room, then shut the door behind him.

A wave of nausea swept over me as I looked around. "You can't make us do anything. We're not streetwalkers."

"I know that. I'm trying to make Mrs. Templeton happy." He stared at us with a piercing look, as if he could see right through us.

"What about the bathing beauties? Was that your doing?"

"Hey, it wasn't my idea. Talk to the pansy at the Galvez. Besides, Mrs. Templeton said it was a one-time thing, only for the weekend." So the snippy hotel clerk was behind this scheme?

"What do you plan to do with us?" Amanda's voice wavered.

"Good question." He lowered his gun. "Look, ladies, I'm no killer and I'm no rapist. I'm just doing my job."

"Your job? What is that exactly? Trying to force young girls to turn tricks?"

"I just recruit the girls, wherever I can find them, on the beach or the street. I don't hurt them." He shrugged, looking apologetic. "They have a choice."

"A choice? What happens to the girls after you get them hooked on opium or booze? How would *you* feel being treated like a piece of meat—or a slave?" I was shaking all over, my heart hammering.

His face fell. "Believe me, I know how it feels." Now his eyes didn't look so menacing, they looked sad, lost. "You don't know me or what I've been through." He looked out the window, as if expecting company. "My parents immigrated here from Ireland, and died in the Great Storm. Mrs. Templeton rescued me from the orphanage when I was a boy. I owe her my life."

"You can find better ways to pay her back," I told him, trading worried looks with Amanda. Why was Colin telling us his sob story if he planned to let us go?

"Who are you to judge me?" He turned and grabbed my wrists, his face inches away. "You must think we're all alike, that we're all monsters." His jade eyes seemed distant. "Bet you think you're too good for me. You like those Joe College types, don't you, Jazz?"

I held my breath. "Prove me wrong, Colin. Prove that you're different from the rest of the Beach Gang."

Giving me a wicked grin, he grabbed my waist and pulled me to him, his mouth covering mine, pressing so hard that I felt suffocated, gasping for air. I jerked back, lips and face on fire.

"Tell me you've been kissed like that before," Colin demanded. "By a man, not a boy."

Amanda's eyes flickered back and forth, not saying a word, waiting to see how I'd respond.

I had trouble breathing, but tried to stay calm. "If you let us go, we won't tell the police. Why not give them inside information about the prostitution racket? They may offer you some kind of deal."

"You're kidding me, right? Most of those numbskulls are in the gangs' back pocket."

"Which gang?" I asked. "The Beach Gang?"

"Both. That way, they get paid twice."

Why was I so surprised? Agent Burton had warned me about dirty cops. Who could you trust on the force, if anyone?

In a flash, Colin grabbed the whip off the bed, circling it around us like a lasso, while Amanda and I cringed.

"Why don't you give me a whipping, like the naughty boy I am? Then you two make a run for the exit."

Was he serious? "What about Mrs. Templeton?"

"I'll take care of her." Colin cracked the whip on the floor, pretending to moan in pain.

I took a hesitant step toward the hall. "How can we trust you?"

"All you have is my word. Now go! I'll cover for you."

I gave him a grateful look as we threw open the door and made a mad dash for the front entrance, breathing hard, giddy with relief. All we cared about now was getting away and making sure the girls were safe. I couldn't figure Colin out, but at least he'd offered us a chance to escape. As we bolted toward the door, I saw Sammy and Dino walking up the front steps.

"Sammy! Dino! Where are the bathing beauties? Are they OK?"

"They're fine." Sammy cocked his head. "But this goon has other ideas."

Then I heard a deep voice bark, "Not so fast, ladies. If you leave now, your friends are goners." I looked up to see a dark-haired hood behind them, a gun pointed at their backs.

As they got closer, I did a double-take. The man looked a lot like Rico, Holly's dead boyfriend. No, it couldn't be Rico. Wasn't he gunned down in front of the Kit Kat Club a couple of days ago?

CHAPTER FORTY-SIX

"Glad you could make it, Rico," Colin grinned. "What took you so long?"

"I had to make sure these saps didn't drive off with our bathing beauties." Rico motioned to Colin with his gun. "Why don't you help me tie them up?" He smirked, glancing around the room. "We use a lot of rope around here, don't we, girls?"

"Where are the bathing beauties now?" Colin asked, retreating to the parlor.

"Sleeping it off in a Roadster. We'll attend to them next. Go ahead, boys, have a seat. You're not going anywhere. Hands behind your heads." Sammy and Dino grumbled, but followed Rico's orders, eyes flashing with anger and humiliation.

Sammy spoke up, thrusting out his chin. "Say, Rico, aren't you supposed to be dead? What happened?"

"Damn thugs set me up, that's what. But those bastards killed my little brother instead." He waved his gun around, his face twisted in rage. "Poor Franco. I sent my baby brother in my place on an errand for Rosario, and he winds up dead?"

"Calm down, Rico." Colin returned with some rope, tying Sammy and Dino's wrists together. "We framed Rose Maceo just like you wanted."

"Says you. He's not in jail yet, is he?" Rico paced the room, his boots thudding on the hardwood floor. "No, Mr. Big Shot is walking around, healthy as a horse, while my brother is pushing up daisies."

"Give it time," Colin said. "You got the perfect cover. You're dead, remember?"

"Yeah, right. I'm a ghost." Rico glanced our way, frowning. "Who are you people?"

"We're friends of Holly's," I said, hoping to pacify him, but instead I hit a nerve.

"Holly? How do you know Holly?" He worked his jaw, clamping his fists tight.

"The bathing beauty contest," I told him, backing away.

"She disappeared and I don't know where she is. Is she OK?" Rico whined. Did he really care?

Before I answered, footsteps pounded on the stairs and a sheepish young man ran down in his bare feet, holding up his pants, carrying his shoes and shirt. He stared at us, puzzled, looking over his shoulder as he bolted out the door. Caught with his pants down. Served the bozo right.

I heard Nathan's voice yell, "Get the hell out!" He followed the john down the stairs, his arm wrapped around a petite gal. At least she seemed alert, despite the fact her hair was mussed, and her nightgown ripped. "What the hell are you trying to do to these girls? He was about to rape her!" he yelled. The girl ran toward Colin and stood behind him, trembling.

"It's not rape if they're being paid." Rico raised his gun in warning. "Maybe they like it."

"Wanna bet? She was screaming her head off. I don't think she was enjoying herself." Nathan crept down the stairs, his face flaming with anger, and leveled his gun at Rico. "I should shoot you right now after what you did to Holly."

"Go ahead, cowboy." Rico aimed his gun at Nathan and fired once. Nathan turned white and collapsed on the stairs.

Amanda and I screamed and rushed toward Nathan, but Rico blocked our way. "Leave him alone or I'll make it three bullets."

A group of half-dressed girls ran out of their rooms clutching their clothes. They took one look at the scene, then raced downstairs and out the door.

Mrs. Templeton marched over to Rico, shaking him by the shoulders. "I didn't invite you into my home so you could shoot up my place and scare away my girls. This isn't some Wild West saloon. There's blood all over my stairway!"

"Listen, old biddy, you better keep your mouth shut or we'll cut off your supply," Rico yelled in her face.

What did he mean—booze, broads or both?

Sammy locked eyes with me, tilting his head toward the door, indicating his intention to escape. I nodded, closely watching Rico's every move.

Dino and Sammy chose that moment to run out the front door, shoving Rico to the ground, knocking the gun out of his hand. "Don't let them get away!" Rico yelled at Colin, scrambling for his gun. "Go after them! Get the girls!"

Colin pressed his worn boot on Rico's arm and picked up his gun. "Hell, I hope they all get away. You had no right to kidnap those bathing beauties."

A shadow crossed the carpet and I saw Nathan standing over Rico, arms shaking. He cocked his pistol, aiming it right between Rico's eyes. "If you don't shoot him, I will."

"Where'd you come from?" I asked him, blinking. "You scared us to death!"

"Ever hear of playing possum?" he said, icy blue eyes focused on Rico's forehead. "I want to make sure this asshole never hurts Holly again."

"Let me do it, pal," Colin told Nathan. "I already got a record. You don't."

"You traitor!" Rico shouted at Colin. "I bet you're the one who killed my brother!"

"It was an accident. As far as the gangs are concerned, you're already dead." Colin aimed his gun at Rico's chest. "Ollie thinks you play too rough with the girls. Maggie didn't deserve to die that way, thrown over the Seawall like a sack of potatoes. She was like my big sister, practically helped raise me!"

Without warning, the young prostitute lunged at Rico, screaming and kicking his legs. "You bastard!" she cried. "Maggie was my best friend!" She suddenly grabbed Colin's gun and pointed it at Rico with trembling hands. "Why'd you have to kill her?"

"Maggie was headstrong. She didn't obey orders," Rico scoffed, his face smug. "Go ahead, Polly. Shoot. I dare you."

In a flash, Polly aimed for his heart, and pulled the trigger.

A shot rang out, the impact reverberating through the old Victorian, shaking the walls. Rico's eyes bulged out as he grabbed his chest, staring at Polly in shock, the same look Maggie had in her photos. Blood seeped through his shirt, and he clutched his sides, writhing in pain.

I stood there dumbstruck, watching while it seemed to play out in slow motion, as if on film. We all stared at Rico, then at the girl, in stunned silence. Tell the truth, I wasn't as frightened or upset as I'd expected, maybe because Rico, of all people, deserved to die.

"Don't be mad," Polly pleaded with Mrs. Templeton. "You know what he did to Maggie."

"Mad? I'm grateful. I just don't want to clean up this mess." Mrs. Templeton gave Rico a hard kick, arms akimbo, shaking her head. "Good riddance, you son-of-a-bitch." Then she turned to Colin, pushing him forward. "Go on, get out of here and take Polly with you. Don't worry, I'll tell the police it was self-defense."

"Thanks." Colin gave her a quick hug, then nodded before he took Polly's arm and rushed out the back exit. What a strange relationship those two had, more like boss and employee than mother and son.

"Let's scram," Nathan told me and Amanda as we slowly regained our senses.

"You need to get your leg checked." I pointed to Nathan's blood-soaked khaki pants. "Want us to drive you to the hospital?"

He stared at his wound as if seeing it for the first time. "Luckily it's my left leg. I think I can make it. I'd have to be half-dead and blind before I let you gals drive my Bessie."

Glad Rico hadn't hurt his sense of humor. On second thought, Nathan wasn't *that* funny.

As we made our way out, my heart leapt when I saw Agent Burton running up the walk. "I heard a gunshot. We've got police cars on their way now." He glanced at Nathan's bloody pants with concern. "What happened in there? Did anyone else get hurt?"

"Ask Mrs. Templeton," I told him, rushing down the steps. "Wait, how'd you know we were here? Who tipped you off?"

"Your ditzy friend, Jo Beth. Gotta admit, she's not as dumb as she looks."

"By the way, where were you today?" I placed my hand on his arm. "I didn't see you at the parades. "

"I was stuck at the Galvez, making sure the girls got to their rides safely. When I realized that Miss Italy and Miss France were missing, I asked Jo Beth what happened. Boy, did she give me an earful. She told me the fancy-pants Galvez clerk approached her about a *job*. Turns out, he acts as the liaison for Mrs. Templeton and provides call girls for out-of-town guests."

I made a face. "What a racket. Wait till you see her photography *studio*. It's a zoo!"

"I'll take the tour myself to make sure the place is clear."

After I gave him a short summary, he studied me. "Sure you're OK? It's not every day you see a shooting close up."

"I'm still numb, so it probably hasn't all sunk in yet," I admitted.

Burton let out a whistle. "I doubt the pageant can top all that excitement, but we both deserve to make a little whoopee after today." He squeezed my hand. "I'll see you Sunday night."

Considering the day we'd had, I could hardly wait. I just hoped Michelle and Antonia had recovered enough from their ordeal to appear in the beauty pageant.

CHAPTER FORTY-SEVEN

By the time we arrived at John Sealy Hospital, Sammy and Dino were already in the waiting room. "How are Michelle and Antonia? Were they hurt?" I wanted to know.

"They're in a stupor, but they'll snap out of it." Sammy's face clouded. "Luckily we got to them before the johns could. No good sons-of-bitches, terrorizing young gals that way."

"You said it," Nathan agreed. "That Polly is some dame."

"Are you OK, Sammy?" Amanda rushed over, giving Sammy a hug. "Rico didn't hurt you, did he?"

"Naw." He shrugged. "Say, Colin's not such a bad guy after all. He loosened the ropes and made it easy for us to escape. Told me he'd keep an eye on you two. Did we miss anything?"

"I'll say! Too bad Rico will have to skip the pageant tonight. He's out cold."

"Cold as a corpse," Nathan cracked, limping over to the counter. The nurses took one look at his bloody leg and pushed him into a wheelchair.

"I'll come back to check on you later," I told Nathan. "But first I want to stop by the *Gazette*, file a couple of stories."

"Need a ride?" I looked up to see Burton strolling through the hospital lobby. "The meat wagon is on its way with Rico, but I doubt he's going to make it. What a bloody mess. I just stopped by to see how the pageant girls are doing."

"They'll be fine," Sammy said. "But I'm not sure about Dino. That love-sick lug is so heartbroken over Antonia, he won't leave her side. He told the nurses he was her uncle so he could stay with her."

"Keep me posted. I know she'll get better—she has to. Italy is depending on her."

Not to mention Dino. I felt guilty for getting him involved in the first place: introducing Dino to Antonia, then asking him to help translate our interview. Poor girls. If I hadn't written those profiles, the bathing beauties wouldn't be lying here in the hospital.

I tugged on Burton's sleeve. "Would you mind dropping me off at the *Gazette?* I've got a lot of work to catch up on."

He seemed alarmed. "Let's wait for official police reports before you jump the gun."

"Don't worry. We'll keep today's events hush-hush, for now."

What would my editors say when they found out the dead "post office prostitute" was actually a bathing beauty? Naturally, it was big news, but some topics were strictly off-limits, especially during tourist season. No doubt they'd give the story to Mack, who'd turn it into the crime of the century and probably end up winning a Pulitzer.

I waved my good-byes to Sammy and Amanda, who were trying to comfort a stricken Dino. Burton escorted me out to his car, and as we drove, I couldn't help but notice he was fidgety, grinding his teeth, tapping his knees.

"What happened at Mrs. Templeton's?" I wondered.

"Mrs. Templeton's is no more. The cops arrested her and a few girls, and a judge slapped a fine on her so huge, she'd never pay it off in her lifetime. I hear the local judges give madams two choices: Leave town or find another line of work."

"That's great news!" I told him. "So what's eating you?"

He shrugged. "I overheard some cops talk around the station. Maybe it's just idle gossip, but they clam up whenever I'm around."

"What sort of talk?"

"Word is, Johnny Jack hired a hit man to do his dirty work while he's locked up."

"A hit man?" I raised my brows. "Guess I shouldn't be surprised. These gang leaders like to keep their hands clean."

"Seems he's got a lot of scores to settle. Jail gives him the perfect alibi." He acted nonchalant, but I heard tension in his voice.

"Any idea what he's planning?" I bit my lip, worried.

His face grew grim as he stared out at the traffic on Beach Boulevard. "Rumor has it, I may be his next target."

"What?" My heart stopped. "Johnny Jack has a hit out on you?" I'd heard Johnny Jack was a hothead with more money than brains, but trying to kill a Prohibition agent was going to extremes. "Please be careful," I told Burton, genuinely afraid for him. "Why don't you leave town for a while and wait till all this mess blows over?"

Strange that it was the same advice I'd recently given Sammy.

Burton looked aghast. "And let him think he's won? He can't get rid of me that easily. Besides, I've got a secret weapon."

"What kind of secret weapon?"

Burton gave me a sly smile. "Your friend Sammy."

What? I almost blurted out, 'My brother'? "Sammy Cook? How's he going to help?"

"I know he's on the outs with Johnny Jack, but he still has friends on the inside. I'm counting on him to find out more about this hit man. Who he is, when and where he plans to strike." He shrugged. "Sammy's the one who put me in this position, so I'd say he owes me."

"I hope Sammy can pull it off." I heaved a sigh. "If the gangs ever found out you two were working together, then you'd both be dead men."

"Now you know why we have to keep it a secret."

"My lips are sealed," I agreed, still stunned. I guess it made sense since—after his bar got raided instead of the Hollywood—Johnny Jack had it out for both men.

In a way, I felt relieved that for once Burton and Sammy might have to join forces against a common enemy. But what weapons did Johnny Jack have in his arsenal?

Burton parked in front of the *Gazette* and turned to face me. "Don't worry about me. Let's just enjoy ourselves Sunday night and pretend Johnny Jack doesn't exist."

My heart dropped, but I tried to lighten the mood. "Please be careful. I'm really looking forward to the pageant, and I hope my handsome date doesn't stand me up."

After Burton dropped me off at the *Gazette*, I saw Finn hawking papers on the front steps, his usual spot. "Hiya Jazz! Who's your fella?" Now it was my turn to blush.

He tipped his cap, then called out: "Bathing beauties galore, here on our fair shore!" Where'd he get that sales pitch, I marveled, straight from the editors?

Golliwog came out of the alley and followed me up to the door, meowing for scraps. I stroked her silky black fur as she circled around my ankles. I'd been too caught up with the bathing beauties lately, and felt guilty for neglecting her these past few days. Poor thing looked skinnier than usual, but she wasn't the only one skipping meals.

"Say, Finn, when was the last time you had something to eat?"

"I had some soda pop this morning. Doesn't that count?"

I handed him a dollar. "Go buy yourself a real lunch, and save something for Golliwog."

"The black cat?" His grin almost swallowed up his freckled face. "Gee, thanks! This'll buy lots of sandwiches. What does she like?"

"Chicken, fish, tuna, ham...the standard stray cat fare. Golly's not that picky."

"Got it. Say, can you watch my papers for me?" He thrust a stack of newspapers at me. "Golly and I are going to lunch."

"Sure, Finn, they'll be under my desk." I smiled at him before he ran off down the street.

I knocked out a couple of stories in an equal number of hours, including the snake scene during the bathing beauties dance routine at the Hollywood. Surely the editors wanted a little spice with their sugar. I decided to wait to write about the kidnappings and the "activities" at Mrs. Templeton's house. First I had to get the OK from Mr. Thomas since I knew Mrs. Harper, and the mayor, wouldn't exactly approve.

By the time I left, Finn and Golly were sharing a tuna fish sandwich in the corner. I could almost hear her purr from the street.

CHAPTER FORTY-EIGHT

Sunday

The next evening, Burton arrived at seven on the dot, looking dashing as ever, his fair hair a sharp contrast to his black evening coat and tails. I'd taken extra pains to get dolled up in a rose-colored silk chiffon gown with ruffles at the hem and neckline, and a big bow on one hip. Amanda even lent me some of her glitter powder for the finishing touch. After all, we had to dress to the nines to shine in a room full of beauty contestants.

"You sure look hotsy-totsy to me." Burton grinned, and gave me a wolf-whistle.

"You're the leopard's spots," I teased, tugging on his bow tie.

Eva came downstairs in a fancy pale sea foam gown. I wished she could come along, but tickets were hard to come by. "I wanted to see the handsome couple off," she beamed.

"Too bad you can't come with us. You look swell."

"Not to worry. I have my own escort." Her eyes twinkled. "One of the fellas from church asked me to go, so how could I refuse the biggest event of the year?"

Burton and I traded smiles. "I know you'll have a great time. Hope to see you there!"

Outside, Burton helped me into his Roadster, all shiny and new. "Glad your aunt met a nice fella," he said. "So where to, milady?"

"How about the Hollywood Dinner Club? I feel safer on the Beach Gang's turf tonight."

As we entered the ritzy nightclub, the diners stopped to stare, all eyes locked on Burton. No one seemed to notice my new silk frock or beaded cloche cap. Clearly word had spread about his raid on the Kit Kat, Johnny Jack's favorite club, and he was gaining quite a reputation as the hotshot Fed agent in town.

Luckily Sam Maceo rushed over, literally welcoming us with open arms, making a big show of seating us at one of his best corner tables. Very romantic and cozy, indeed.

The diners visibly relaxed and returned to their conversations and cocktails. Tonight the floor show was cancelled since all the country club types, bigwigs and newshawks, would be crammed into the Grand Opera House watching the Miss Universe and Miss United States pageants.

How in the world would they manage to pull off two beauty contests, both on the same stage, in one evening? That feat alone was worth the price of admission.

After we ordered dinner, Burton looked me up and down. "Why don't you tell me what *really* happened at Mrs. Templeton's today?"

My back stiffened. "What did she tell you?"

"Oh, the usual hogwash. How Rico was threatening everyone, waving his gun around, how he was shot in self-defense, but she didn't mention any names. Funny thing is, the cops couldn't find a murder weapon. Worse, they don't have a list of suspects, just a houseful of working girls who claim they saw nothing."

I tried to act nonchalant. How much could I tell Burton without incriminating Polly or Colin?

"Can you blame them? They were scared to death." I leaned forward, lowering my voice. "Rico was ranting and raving, swearing that the Beach Gang set him up and killed his kid brother, Franco, by accident. He'd tied up Sammy and Dino, and was holding us hostage in there. He was so angry, he was acting like a hit man, ready to shoot anyone who moved. He shot Nathan without even blinking."

"Since you mentioned it, what about your pal Colin? Did he shoot Rico and his brother—or was it an *accident?*"

What had he heard? "How would I know? I'm not his keeper or his friend, despite what you think. Besides, I thought he left town."

"Is that so? Any idea where he is?" Burton raised his brows. "We've looked all over for him."

Me and my big trap. "Hey, I thought this was a date, not an interrogation."

"Sorry, Jazz. Hard to turn off work sometimes, but you provide a swell distraction."

When he put it that way, I couldn't be upset. Still, I was playing it safe. Since he was a Fed agent, I knew this case was out of his area, and I didn't trust the cops who worked in Homicide.

The waiter arrived with our salmon dinners, and Burton carefully checked his fish for bones while I dug into the meal with gusto. I tried to make small talk, but Burton seemed preoccupied, purposely avoiding my questions and my eyes.

Why didn't I just tell him the truth?

At the Opera House, a valet parked Burton's Roadster and a tuxedoed attendant led us to our plush velvet seats. A few well-heeled couples eyed us with curiosity, perhaps wondering who we were since we didn't register on their social register.

The Victorian Rococo building looked completely different at night, all lit up with elegant chandeliers and candelabras in the aisles. An orchestra played a medley of classics as the audience filled the seats. I turned to admire the majestic theatre, waving to a few familiar faces, noting the elegant dresses and suits of the nouveau riche and the moneyed set whose names filled the society pages. It was so crowded, I didn't see Amanda or Eva or Nathan.

The music quieted and the mayor commanded the stage, giving a brief introduction to the pageant: "Ladies and gentleman, you're in for a double treat tonight. First, we'll have our usual tradition, the international bathing beauties competition. Then we'll introduce our first ever Miss United States pageant. The two lucky winners of both pageants will then compete for the crown of Miss Universe."

One by one, the contestants strutted across the stage in no particular order, and said a few words of welcome in her native tongue. I held my breath, hoping that Michelle and Antonia were strong enough to make an appearance.

The international pageant came first and as the lights dimmed, the orchestra began to play songs from each girl's native country. After the first contestant came out, Miss Egypt, a pale, exotic beauty, she received a standing ovation.

As the names were called, everyone applauded while the beauties twirled in their sumptuous ball gowns for the crowd's approval. My heart leapt whenever one of my favorites appeared, and I stood up, applauding like a proud mother hen. The gowns glowed and glimmered like gossamer wings, some with feathers and sequins or ruffles and bows, while others appeared in sleek designs reminiscent of *Erté's Ballet Russe* costumes.

When they played an Italian opera, I was overjoyed to see Antonia proudly cross the stage, radiant in a ruby gown that set off her long, raven hair. Thank goodness she'd recuperated in time for the pageant. I even heard Dino cheering across the room and soon everyone in the theatre gave her a standing ovation. If they only knew what she'd endured to be here tonight.

Next came Michelle, graceful in a flowing floral frock, her long hair adorned with ribbons, colorful as a maypole. I stood up, clapping wildly. The crowd joined in with loud applause and also gave her a standing ovation. "Merci beaucoup," she said, bowing.

Had they heard about Mrs. Templeton's? I nudged Burton, smiling with relief. Hard to believe we'd rescued the girls only yesterday afternoon.

The Miss United States pageant followed with the orchestra playing the "Star-Spangled Banner" and a few upbeat Gershwin tunes. I enjoyed seeing the contrast of the flamboyant frocks juxtaposed with the latest elegant European fashions. Even the jaunty way the home-grown girls walked screamed "all-American."

Each of the contestants came out with dazzling smiles, twirling this way and that, swishing their long gowns as they pranced across the stage. I waved at Miss New Orleans and Miss Palestine from my seat, admiring their sultry stride, as if they were professional Paris fashion models.

When Jo Beth appeared, she stood out in a soft, floral print frock and a wide-brimmed hat, and posed for a minute, right hand on her hip. As I watched her swish around the stage like a true Texas gal, a gleam caught my eye and I almost jumped out of my seat.

Maybe I was seeing things, but I could've sworn she was wearing the dead bathing beauty's gold charm bracelet on her right wrist.

CHAPTER FORTY-NINE

"What's wrong?" Burton leaned against me, touching my knee.

I squinted in the dark, wondering if it was my imagination. "Did you see Jo Beth's gold charm bracelet?" I cupped my hand by his ear. "It looks exactly like the victim's bracelet."

"Are you sure? Maybe she bought it from the jeweler. Or it could be a gift from an admirer."

"That's true," I nodded, trying to think. "I doubt she could afford such a bauble herself, so it was probably from a rich sugar daddy." Surely Jo Beth had no idea it belonged to a murdered bathing beauty. So how did she end up wearing the bracelet tonight?

I watched the rest of the pageant in a daze, wondering how to approach Jo Beth about the bracelet. What could I say? "You look wonderful tonight, and by the way, how did you get your hands on that gold bracelet?"

After a song and dance number from the Hollywood Dinner Club performance, the finalists lined the stage, and the drum roll began. As they paraded across the stage one last time, the mayor began calling the runners-up.

Miss Luxembourg won the international competition, regal and radiant in her flowing gown, while Miss New York was given the Miss United States title. Now the two finalists stood holding hands on the stage, as the orchestra played a crescendo to stir up the crowd.

Finally when Miss New York was crowned Miss Universe, she burst into tears while the crowd cheered and gave her a long standing ovation. I admit, I was disappointed that none of my friends had won, but I knew Miss New York had a great camaraderie with the other contestants, who seemed genuinely happy for her.

After the pageant, I led Burton down the aisle toward the girls who were circulating around the theatre, my heart beating wildly.

To be honest, I didn't even want to make small talk or mingle with the guests until I'd confronted Jo Beth. How could I bring up the bracelet without making her mad or suspicious?

As I walked over, I saw her arguing with a tall, dignified, middle-aged man with a handlebar moustache who was yanking on her arm. Was that her sugar daddy or a pushy masher?

"What's he doing?" I said to Burton in alarm. "Is that her father or her fella? Why is he trying to pull off her bracelet?"

"Let's find out," Burton said, pushing past the crowd gathered around the contestants.

As we approached, I held back to watch their interaction, wondering what was the nature of their relationship. From the looks of it, the man appeared to be quite angry, digging at the bracelet with his nails, roughly twisting Jo Beth's arm until her face twisted in pain.

"Jo Beth!" I called out and rushed to give her a big hug. "You look beautiful tonight!"

"Thanks, Jazz," she whispered, panic in her voice, her arms clenched around me. "That strange man is trying to steal my bracelet. Can y'all help?" You'd think we were long-lost best friends, we were holding on so tight.

Out of the corner of my eye, I saw Burton shaking the man's hand. "Good evening, Senator O'Reilly," I heard him say.

Senator? What was Jo Beth doing with a senator?

"Agent Burton." He gave a nod, his face flushed. "And what may I do for you?"

Jo Beth and I stared in surprise. "I swear, I've never seen that man before in my life. Wait, I did see him once, during the first day of rehearsals, watching us gals like a hawk." She frowned. "I figured he was some big shot, but I had no idea he's a senator."

"What does he want with your bracelet?" I asked, watching her reaction closely.

"Who knows? He can afford to buy his own damn bracelet, so why does he want mine? I got it as a gift from a fella." She blushed like a new bride.

"He told me to be sure to wear it tonight, that all the charms would bring me good luck. OK, so I didn't win the pageant, I still feel like a winner." She twirled the bracelet on her arm, playing with the charms like a kid, smiling with delight. "I just adore this bracelet."

"How thoughtful. Can I see it?"

Jo Beth held up the charm bracelet proudly, the gold glittering under the theatre spotlights, the charms dangling like wind chimes. Yes, it was the exact bracelet I'd seen at the jeweler's only a few days ago, with one missing charm.

"So who's the lucky fella?" I wondered. "Anyone I know?"

She nodded, cheeks pink. "Remember Colin Ferris? I know you warned me about him, but I can't help myself. I always fall for rascals and scoundrels, especially the good-looking ones."

Colin? How did he get the bracelet—and if it was so valuable, why did he give it to Jo Beth?

Burton reappeared with O'Reilly, whose face had broken out in a sweat. "Senator, please explain to Jo Beth what you told me, that the bracelet belongs to your wife."

"That's right," the senator stammered, stroking his moustache. "She'll be very upset to find it missing."

"Sir, that's a serious accusation." Burton played it cool. "Why don't we ask your wife to confirm it's the same bracelet she lost?"

"No, that's not necessary," he said, blanching. "I bought it as a gift, so I know it's hers."

"That's not true! My boyfriend gave it to me for good luck." Jo Beth stomped her foot and faced the senator. "Are you accusing him of stealing?"

"Who's your boyfriend?" Burton demanded. "When did he give you the bracelet?"

"Colin. He gave it to me right after the parades and insisted that I wear it during the pageant." Her eyes misted. "Colin told me he'd think of me, even though he couldn't be here tonight."

"Colin Ferris?" Burton raised his brows, glancing at me in surprise. "Why don't we discuss this outside, away from the crowd?"

By now, a small arc of gawkers had gathered around us to watch, eyes and mouths wide open. I'd be eavesdropping too, if I didn't already have a front-row seat.

"There's nothing more to discuss." The senator turned to go. "Good night, sir. I'll file charges against this woman Monday morning. Who will they believe? Me or this tart?"

"Tart?" Jo Beth drew back her fist, charms gleaming, ready to slug him. "Who are you calling a tart? I'm Miss Dallas!"

"Let's step outside, shall we?" Burton repeated. When the senator resisted, Burton cocked his head toward the front, where Sam and Rose Maceo were holding court. "Perhaps the Maceos would like to assist you?"

Senator O'Reilly looked alarmed, and Burton firmly gripped his arm and led him out the front door. I followed Jo Beth to make sure she wouldn't run away, but she was as curious as I was. Better to pretend we were best friends, not foes.

Outside, the noise and cars and music drowned out our conversation. "What's going on?" The senator acted baffled. "I just want my bracelet back."

"When did you buy it for your wife?" Burton eyed him.

"About a week ago," the senator mumbled, loosening his collar.

"That's not true," I piped up. "I saw it for sale in a jewelry shop a couple of days ago."

"Young lady, are you calling me a liar?" he huffed.

"Senator, I think you should come downtown with me." Burton took his elbow. "Now."

"I'm at the social event of the year. Why would I go downtown with you now? So you can falsely accuse me of theft?" He bristled.

"This bracelet is evidence in a murder investigation. I'm sorry, Jo Beth, but you'll need to turn it over to the police."

Jo Beth's face fell, her voice wavering. "Do I have to? It's supposed to be a present!"

"I'm afraid so. We believe it belonged to a bathing beauty who was killed a week ago." Burton glared at the senator. "Roughly the period when you said you *bought* the bracelet."

O'Reilly crumpled before our eyes. "Please don't treat me like a common criminal. Believe me, it was all an accident."

Burton raised his brows. "An accident?"

"Her name was Maria Costa, Miss Venezuela. A lovely girl, so full of fun and life. How could I resist her?"

Now the poor victim had a name, at least.

"I thought we were getting along great, but I have needs, you see." O'Reilly blinked rapidly, holding back tears, or else he was a damn good actor. "For some reason, she got scared and started screaming and I..I...tried to keep her quiet."

The senator tugged at his tie, as if gasping for breath, his voice cracking. "I swear, I'm no killer. It wasn't supposed to happen."

Shaking with fury, he flared up at Jo Beth. "I asked your pals to get rid of the bracelet, and it turns up tonight, *here* of all places, for all the world to see?"

Burton and I traded smiles. "I think that's just what Colin wanted when he gave Jo Beth the bracelet." I gave Senator O'Reilly the once-over. "A killer's confession."

"Where's Colin now?" Burton asked Jo Beth, glancing around.

"I don't know." Jo Beth looked downcast. "He didn't tell me anything else."

"Colin's in the wind," I told them. "As far as I know, he's gone for good."

"Too bad." Burton shrugged. "We could have used his testimony. Jazz, do you mind if I run a quick errand downtown? Mingle a while, and I'll be back in half an hour." He yanked the senator up by his collar. "I have to go take out the garbage."

CHAPTER FIFTY

An hour later, Burton and I were walking along the Seawall, the moon lighting up the pale beach while tourists took their nighttime strolls. Then he took my hand as we talked, as casual as sweethearts.

"What happened at the police station?" I was dying to know.

"The senator is in lock-up now, but he confessed to everything. He says he wants to cooperate with authorities so he'll get a lighter sentence. But I don't think our mayor or the Venezuelan government will let him off that easily."

In the moonlight, I could see his sly smile. "If they do, we can always contact the Maceos. I doubt the sponsors will appreciate the fact that Senator O'Reilly gave their beloved bathing beauty *and* their pageant a black eye."

"Good. I hate to sound like a gangster, but that senator deserves any punishment he gets. I'm sure Mrs. Wembley and the bathing beauties will be willing to testify. I almost talked to her after the pageant, but I didn't want to spoil such a happy occasion."

I faced him, enjoying the warm sea breeze whipping through my hair. "So how did they get together? I didn't expect a bathing beauty to wind up with such an old masher. A killer, no less."

Burton stopped walking, working his jaw. "Remember that cake-eater at the hotel? Turns out he was trying to run an escort service out of the Galvez, and give Mrs. Templeton's some competition. When the clerk, Mr. Whipple, found out the bathing beauties were staying at the Galvez for a week, he thought he'd hit the jackpot."

"What?" I whirled around, my head spinning. "That sick, twisted lowlife. How could anyone be so cruel, so heartless?"

"You said it." Burton nodded. "Seems he tried to convince the chaperones to work their charges, so to speak, especially the foreign girls, to help pay for their travel expenses. Luckily, after Miss Venezuela disappeared, he held off on his get-rich-quick scheme."

"These poor girls come so far from home, only to be raped and mauled for *money?*" I stomped around the Seawall, trying to work off some steam. "Let's go there right now and nail the bastard. How dare he treat these poor girls like cattle!"

"Calm down, Jazz." Burton took my hands. "I stopped by the hotel, but he's off tonight. So we sent an undercover cop there to watch the lobby. We'll be ready to nab Whipple the moment he steps foot in the Galvez. Don't worry, the cop will make sure he doesn't try to pull anything before we arrest him. Frankly, from the looks of him, I doubt he'll last long in prison."

"That lecher belongs in the jail cell next to Senator O'Reilly and Johnny Jack." I breathed a sigh of relief, shaking my head, trying to make sense of it all. "Did any of the bathing beauties know? I wish someone had turned him in before Miss Venezuela was killed."

"I don't think the girls knew or they were too afraid to speak up. It's no secret that the pageant is run by gangsters. I heard Whipple was trying to cut a deal so the chaperones could stay in town an extra week, and rent their girls out by the hour. Only the losers, of course."

"Naturally," I fumed, stomping around the Seawall. "No nice girl in her right mind would agree to turn tricks so their *chaperones* can make a profit." I wanted to write an exposé about the cathouses in Galveston—and the murders—but I knew it'd never make it into print. Maybe Mack could cover the story, with my help?

Burton looked concerned, and started rubbing my shoulders. "You need to relax, Jazz, take your mind off this fiasco."

"You're right. I've been so tense lately, worried about you and Sammy and the bathing beauties."

Like a kid, I brightened when I saw an ice cream vendor down by Murdoch's. "How about some ice cream? I could go for a big chocolate cone with sprinkles."

"I was thinking of something more personal." Burton pulled me toward him and I felt warm lips pressed against mine, firm then soft.

So different from the hard, rough way Colin had kissed me, if you call that an actual kiss. More like manhandling.

For a few moments, I forgot all about deadlines and death threats and bathing beauties and murdered prostitutes.

"Well, what do you know?" Burton grinned at me, gently stroking my wild, windblown hair. "I think it worked."

I smiled back, watching the foamy waves hit the shore, trying to catch my breath, unable to speak. The stars seemed extra-bright tonight, sparkling like marquee lights.

As I admired the peaceful beach scene, I couldn't help but savor the irony of the situation: Thanks to Agent Burton, a ruthless senator and gang leader would spend the night side by side, locked up in a Galveston jail cell. I knew they wouldn't remain behind bars forever, but at least we were safe, for now.

1920s JAZZ AGE SLANG

All wet - Wrong, incorrect ("You're all wet!" "That's nuts!")

And how! - I strongly agree!

Applesauce! – Nonsense, Horsefeathers (e.g. "That's ridiculous!")

Attaboy! - Well done! Bravo! Also: Attagirl!

Baby grand - A heavily-built man

Balled up - Confused, Unsure

Baloney - Nonsense, Hogwash, Bullshit

Bathtub Booze - Home-brewed liquor, Hooch (often in tubs)

Bearcat - A hot-blooded or fiery girl

"Beat it!" - Scram, Get lost

Bee's Knees - An extraordinary person, thing or idea

Berries - Attractive or pleasing; Swell ("It's the berries!")

Big Cheese - Big shot, an important or influential person

Blotto - Very drunk, Smashed

Blow - (a) A wild, crazy party (b) To leave

Bluenose - A prim, puritanical person; a prude, a killjoy

Bootleg - Illegal liquor, Hooch, Booze

Breezer (1925) - A convertible car

Bruno - Tough guy, enforcer

Bug-eyed Betty - An unattractive girl or student

Bum's rush - Ejection by force from an establishment

Bump Off - To murder, to kill

Bunk – Bullshit, Hooey, Wrong as in : "That's Bunk!"

Cake-eater - A lady's man, a gigolo; an effeminate male

Carry a Torch - To have a crush on someone

Cat's Meow/Whiskers - Splendid, Stylish, Swell

Cat's Pajamas - Terrific, Wonderful, Great

Clams - Money, Dollars, Bucks

Coffin varnish - Bootleg liquor, Hooch (often poisonous)

Copacetic - Excellent, all in order

Dame/Doll - A female, woman, girl (usually attractive)

Dogs - Feet

Dolled up - Dressed up in "glad rags"

Don't know from nothing - Don't have any information

Don't take any wooden nickels - Don't do anything stupid

Dough - Money, Cash

Drugstore Cowboy - A guy who picks up girls in public places

Dry up - Shut up; Get lost

Ducky - Fine, very good (Also: Peachy)

Dumb Dora - An idiot, a dumbbell; a stupid female

Egg - Nice person, One who likes the big life

Fall Guy - Victim of a frame

Fella - Fellow, man, guy (very common in the 1920s)

Fire extinguisher - A chaperone, a fifth wheel

Flat Tire - A dull, boring date (Also: Pill, Pickle, Oilcan)

Frame - To give false evidence, to set up someone

Gams - A woman's legs

Gate Crasher - A party crasher, an uninvited guest

Giggle Water - Liquor, Hooch, Booze, Alcohol

Gin Joint/Gin Mill - A bar, a speakeasy

Glad rags - "Going out on the town" clothes, Fancy dress attire

Go chase yourself - "Get lost, beat it, scram"

Hard-Boiled - A tough, strong guy (e.g. "He sure is hard-boiled!")

Hayburner - (a) A gas-guzzling car (b) A losing racehorse

Heebie-jeebies (1926) - The shakes, the jitters, (from a hit song)

High-hat - Snobby, snooty

Holding the bag - To be cheated or blamed for something

Hooch - Bootleg liquor, illegal alcohol

Hood - Hoodlum, Gangster, Thug

Hooey - Bullshit, Nonsense, Baloney (1925 to 1930)

Hoofer - Dancer, Chorus girl

Hotsy-Totsy - Attractive, Pleasing

Jack - Cash, Money

Jake - Great, Fine, OK (i.e. "Everything's jake.")

Jeepers creepers – Exclamation of surprise ("Jesus Christ!")

Joe Brooks - A well-groomed man, natty dresser, student

Juice Joint - A speakeasy, bar

Keen - Attractive or appealing

Killjoy - Dud, a dull, boring person, a party pooper, a spoilsport

Lollygagger - (a) A flirtatious male (b) A lazy or idle person

Lounge Lizard - A gigolo; a flirtatious, sexually-active male

Mick - A derogatory term for an Irishman

Milquetoast (1924): A very timid person; a hen-pecked male
(from the comic book character Casper Milquetoast)

Mrs. Grundy - A prude or killjoy; a prim, prissy (older) woman

Moll - (Gun Moll) A gangster's girlfriend

Neck - Make-out, kiss with passion

"Oh yeah?" - Expression of doubt ("Is that so?")

On a toot – On a drinking binge, Bar-hopping

On the lam - Fleeing from police

On the level - Legitimate, Honest

On the trolley – In the know, Savvy ("You're on the trolley!")

On the up and up - Trustworthy, Honest

Ossified – Drunk, Plastered

Palooka - A derogatory term for a low-class or dumb person
   (Re: Comic strip character Joe Palooka, a poor immigrant)

Piker - (a) Cheapskate (b) Coward

Pitch a little woo - To flirt, try to charm and attract the opposite sex

Rag-a-muffin - An unkempt, dirty and disheveled person/child

Razz - To tease, to insult or make fun of

Rhatz! - "Too bad!" or "Darn it!"

Ritzy - Elegant, High-class, "Putting on the Ritz" (Re: Ritz Hotel)

Rotgut - Cheap hooch, inferior alcohol, poisonous bootleg liquor

Rummy - A drunken bum, an intoxicated man, a wino

Sap - A fool, an idiot; very common term in the 1920s

"Says you!" - A reaction of disbelief or doubt (also "Hogwash!")

Screaming meemies - The shakes, the jitters, to be afraid

Screwy - Crazy, Nuts ("You're screwy!")

Sheba - An attractive and sexy woman; girlfriend
   (popularized by the film "Queen of Sheba")

Sheik - A handsome man with sex appeal
   (from Rudolph Valentino's film "The Sheik")

Scram – "Get out," "Beat it"; to leave immediately

Speakeasy - An illicit bar selling bootleg liquor

Spiffy - An elegant appearance, well-dressed, fine

Stuck On - Having a crush on, attracted to

Sugar Daddy - A rich, older gentleman (usually married)

Swanky - Elegant, Ritzy

Swell - Wonderful, Great, Fine, A-OK

Take for a Ride -To try to kill someone (bump them off)

Torpedo - A hired gun, a hit man

Upchuck - To vomit, especially after drinking too much

Wet Blanket - A dud, a dull date or person, a party pooper

Whoopee - (Make whoopee) To have fun/a good time, to party

"You don't say!" – i.e. "Is that so?" "Oh, really? I didn't know"

"You slay me!" -"You're hilarious!" or "That's funny!"

Zozzled - Drunk, intoxicated, (Also: Plastered, Smashed)

BIOGRAPHY

Ellen Mansoor Collier is a Houston-based freelance writer and editor whose articles and essays have been published in several national magazines including: FAMILY CIRCLE, MODERN BRIDE, FIRST, GLAMOUR, BIOGRAPHY, COSMOPOLITAN, COUNTRY ACCENTS, THE WRITER, PLAYGIRL, etc. Several of her short stories have appeared in WOMAN'S WORLD.

A flapper at heart, she loves all things Deco and runs MODERNEMILLIE on Etsy, specializing in vintage accessories.

Formerly she worked as a magazine editor and freelance writer, and in advertising/marketing and public relations. Collier graduated from the University of Texas at Austin with a degree in Magazine Journalism, where she lived in a 1926 dorm her freshman year. She served as an editor on UTmost magazine and was active in Women in Communications (W.I.C.I.), acting as President her senior year. During college summers, she worked as a reporter on a community newspaper and once as a cocktail waitress, both jobs providing background experience for her Jazz Age mystery series.

FLAPPERS, FLASKS AND FOUL PLAY is the first novel in her Jazz Age Mystery series, first released in 2012. BATHING BEAUTIES, BOOZE AND BULLETS, the sequel, was published in 2013. GOLD DIGGERS, GAMBLERS AND GUNS was released in 2014, followed by VAMPS, VILLAINS AND VAUDEVILLE in 2015, all set in 1920s Galveston.

"When you grow up in Houston, Galveston is like a second home. I had no idea this sleepy beach town had such a wild and colorful past until we visited a former speakeasy-turned-diner and heard some colorful gangster stories. Curious, I began doing research and became fascinated by the real-life legends and landmarks of 1920s Galveston. In my series, I tried to recreate that exciting era from an ambitious, adventurous young reporter's point of view."

DEDICATION

Thanks to Gary, my supportive husband, who has helped me from day one and read several drafts of this novel.

To my mother, May Mansoor Munn, also a writer, who inspired me to write at a young age and often offered words of wisdom, and to my late father, Isa Mansoor, a kind and generous man who always encouraged me to do my best.

ACKNOWLEDGEMENTS

I owe a debt of gratitude to Noreen Marcus who read and edited various drafts of BATHING BEAUTIES, and to Karen Muller, whose eagle eye helped me make some final changes and improvements.

Many thanks go to *Texas Monthly* contributor Gary Cartwright, author of *Galveston: A History of the Island*, whose painstaking research made Galveston's past come alive.

For my cover art, I'm delighted to thank my brother, Jeff J. Mansoor, who created the graphics for both covers. Sadly, the Deco illustrator and photographer are unknown.

Also I'm grateful to my friends and family members for their support. I especially want to thank my swell husband Gary, who not only read several drafts and formatted the print versions of each novel, he always offered his help and encouragement.

56031075R00151

Made in the USA
Charleston, SC
12 May 2016